P9-DNS-530

Praise for **ANNE GEORGE's** Southern Sisters Mysteries

"A sassy series."
Chicago Tribune

"Anne George may be my favorite discovery of the year . . . The Patricia Anne and Mary Alice mysteries are wonderful confections that prove life is funny and poignant on the other side of 60."
New Orleans Times-Picayune

"George's low-key humor and engaging characters keep you flipping pages."
Orlando Sentinel

"Great fun . . . George portrays a Southern family and all the connections that go along with it perfectly."
Greensboro News & Record

"The characters are so opinionated you half expect them to fire your babysitter, and the action so real you think it's happening next door."
Los Angeles Times

"I haven't been this excited about a series since the Hardy Boys."
Birmingham Magazine

"I wish Patricia Anne and Mary Alice were *my* sisters. I'd love to hang out with them."
Jill Churchill, author of the *Jane Jeffry* Mysteries

Other Avon Books by
Anne George

MURDER ON A GIRLS' NIGHT OUT
MURDER RUNS IN THE FAMILY
MURDER MAKES WAVES
MURDER GETS A LIFE
MURDER SHOOTS THE BULL
MURDER CARRIES A TORCH

And

THIS ONE AND MAGIC LIFE

Coming Soon in Hardcover

MURDER BOOGIES WITH ELVIS

ATTENTION: ORGANIZATIONS AND CORPORATIONS
Most Avon Books paperbacks are available at special quantity
discounts for bulk purchases for sales promotions, premiums, or
fund-raising. For information, please call or write:

**Special Markets Department, HarperCollins Publishers Inc.
10 East 53rd Street, New York, New York 10022-5299.
Telephone: (212) 207-7528.   Fax: (212) 207-7222.**

ANNE GEORGE

Murder on a Bad Hair Day

A SOUTHERN SISTERS MYSTERY

AVON BOOKS
An Imprint of HarperCollinsPublishers

This is a work of fiction. Names, characters, places, and incidents are products of the author's imagination or are used fictitiously and are not to be construed as real. Any resemblance to actual events, locales, organizations, or persons, living or dead, is entirely coincidental.

AVON BOOKS
An Imprint of HarperCollins*Publishers*
10 East 53rd Street
New York, New York 10022-5299

Copyright © 1996 by Anne George
ISBN: 0-380-78087-9
www.avonbooks.com

All rights reserved. No part of this book may be used or reproduced in any manner whatsoever without written permission, except in the case of brief quotations embodied in critical articles and reviews. For information address Avon Books, an Imprint of HarperCollins Publishers.

First Avon Books paperback printing: September 1996

Avon Trademark Reg. U.S. Pat. Off. and in Other Countries, Marca Registrada, Hecho en U.S.A.
HarperCollins® is a trademark of HarperCollins Publishers Inc.

Printed in the U.S.A.

20 19 18 17 16 15 14 13 12 11

If you purchased this book without a cover, you should be aware that this book is stolen property. It was reported as "unsold and destroyed" to the publisher, and neither the author nor the publisher has received any payment for this "stripped book."

For Tina, my daughter

Acknowledgments

My thanks to Dr. Chandler McGee and Dr. Christina Duffey for their ideas and interest and for generously sharing their knowledge of chemistry with me. And thanks to the "Center Point" group—Jean Burnett, Elsie McKibben, and Virginia Martin—for their patience, suggestions, and laughter.

One

"I tell you, Patricia Anne, I'm sick and tired of always being some man's sex slave." Mary Alice shut the kitchen door firmly and headed for the stove. "Is this fresh coffee?"

I looked up from the morning paper and nodded. I also grinned. My sister is sixty-five years old, six feet tall, and admits to weighing two hundred fifty pounds. The idea of her as a sex slave is mind-boggling.

"You look like a jackass eating briars," she said. "But I'm telling you the truth." She got a cup from the cabinet, poured her coffee, and helped herself to a muffin from a plate on the counter. "What kind are these?"

"Blueberry."

She took a second one and came to the table in the bay window where I was reading the paper and having a second cup of coffee. "What are you doing?"

"Reading Omar Sharif's bridge column."

"Oh, God, I love that man. Those daffodils!"

"I know." For a moment it was not December in Birmingham, Alabama, but springtime in Russia with "Lara's Theme" soaring. "How many times have you seen *Dr. Zhivago*?" I asked.

Mary Alice took a bite of blueberry muffin. "Maybe twenty. I still keep hoping they'll get back together."

"But they did in a way."

"Don't be ridiculous. He dies every time. Splat. Right there in the street." She took another bite of muffin. "You know, being his sex slave wouldn't be so bad. Unless he plays bridge all the time."

I folded the paper. "Why don't you pull off your coat? And what is this sex slave bit?"

"I'm just staying a minute. And it's what all of us women are. You. Me. Working our butts off to please some man."

I could have pointed out that my husband, Fred, was at work while I was sitting in the kitchen in my bathrobe reading the paper, but I decided not to push my luck.

"We iron their clothes, cook their food, mop their floors, and do God knows what just to please them."

"Sister," I said, "I think a sex slave is used sexually."

"That, too," she said.

I decided not to pursue this line of conversation. "You want some more coffee?" I asked.

Mary Alice shook her head no. "Mouse," she said, using her old childhood nickname for me, "I want to show you something, but you have to promise not to laugh."

"Sure," I agreed.

"You promise?"

"I promise."

She stood up and unbuttoned her coat but still clutched it around her. "Swear."

"I told you I wouldn't laugh."

She pulled her coat off and all promises were off; I laughed like hell. Mary Alice was Mrs. Santa Claus, complete with a short red skirt, red leggings, and a white knit shirt decorated with the words "Mrs. Santa" that flashed sporadically with lights that apparently were beyond Sister's power to control.

"I knew you would laugh," she said morosely. "There's a wig that goes with it, though." She reached into the pocket of her coat, brought out what looked like a dead white poodle, and placed it over her own short pinkish hair. "You think anyone will recognize me?"

"Oh, Lord," I laughed. "I have to go to the bathroom."

"Well, maybe they won't," she called as I rushed down the hall.

When I got back to the kitchen, she had her coat on again and, except for an occasional giggle, I was in control. "What's this about?" I asked.

"Bill's got a job as Santa Claus down at the Rosedale Mall. They wanted a couple. It's supposed to keep the kids from being so scared." Mary Alice shrugged. "See? I told you I was a sex slave."

Seventy-two-year-old Bill Adams is Sister's current "boyfriend." He has lasted for several months, probably because he can dip her when they dance. Or at least that's what Fred and I thought. There just might be more to the relationship if she was willing to go along with him on this.

"Rosedale Mall's on the other side of town," I assured her. "You won't see a soul you know. Besides, what does it matter? You're being a good sport."

"You think so?"

"I know so. Just think of all the kids you'll make happy."

"That's true." Mary Alice looked at her watch. "I've got to go. I just wanted to remind you of the gallery opening tonight. It's from five until eight, drop in, and I won't get off work until six, so I won't pick you up until seven. Okay?"

"Why don't I meet you there?"

"The way you drive? Don't be silly. And wear that sweater I gave you last Christmas, the off-white with the pearls on it."

"And which skirt should I wear?" Mary Alice is immune to sarcasm, which can be both a blessing and a curse for a sister.

"The off-white, of course. And for goodness sakes don't wear those shoes you bought that are supposed to be 'winter white.' I can't believe you were suckered like that."

"One every minute," I said, grinning again.

"I'll see you at seven." Mrs. Claus picked up another muffin on her way out.

"See you." Sooner than she thought. I had a date for lunch at the Rosedale Mall.

As soon as Omar Sharif made his impossible six no-trump bid, I threw on some sweats and went out to take my old Woofer for his walk. It was a beautiful morning, crisp but not cold, and though it was just three weeks until Christmas, a few pink geraniums still bloomed in the containers on the deck. Woofer was sleeping late. The year before, I had paid a fortune for an insulated doghouse that looked like an igloo, but it had been money well spent. The problem was getting Woofer out of it.

I lifted the flap and poked him. "Hey, lazy."

He came out stretching, looking a little sheepish that I had sneaked up on him, and smelling mightily of warm dog.

"Walk time," I said, rubbing his head and noticing how gray he was getting. Well, weren't we all. I put his leash on and we started out.

Our neighborhood is an old one of front porches and sidewalks. We have a saying here, "On a clear day, you can see the moon." This refers to the huge statue of Vulcan, the god of the forge, placed on top of Red Mountain about a hundred years ago as a symbol of Birmingham's iron and steel industries. Which is fine. I've got no quarrel with the big iron man. Tourists climb him as they would a lighthouse to get a great view of downtown, and they buy postcards and souvenirs. The postcards are always pictures of the front, though.

Wisely, given his trade, Vulcan is wearing an apron. Unfortunately for the tree-lined residential streets on the other side of the mountain, that's all he's wearing. As long as I can remember, there have been petitions floating around to cover up Vulcan's rear end. But nothing has come of them. If they decided to put a wraparound apron on him, we would lose, as Mary Alice says, the butt of most of our jokes.

I grew up by the light of this moon and thought nothing about it until a small cousin visiting from Atlanta stood on our front porch and, eyes round with awe, announced, "There's a nekkid man up yonder."

"With a great ass," Mary Alice said. She couldn't have been more than ten at the time.

The moon was very clear today. Woofer and I walked under a bright blue sky, moseying along, taking our time. When I retired in May, right after my sixtieth birthday, this was the sort of morning I had in mind.

I admired the Christmas decorations that had begun to appear Thanksgiving afternoon. Our neighborhood is nothing if not gaudy at Christmastime. We don't go for those little white lights. The big colored ones strung around the eaves of the houses suit us just fine. Add a few life-size nativity scenes in the yards and a lot of Rudolphs and Santas sprinting across roofs and we're ready for the season.

When we got home, I gave Woofer a treat, took a quick shower, and put on my red suit in honor of the season. I was meeting Bonnie Blue Butler for lunch at Rosedale Mall. She was going to get a kick out of Mrs. Santa. And it was the first thing I was going to tell her about.

Meeting Bonnie Blue was one of the few good things to come out of Mary Alice's purchase a few months back of the Skoot 'n' Boot, a country-western bar out Highway 78. Mary Alice still swears it was a good idea and everybody in Birmingham would be up there today line dancing up a storm if it hadn't been for all those unfortunate murders. Of which I was almost one. I shivered thinking what a close call it had been. But today was a beautiful day, I had on my red suit, and it was three weeks until Christmas. Fiddle-dee-dee, Miss Scarlett!

I got to the Blue Moon Tea Room first, and had just started on my first cup of decaf when I heard "Yoo-hoo, Patricia Anne!" and saw Bonnie Blue working her way toward the table with a large package wrapped in Christmas paper.

Every time I see her, I am amazed at how much she reminds me of Mary Alice. They are the same size. They dress alike, walk alike, even their personalities are alike. But Bonnie Blue is black and about fifteen years younger. Still, it's like looking at a negative image when they are together. I got up to help her with the package and we hugged each other.

"Whoa," she said, easing into her wrought iron chair. "This place is a tight fit."

"You want to go somewhere else?"

"Lord no. I picked the place, didn't I? Their chicken salad and orange rolls are worth a little squeezing in." She looked over at me. "You still weigh a hundred five?"

I admitted that I did. "But I'm just five foot one, remember."

"You eating?"

I said that, indeed, I was eating. Mary Alice tells everyone I'm anorexic and has convinced Bonnie Blue, apparently.

"How are Fred and Haley?"

I said that my husband and daughter were fine.

"She still dating that Sheriff Reuse?"

"Some," I admitted.

"Hmmm." Sheriff Reuse had been the main investigator at the Skoot 'n' Boot. He was not one of Bonnie Blue's favorite people.

The waitress came and got our orders, chicken salad and orange rolls for both of us. When she left, Bonnie Blue reached down for the Christmas package that was propped against the wall.

"This is with my thanks," she said.

"Oh, Bonnie Blue, whatever for?" I asked.

"The job." She held the package toward me. "All sorts of things."

Tears filled my eyes. "You got the job yourself."

"But you told them about me. And it's a good job, Patricia Anne. Nice people."

After the fiasco at the Skoot 'n' Boot, Bonnie Blue had been working at a truck stop, which would be hard work for a young, skinny girl—which Bonnie Blue definitely is not—and I was worried about her. I was in the Big, Bold, and Beautiful Shop buying Sister a present and got to talking to the owner, who said she was looking for a saleslady. One phone call and Bonnie Blue had the job. It was still hard work, and she was still on her feet a lot, but compared to the truck stop, it was a snap.

"With my thanks," she said.

I took the package, which was poster size, and began to peel the wrapper off. A piece of painted plywood came into view, and the signature "ABE" with the *E* backwards. I looked at Bonnie Blue in shock.

"It can't be," I said.

"Go ahead." She smiled. "Be careful."

I tore the rest of the paper off and saw the painting of an old black man dressed in a black suit with a blue shirt. He held a cane in his hand. The legs were too long, the arms too short, the feet both pointed toward the left. The background was white, and around that, around the edge of the plywood, the artist had painted a black border as a frame. A pop-top opener served as a hanger. The man was smiling, two tiny rows of white dots, and what looked like gray cotton had been glued to his head. On the back of the plywood was printed "ME" with the *E* going the wrong way. What I was holding, I knew, was an original Abraham, a picture by the most famous of Alabama's "Outsider" or folk artists.

The tears spilled over. "My God, Bonnie Blue. This is unbelievable!"

She was smiling proudly. "You like it?"

"Like it? I can't believe it. I bought a little one of his paintings a couple of years ago of children on a bus but he's gotten way out of my range."

"He's my daddy," Bonnie Blue said.

"Abraham's your daddy?"

"Abraham Butler. That's my daddy." Bonnie Blue pointed to the hair on the painting. "You see that? That's his real hair. I said, 'Daddy, this is for a friend of mine,' and he said, 'Hand me the scissors, Bonnie Blue.' "

I wiped my eyes with a napkin and held the painting to me. "It's the best present I've ever gotten," I said. "I may have to sleep with it."

"Well, watch that hair. I don't know how good it's on there. Daddy uses whatever's around."

"That's the most special thing of all," I said. "I'll be careful."

Bonnie Blue gathered up the wrappings.

"So Abraham is the man who got so carried away during *Gone with the Wind* that your mama got pregnant with you."

"Tell me I'm not glad. My sisters' names are Myrtice, Viola, and Gladys."

I held the picture out to look at it again.

"He has to use that cane all the time now," Bonnie Blue said. "Sometimes a walker. He still gets around, though. He's eighty-four."

"I'd love to meet him," I said.

"Anytime. About all he does is sit there and paint. Keeps us busy finding the stuff for him to paint on."

"Mary Alice is going to have a fit," I said. "She and I are going to a gallery opening tonight for the Outsiders."

"At Mercy Armistead's?"

"I think so. Why?"

"We'll be there. My brother, James, and I are taking Daddy."

"That's wonderful," I said. "We'll see you there."

"And I've got a picture for Mary Alice, too."

"Does it have real hair?"

"No."

"Good."

Our lunch came just then and we each buttered two orange rolls. Just as I took my first bite of chicken salad, though, I felt a presence looming over me. I looked up into the blinking chest of Mrs. Santa Claus.

"What are you two doing here?" Mary Alice said.

"Having lunch," I said. I'm not sure Bonnie Blue believed it was Sister. Her fork was frozen halfway to her mouth.

"You are not. You brought Bonnie Blue to see me in this outfit, didn't you? Well, I don't care. I'm getting used to it." Mary Alice pulled up a chair and helped herself to a roll. "I'm starving. Bill keeps getting arrested for shoplifting. Half the children in Birmingham are going to be traumatized for life if the security guards don't quit grabbing Santa Claus.'' She took a bite of roll. ''Hey, Bonnie Blue.''

''What's he shoplifting?'' I wanted to know.

''Nothing, Patricia Anne. Bill's not a *thief.* Something on his outfit keeps setting off alarms every time he walks through the rest room doors. He's really getting upset about it, poor baby.''

Bonnie Blue looked at Mrs. Claus's chest. ''Is he electrified, too?''

''No. It's a tag somewhere on the outfit. I told him to just quit going to the bathroom, but he says some of those kids are *big*.'' Mary Alice drew a huge box with her hands and at the same time discovered my painting. ''Oh, my. That can't be an Abraham.''

''Yes, it can,'' I said, pulling the picture out so Sister could see it. ''He's Bonnie Blue's daddy.''

''Are you serious?'' She held the picture up. ''Bonnie Blue, this is wonderful. Is it for sale?''

''It's mine,'' I said. ''Bonnie Blue gave it to me. That's his real hair.''

''I've got one for you, too, Mary Alice, but I didn't think I'd see you today.''

''Mrs. Santa hits all the malls at Christmastime,'' I said.

Mary Alice kicked my foot. ''I'm helping Bill,'' she explained to Bonnie Blue. ''I just wish they wouldn't keep arresting him. It's unnerving.''

''Gives you a chance to stand by your man,'' I said, moving my foot before she could get to it.

''Shut up, Mouse.'' She picked up a spoon and helped herself to the chicken salad on my plate. ''Umm. That's good.''

''Where's Bill now?'' Bonnie Blue asked.

''Taking off his outfit. This is our lunch break. They have a cute sign that says we've gone to feed the reindeer.'' She took another bite of my salad.

''Bonnie Blue's going to be at the gallery opening tonight,'' I said, moving my plate as far as I could from Sister's reach.

"That's great." She held the picture up again. "Why didn't you tell us Abraham was your daddy, Bonnie Blue?"

"It just didn't come up."

"Well, I know you're proud of him. He's getting more famous every day, you know."

"Seems like it."

"And I can't wait to see my picture."

"I'll bring it tonight," Bonnie Blue promised.

"Yours doesn't have Abraham's hair on it," I said.

Just then, fortunately, Bill came into the tea room. He's a handsome man, large but not paunchy, with a ruddy complexion and a lot of white hair. Even at seventy-two, he can turn women's heads, a fact that was obvious as he walked toward us through the lunch crowd at the restaurant.

"Hey, Patricia Anne. Hey, Bonnie Blue." Bill put his hand on Sister's shoulder, a gesture which didn't escape me. Her hand went up to cover his.

"Unh-huh," I said to myself. This was beginning to look serious. Mr. Bill Adams just might be husband number four, though he didn't fit the mold: Mary Alice's three husbands had all been at least twenty-five years older than she was and extremely wealthy. And she had had a child by each. At sixty-five I suppose it was time to break the pattern. There weren't too many available men twenty-five years older, she would have to be a biblical character to give birth, and she had more money than she knew what to do with from the first three.

Bonnie Blue and I both greeted Bill, and I showed him my painting, which he admired.

"I can't believe you didn't tell us Abraham was your daddy," he said to Bonnie Blue. "I have a sweatshirt with one of his snowmen on it."

"He'll be at the gallery tonight," Mary Alice said. "You want to come with Patricia Anne and I?"

"Me," I corrected. "Come with Patricia Anne and *me*." I automatically jerked my leg back so Mary Alice couldn't make contact, so all I got was a dirty look.

"Can't, Babe. I'm playing poker tonight, remember?" Bill

patted her shoulder. "Come on, let's leave these ladies to their lunch and go find a McDonald's."

"Only if you'll order a McLean," Mary Alice said.

Babe? A McLean? "What's with them?" I asked Bonnie Blue as they walked out of the restaurant holding hands. "They're looking mighty cozy."

"Don't ask me," she said. "I'm too old to know everything."

I laughed and pulled my plate back in front of me. "Do you have time to come look at the coat I'm thinking about getting Haley for Christmas?"

"One more orange roll," she said.

I love malls at Christmastime. Rosedale was especially pretty with Christmas trees sparkling with tiny lights down both sides of the wide corridor of the first floor and the balcony of the second. Santa's throne was in the center of the food court, and children were milling around, waiting for Santa to finish feeding his reindeer. It was crowded, but not as crowded as it would be the next week. I had no trouble maneuvering with the picture.

Bonnie Blue and I went into Macy's and headed toward the coat department.

"I saw it out at the Galleria," I explained, "but I'm sure they'll have it here, too."

And they did. A white trench coat made out of a light wool gabardine that would be perfect for our southern winters. I had seen Haley admiring it in the Christmas catalog and I thought, Why not? It had been two years since her husband Tom's death, two years when all she seemed to be interested in was her work as a scrub nurse in an open-heart unit. Recently, though, she seemed to be coming out of her shell. She was beginning to take an interest in clothes again and had even had a few dates with Sheriff Reuse.

I looked at the price tag again; it was way over my budget.

"That's beautiful. What size does she wear?" Bonnie Blue asked.

"Six petite. Same as me."

Bonnie Blue shook her head. "No way you and Mary Alice could be sisters."

"We were born at home, Bonnie Blue."

"But whose home?"

"I look like Mama, blond and little, and Sister looks like Daddy, big and brunette."

"Mary Alice was brunette?"

"Best I can remember."

Bonnie Blue took the painting from me. "Try the coat on," she said.

It did exactly what I had known it would. The material curved to my body in all the right places. Just as it would Haley's. Even my mousy hair seemed to pick up highlights.

"Buy it for yourself," Bonnie Blue said. "That thing's a work of art."

"I'll just borrow it," I said, whipping out my charge card without another moment's hesitation. Sixteen more presents to buy and I was already over budget. Lord, I love Christmas!

TWO

I drove home through the mildness of the early winter day. Not all the leaves had fallen from the trees, and there were still a few splashes of color, the deep of the last reds and oranges. Cold weather up north was poised, waiting to pour over us. But not yet. Sister and I have lived here all our lives and have never seen a white Christmas. Which is just as well, considering what happens in Birmingham when a few flakes of snow fall. Old Vulcan, the god of the forge up there on Red Mountain, looks down on a totally paralyzed city on one side and moons an equally paralyzed one on the other. Lights go out; roads are impassable. When the citizens of this very southern town sing ''White Christmas,'' they keep their fingers crossed.

I stopped by the Piggly Wiggly and picked up a barbecued chicken and some tossed salad. A couple of potatoes in the microwave, and supper would be done. Where had all the wonderful fast foods and salad bars been when I was teaching and raising three children? Back then I'd get home from school and start cooking. Of course, there were some shortcuts then, too. My daughter-in-law, Lisa, is still begging me for my cherry pie recipe that Alan remembers as being remarkable and which I am embarrassed to tell her consists of Jiffy Pie Crust Mix and Lucky Leaf Cherry Pie Filling. So I tell her I'm still trying to remember all the ingredients. She knows I'm lying but forgives me, probably thinking it's some great secret like the formula for Coca-Cola and that someday I will break down and confess all. Maybe I should. A slice of that pie with a dab of Cool Whip is something no boy should miss, and Lisa and Alan have two, our only grand-children. Fred Jr., at thirty-nine, is not married but is living with a woman named Celia who is startlingly lovely and startlingly strange. She can, so she claims, put a "hex" on people. My darling husband made out a list of names and sent it to her with a note saying "Not too much." So far all of them are still healthy and still beating Fred at golf and pinochle. He says he's going to drop Celia another note say-ing "Just a tad more." Somehow, I don't think Celia and Freddie are planning on children. And Haley, who does want children badly, lost her beloved Tom to a drunk driver.

When I got home, I walked around with the painting, fi-nally deciding that it would look great on the den wall where we could also see it from the kitchen. I hung Haley's coat carefully in the guest bedroom closet and straightened up the house some before I went out to take Woofer for his late-afternoon walk. Lights were coming on when we got back. I fed him and went in to fix our own supper. We would have to eat early since I was going to the gallery opening with Mary Alice.

The message light was blinking on the telephone. I turned it on and heard Sister's voice: "His beard, Mouse."

His beard? Bill's Santa Claus beard?

Fred came in while I was trying to figure out what she was talking about. So at sixty-three he has a little paunch and maybe not quite as much hair. He still looks mighty good to me. He leaned over and kissed me.

"Listen," I said, running the tape back.

Mary Alice's voice said, "His beard, Mouse."

Fred patted me on the behind and said, "What's the prob-lem? That's just Mary Alice."

"But I don't know what she's talking about."

"I never do." Fred went to the refrigerator and got a beer.

"Maybe it's about Bill getting arrested," I said.

"Bill got arrested?"

"Not really. Just sort of." I explained about Mrs. Santa and her chest that lit up, and Bill's job at the mall where he set off alarms, and lunch with Bonnie Blue and the Abraham picture, and Haley's coat. I left the price of the coat out.

"Where's the picture?" Fred asked.

I went into the den and he followed me.

"Isn't this wonderful?" I said, holding it up. "An Abraham. That's his real hair, too. He cut it off and glued it on."

Fred looked at the picture. "His feet are going the same way," he said. "And how come his nose starts in his hair?"

"He's a primitive painter, Fred. One of the best folk artists in the state. You'd pay a thousand dollars for this painting in a gallery in Nashville or Atlanta."

"No, I wouldn't." Fred took the picture from me. "Where are you going to hang it?"

"I thought right here"—I pointed—"so we could see it from the kitchen."

"I don't think so," Fred said. He looked at the picture more carefully. "There's a pop-top opener here for a hanger and it's not even in the middle. I'll put a regular hanger on it tonight while you're gone and we'll decide where to put it."

I snatched the picture back. "You'll do no such thing! That pop-top hanger is part of the authenticity. Part of the charm, damn it. Don't you dare touch it."

"Well, Lord, Patricia Anne. It looks funny."

"Put a finger on my painting and you'll pull back a nub!" I clutched the painting to me, being careful not to smush the hair, and marched back into the kitchen. I propped my treasure carefully against the table and began to scrub the potatoes.

In a few minutes, Fred was standing in the den door. "Well, look, honey. I didn't mean to make you mad. It's just not a real pretty picture, that's all."

I didn't answer, and he took a few steps into the kitchen.

"I'll hang it for you tonight, okay? Right there in the den. You just tell me where."

I nodded reluctantly.

"Just one thing." By this time he had made it over to the table and was looking at the picture. "Can I move the pop-top to the middle so it'll hang straight?"

Mary Alice blew the horn for me at seven o'clock, right on time. She is always punctual, a trait that doesn't match the rest of her personality and one I'm grateful for. When I slid into the car, she wanted to know which shoes I had on.

"Taupe. Okay?"

"Just so they're not those winter white."

"Shut up about my shoes, Mary Alice. I'll wear what I want."

"Temper, temper."

We rode without talking for a few blocks. Mary Alice was halfway singing, halfway humming "Joy to the World."

"Fred like your picture?" she asked as we turned up the interstate ramp.

"He wanted to know why both feet were at a ninety-degree angle turned to the left."

"Fred has no imagination." She blended easily into the traffic. "That's why he needs you."

"He does, too, have an imagination."

"No, he doesn't. And you don't have any common sense, and that's why you need him."

"Of course I have common sense. A lot of it." A light was beginning to dawn. "You've been watching a lot of Oprah, haven't you?"

"Bill and I are taking a course at UAB called 'The Real You.' I'm the ETJ type and so is Bill. That's extroverted, thinking, judgmental." She looked over at me. "You're introverted, intuitive, feeling. Sure as anything. And Fred's ITJ, I'll bet you."

"Hey," I said, "we get along. Okay?"

"Of course you do, and that's why."

Mary Alice went on explaining the personality tests she and Bill had taken, and I looked out of the window and let my mind drift. We were on part of the highway that is elevated above downtown and I could see the decorated trees sparkling in the park at the library, and the Sonat Building that has colored blinds in certain windows to create a seasonal picture. On one side is a Christmas tree, on one a stocking. A third side has a wreath on it, and the fourth side has "Joy" spelled in huge letters. Fred and I flew in from Philadelphia once just before Christmas and we could see that building's Christmas greeting miles before we landed.

"He tends not to notice things, though." Sister was still talking about Bill and the personality tests. "That's why the alarms kept going off. I said, 'Bill,' I said, 'how come you didn't notice that big chunk of plastic in that beard? It had to be hitting you on the chest.' You know how big those things are. And he said he thought it was supposed to be there." Mary Alice turned on her right turn signal and we exited the interstate. "I can't imagine what one of those plastic shoplifting things was doing on a Santa Claus outfit anyway. Doesn't make sense."

I agreed that it didn't.

"Start watching for Sixth Avenue, Mouse. What's this? Fourth?"

"Yes," I said. Actually, I didn't know. I didn't have on my glasses. But if I'd said I couldn't see the street signs, I would have gotten a lecture on contact lenses, which I had tried once and kept losing.

There was no question of our finding the place. The Mercy Armistead Gallery was located in an old bottling plant that someone had been smart enough to divide into spaces for boutiques and gift shops. Several artists had studios there, and there was at least one other gallery. The building looked festive with my kind of Christmas lights strung around it, and the parking lot was almost full.

"This is great," Mary Alice said. "Mercy's got a good turnout."

"Who is she, anyway?"

"You know who she is, Patricia Anne. Her mother was

Betty Bedsole. Remember? The Miss Alabama that married that big movie guy."

"Oh. Okay."

"Anyway, she used to spend her summers here with her grandparents. You know the Bedsole Steel Company? That's her family. And about a year ago she moved here for good. You obviously don't read the society page."

"Am I missing something?"

Mary Alice ignored this. "I met her a couple of times at fund-raisers and things, and now that she's moved here, she's on the Museum Board of Directors with me. She's real interested in folk art. Thinks the Outsiders are the hottest thing since sliced bread."

"Is that what she said? How old is this woman?"

Mary Alice got out and slammed the door. "It just so happens I was planning on buying your Christmas present here. Don't push your luck."

I hopped out and rushed in behind her.

My first impression of the gallery was a riot of color, so much color that it was dizzying. The soft gray of the walls and floors couldn't mute the vibrancy of the quilts and paintings that hung there. And the cheerfulness of the works was reflected by the people admiring them. Christmas music played softly while glasses clinked. This was a party. Merry Christmas!

Mary Alice held up her arms as if she were blessing the gathering. "Would you look at this, Mouse!"

"Welcome, ladies. Would you sign our book, please?" The voice belonged to a beautiful young woman with very black shiny hair cut like a flapper's, straight bangs that ended just above black eyebrows, and straight sides that were longer than the back and which swung against her cheek. She could have been Rudolph Valentino's co-star. The gray, floor length knit sheath she wore showed a body that was as sleek as her head.

"I'm Claire Moon," she said, holding out a very white hand.

"Mary Alice Crane," Sister said, shaking the proferred

hand, "and my sister, Patricia Anne Hollowell."

"Mrs. Hollowell," Claire Moon said. "I was Claire Needham. You taught me about twelve years ago."

This happens frequently when you've taught school as long as I have. Sometimes I remember the students, sometimes I don't. But I am seldom so astonished at what has happened to them that my mouth falls open.

Claire Needham Moon took pity on me. "I know I've changed a lot." She laughed a little tinkly laugh.

"Just your hair," I said. We both knew I was lying.

"Your hair is fantastic," Sister said.

Claire Moon ran both hands over her sleek head. "Delta," she said, "at Delta Hairlines. She can do anything."

I was still confused at Claire's metamorphosis. I had no idea what she was talking about. She got her hair done on a plane?

"I'll have to look her up," Sister said.

"You'll be pleased." Claire handed Sister a pen. "When you sign the book, just make yourselves at home. Mercy's around here somewhere. It's good seeing you, Mrs. Hollowell, Mrs. Crane." She seemed to fade away into the gray carpet and gray walls like the Cheshire cat. Only it was her white face we continued to see for a while.

"Who's she?" Sister asked. "She's gorgeous."

"When I taught her she was Clarissey Mae Needham, one of the most pitiful children you could imagine. Came from a very abusive family, alcoholic father, mother totally unable to protect herself or the children. Youth Services finally took the children away, and by the time I taught her, she was in a foster home. Timid, frail. Cried all the time."

"Are you sure it's the same one?"

"Hard to believe. But I hope so. I've often wondered about that poor child. The boys, and the girls, too, used to tease her, saying, 'Clarissey may, Clarissey may not.' Then one day she handed in a paper that just had 'Claire Needham' on it."

"She'd had enough."

"She'd had more than enough."

"Well, bless her heart, she's a knockout now. I'm going to look Delta up. Don't you think my hair would look good like that?"

"You mean black?"

"Why not?"

I've learned it's best not to answer these questions. "Let's go find Bonnie Blue," I said.

The floor of the gallery was crowded, but people were gathered in groups so it was easy to move around. I spotted some of Abraham's work against the far wall, and we worked our way over. Bonnie Blue wore a bright blue caftan and was standing guard over her frail old father, who was sitting in a chair with a glass of champagne in his hand.

"Hey, y'all," Bonnie Blue said. "This is my daddy, Abraham Butler. Daddy, this is Patricia Anne Hollowell and Mary Alice Crane. They're sisters."

Abraham Butler tilted his head back so he could study us through the bottoms of his bifocals. "Can't be."

"We were born at home," Mary Alice said. "Same mama, same daddy."

"No, no. It's just surprising to see two such beautiful young ladies in one family."

Behind him, Bonnie Blue rolled her eyes and made a shoveling motion.

"Why, Mr. Butler." Mary Alice beamed. "What a nice thing to say."

"Call me Abe," he said.

I love the way old Southern men flirt. It's an art form I'm afraid is dying out and which, when it is gone, will leave the world less fun. Even men in their sixties like Fred haven't mastered it. Chances are the younger men would have learned from the old masters if they had realized how wildly successful it is. I've always figured this as part of Mary Alice's fascination for older men.

"Abe," she said, taking the hand that wasn't holding the champagne. "Now, you just call me Mary Alice."

Bonnie Blue looked at me and grinned. "You want some

food, Daddy? Patricia Anne and I are going to go get some refreshments.''

"Just anything," Abe Butler said.

"Me, too," said my sister. "And bring me some champagne."

"They'll be busy a while," Bonnie Blue said as we headed across the gallery to the food table.

"Which one is Mercy Armistead?" I asked her. "Mary Alice knows her, but I don't."

"You can't miss her." Bonnie Blue looked around. "She's got red hair she wears in long curls kind of like Miss Pitty Pat. Sort of strange-looking, but pretty. But when Daddy and I got here she looked like the Bride of Frankenstein. You remember that movie?"

"The one with Elsa somebody that Charles Laughton was married to?"

"Yeah. The one where her hair stands straight out. I expect Mercy's still somewhere trying to comb it."

"What happened?"

"Some kind of curling mousse she used."

"I'll bet it was the extra curly. I bought some by accident once and it was like glue."

"You poor thing." Bonnie Blue grinned, running her hand over her elegant modified Afro. "That's Mercy's husband, Thurman Beatty." She motioned toward a large, blond man who looked to be in his early forties and who had the thick neck of a professional athlete. He was walking around with a bottle of champagne, filling glasses.

"I remember him!"

"Sure you do. Mr. Roll Tide. Yeah, Alabama."

"He was great."

"Sure was."

Fred would have loved seeing Thurman Beatty. Mention the name, and he still goes into a harangue about how Thurman was gypped out of the Heisman.

"And that's Mercy's aunt Liliane Bedsole."

I looked around.

"The old lady with the stiff face," Bonnie Blue added. "And orange hair."

Aunt Liliane was easy to spot. She was talking to a middle-aged man dressed in a jacket that was so red his face and bald head glowed pink.

"How many face-lifts do you reckon she's had?" I asked, looking at Aunt Liliane.

"I doubt she closes her eyes to sleep." Bonnie Blue giggled. "That's Ross Perry, the art critic, she's talking to. He's writing a book about the Outsiders. He's been over to the house to talk to Daddy."

We had reached the refreshment table.

"Would you look at this!" Bonnie Blue said. "I think I'm going to have to splurge tonight." She took a plate and helped herself to strawberry cheesecake, pecan pie, and blueberry trifle. "Fruits and nuts," she said. "Not too far off my diet."

I had just eaten a big supper, but everything on the table looked delicious. I took some strawberries dusted with sugar. Bonnie Blue eyed my selection thinking, I knew, anorexia. So I filled the plate up with little quiches and nuts and sandwiches. Mary Alice liked to eat off my plate anyway.

"Hey, Bonnie Blue. Where's James?" We turned and saw Thurman Beatty standing behind us.

"He'll be here in a little while." Bonnie Blue introduced us. "My brother James and Thurman played football together," she explained.

"Best tight end Alabama ever had." Thurman held out the champagne bottle. "Y'all got glasses?"

"Not yet."

"I'll get you some, then." He disappeared for a moment and then was back with two fluted glasses and a big grin. "Ladies."

I'm allergic to alcohol, but I took the glass for Mary Alice. I probably would have taken it, anyway, Thurman Beatty was so charming. Maybe I shouldn't write the younger generation off just yet.

"Where's Mercy?" Bonnie Blue asked.

"Around. Wheeling and dealing." Someone called Thurman's name. "Tell James I want to see him when he gets here."

"He's a pretty good tight end himself," Bonnie Blue said, watching him walk away. I agreed.

Mary Alice had found a chair somewhere and pulled it up beside Abe Butler. They were deep in conversation when we came up. I handed her the champagne and told her she could eat off my plate.

"Thanks," she said, not even looking my way. I took the strawberries, put the plate on her lap, and walked around the gallery, munching and admiring.

Quilts can hold their own in any art gallery or museum. The ones I particularly admired that night were what the artist called "story quilts." Appliquéd, embroidered, and even painted on the patchwork quilts were historic figures or scenes of family life such as a picnic or children playing in a yard. I yearned for one called "The '60s" with Martin Luther King and John and Robert Kennedy greeting Freedom Riders as they got off a bus. From the window of the bus, Rosa Parks looked out with an expression of surprise on her face. I checked the price and discovered that the Outsiders were learning the value of their work. Which was as it should be. I would just have to take the lady's name and start saving my money.

"Finding what you want, Mrs. Hollowell?" Claire Moon stood beside me.

"Everything's beautiful, Claire. Do you work here?"

"I'm Mercy's assistant."

"Do you like your work?"

Her pale face became animated for the first time. "I love it." She smiled. "Mercy is an artist herself, you know, probably better known in Europe than here. That'll change, though."

"But she grew up here in Birmingham?"

"Her mother did, and Mercy visited a lot. Birmingham is Thurman's home, though."

"And he's delighted to be here after being dragged all

over the globe for years.'' The speaker who had come up behind us was a tall, thin woman with delicate features and reddish gold hair pulled back into a single long braid. She reminded me of a young Vanessa Redgrave.

Claire Moon introduced us and I congratulated Mercy on the gallery and the showing.

"I'm proud of it,'' she said. "But Claire did most of the show.''

Claire looked startled and pleased. "Oh, Mercy, you know I didn't.''

Mercy put her arm around Claire's shoulders. "Now, Claire, you're the one who located most of these artists.'' There was a slight pause before the word *artists*. Enough to catch my attention and dim the smile on Claire's face. Enough to make me immediately defensive.

"I've never seen more beautiful art,'' I said. "I think it's a shame the Outsiders' talents aren't appreciated more.''

"Of course.'' Mercy Armistead looked straight at me with eyes not green, not brown, but an amber color somewhere in between.

I gave her back my schoolteacher look, which still works like a charm.

"Well,'' she said, "let me mingle.'' She patted Claire on the shoulder, said "It was nice meeting you, Mrs. Hollowell,'' and disappeared into the crowd.

"So much for folk art,'' I said, watching Mercy greet a couple who had just come in.

"She's really very nice, Mrs. Hollowell. She's just still in a tizzy because there were so many last-minute things to do. The caterer was late, and she was in a rush to get ready. And then her hair got all messed up with people already beginning to arrive.'' Two vertical lines had appeared between Claire's black eyebrows.

"Don't worry about it,'' I said. "I guarantee you everybody here is impressed with the exhibit. Come let me show you the quilt I'd love to buy. All I need is a line of credit from AmSouth Bank.''

The lines disappeared and she smiled. "It must be one of Leota Wood's." •

"Does the gallery get a certain percentage?"

"Forty, usually. Mercy needs the money like she needs a hole in her head, though. Her father is Samuel Armistead, the movie producer."

"Claire, Claire. Claire." To my surprise, Claire was suddenly airborne and hoisted over a large black man's shoulder. "Where's the hooch, Claire, the real stuff? Thurman says you got some."

"Jack Daniel, Claire. Mercy's got it hidden somewhere. Here, James, throw her to me."

James tossed the squealing Claire lightly into Thurman's outstretched arms. "Now throw her back." Bonnie Blue's brother was a giant of a man dressed in a conservative dark suit and a Mickey Mouse Christmas tie.

"No! I'll tell." Claire's white face showed a tinge of pink. I could tell she was enjoying the game, that it was a familiar one.

Thurman set her down. "Bourbon, Claire. A man's drink."

"Looks like you've already been into it."

Thurman moved to pick her up again.

"No!" She jumped back, straightened her dress, and ran her hand over her hair. "I'll get it for you."

"My man!" James slapped Thurman on the shoulder and they followed Claire through a side door.

Mary Alice was cruising the room and Bonnie Blue was showing one of Abe's paintings to a prospective buyer when I got back. I thanked the old man for the picture Bonnie Blue had given me and told him how much I admired his work.

"You got any extra plywood?" he asked.

I told him I didn't, but that I would be on the lookout for some.

"Plywood paints good," he said. "Don't bend like canvas."

I told him I could see that was an advantage.

"Cardboard's okay. You got some, I can use it."

I nodded and looked around for Sister. My feet were beginning to hurt.

"A drink would be nice," Abe said.

"What?"

He held up his glass. "Champagne."

I took the glass and started for the refreshment table. On the way, I spotted Sister admiring Leota Wood's quilts and made a detour.

"You said you were buying my Christmas present," I said. "I want that one." I pointed to the one titled "The '60s."

Mary Alice went over and looked at the price. "I'll tell Fred," she said.

I assured her I wouldn't hold my breath.

She looked at the glass in my hand. "For Abe," I explained.

"Lord, he's inhaling that stuff. Someone's going to have to carry him home."

"His sweet chariot has just swung low," I said. "His name is James."

Mary Alice looked at me. "Patricia Anne," she said, "that was *so* bad."

Actually, I thought it was kind of clever.

"Come look at these wood carvings," she said. "They're little totem poles made out of chair legs."

We worked our way through the crowd. I spotted Mercy talking to her aunt Liliane Bedsole, the woman with orange hair. I poked Sister in the back. "I met Mercy. I got the impression she doesn't think the Outsiders are such hot artists. I wonder why she's opening her gallery with a showing of their work."

We had arrived at the wood carvings. Most of them were charming, brightly colored single figures. Some of them, however, were definitely sexual. And humorous. The artist had painted expressions on the entwined figures' faces that said plainly, "Well, how about this!" On nearly every carving was a small pink "Sold" tag.

"Those pink tags are why. It's going to be a sellout."

Mary Alice picked up one of the figures. "Does this remind you of Bill?"

"In your dreams."

"Sure it does. I've got to have this." Sister turned the carving over and looked at the price. "Wow."

"Claire Moon said Mercy didn't need money."

"And you said Claire was one of your advanced students?" Sister opened her purse, took out her checkbook, and patted it fondly. "Ha! Ask me, the girl hasn't got biddy brains." And with that, my sister proceeded to buy two carved chair legs which kept falling over and which the artist swore were a pair.

Three

Fred was sound asleep when I got home. I undressed quietly and went into the den to read and wind down. By the time I slipped in beside him, he was snoring slightly and it was almost one o'clock. I snuggled against him and didn't know anything else until I heard the sound of the shower. Seven-twenty. I yawned and turned over, trying to will myself back into the dream I had been having, which had been a good one and which was already gone. No use. I was awake.

I turned on the TV to see what the weather was going to do and got the local news. "An apparent heart attack," the announcer was saying. As I leaned over to get my robe, I glanced at the screen and did a double take. Mercy Armistead was smiling at me. I grabbed the remote and turned up the volume.

"Ms. Armistead's body was found by her husband, former football great Thurman Beatty, at the gallery Ms. Armistead owned and where she had hosted a gala opening just last night."

Fred came into the room with a towel around him.

"Mercy is dead," I said.

"Are you quoting Shakespeare or just making a statement?" Fred did a playful bump-and-grind strip.

"Get dressed," I said. "A lot you know about Shake-speare."

He grinned and stepped into his shorts, making a little flipping motion as he pulled them up.

"The woman whose gallery we went to last night. Mercy Armistead. She had a heart attack and died."

"How old was she?"

"I don't know. Mid-thirties, maybe. Her husband's Thurman Beatty."

"Good Lord!" The mention of Thurman Beatty's name got Fred's attention. He sat down on the side of the bed. "Was she all right at the party?"

"Seemed to be. I never met her before."

"A heart attack?"

"That's what they said. An apparent heart attack."

"That's awfully young." Fred was thinking the same thing I was. That was the age of our children. He got up, went to the closet, and took out a shirt and pants. I reached over and got the phone and dialed Sister's number.

"Hello," Bill Adams said.

I looked at the clock. Seven-thirty. That answered that question.

"May I speak to Mary Alice, Bill?"

"She's still asleep, Patricia Anne."

"Well, tell her Mercy's dead and to call me soon as she wakes up."

"Mercy's dead. Got it." There was silence for a few seconds.

"Bill?"

"Just looking for something to write with. There's nothing here to write with."

"I'll call her later," I said. "Bill's at Sister's," I told Fred, who by now was buttoning his shirt.

"Are you surprised?"

"Nope." I started to get up. "You want some cereal?"

"I'll get it and I'll get you a cup of coffee. How about that?"

"How about you put the towel on again."

He laughed and headed toward the kitchen. "You missed your chance."

I went into the bathroom, automatically put the toilet seat down like every other female in America was doing that morning, splashed some cold water on my face, brushed my teeth, and was back in the bed by the time Fred arrived with the coffee.

"You think Mercy's death would be in the paper?" I asked.

"What time did she die?"

"I don't know. They said Thurman found the body at the gallery."

"Depends on how early it was. I'll stick the paper in the kitchen door for you."

"Thanks." I sipped coffee while Fred ate cereal. "You want to go Christmas shopping tonight?"

"We need to, don't we?"

Pictures of wars, floods, and famines flashed across the TV screen while we sat in our small bedroom and talked of children and Christmas presents. Keeping the world at bay. Keeping our fingers crossed.

"I've got to go," Fred said. "The traffic's going to be impossible." He leaned over and kissed me. On the way out of the door, he turned. "Dying in your thirties is so unfair."

Tears sprang to my eyes. I was thinking about Mercy, of course, but I was also thinking of our son-in-law, Tom Buchanan, who was thirty-four when he died. "Yes," I said.

The phone rang while I was getting my second cup of coffee.

"Mercy's dead? Did Bill get the message right? What happened?"

"I heard it on the local news. They said she died of an apparent heart attack at the gallery and Thurman Beatty found her."

"I can't believe this," Mary Alice said. "She was fine when we left. What did she do? Just keel over?"

"How do I know? I never met the woman until last night,

and the only time I talked to her she was in a snit about her bad hair.''

''Her hair looked fine.''

''Bonnie Blue said she looked like the Bride of Frankenstein when they got there. Some kind of curling mousse she'd used.''

''Maybe that's what killed her,'' Mary Alice said. ''Maybe she was allergic to the stuff and had one of those fatal attacks like Molly Dodd's boyfriend had just before they got married. Remember that? She was pregnant and they were going to the opera. What do you call it? Some kind of shock.''

''Anaphylactic. And who died of it?''

''On *The Days and Nights of Molly Dodd*. You remember. Didn't have a laugh track. Her boyfriend.''

''Of course. Ate some shrimp by mistake.''

''Was it shrimp? You ought to be able to spot shrimp.''

''Maybe it was something else,'' I said. ''You die right away with that stuff, though. If Mercy was allergic to the hair spray she'd have been dead when we got there.''

''Well, this is just unbelievable. And so sad.''

''Did she have any children?''

''I don't think so. I've never heard any mentioned.''

We were both silent for a moment, thinking.

''You got anything special planned today?'' Sister asked.

''No. I was thinking about getting the Christmas decorations down from the attic.''

''Then let's go see Fay and May.'' These precious identical twins belong to Mary Alice's daughter, Debbie. They are almost two years old and are their grandmother's heart. Mine, too. Mary Alice says a trip to see the babies is better than Prozac. She's even resigned herself to the fact that Debbie, a successful single lawyer in her mid-thirties, opted for a sperm bank instead of a husband.

''What about Mrs. Claus? The sex slave?'' I asked.

''Oh, God. I forgot that. Damn.''

''Maybe I could bring them to see Santa Claus.''

''That would totally confuse them.''

''Kids are always confused about Santa Claus anyway.''

"That's true. I'll check with Debbie and call you back."

I got the paper out of the kitchen door and looked to see if there was anything about Mercy's death. There wasn't. I put on my sweats, grabbed a handful of dog treats, and went to walk Woofer.

The weather was changing. The cold front that had been sitting over the Midwest was rapidly approaching. High clouds of moisture from the Gulf were already dimming the sunlight. By nightfall, we would probably have thunderstorms.

I walked along and thought of the party the night before. It had been so cheerful, so fitting for the holidays. I thought of Claire Moon and how she had changed, and of Thurman Beatty. Had he loved his wife deeply? Was he devastated by her death? I would call Bonnie Blue when I got home and see if she knew any more of the details.

And then I saw it, the mother lode of plywood! A neighbor making a nativity scene had piled the leftovers by his garbage can. I looped Woofer's leash around my arm and picked up several pieces. The Wise Men were empty spaces surrounded by plywood. As were the manger and Mary and Joseph. It was slightly eerie that they were so recognizable. A little Christmas Zen.

There was enough for two trips. Abe Butler was going to love this.

"We're not through with our walk, old boy," I assured Woofer. Bless his heart.

As we came around the house, he started barking. "We're going back," I said as he began to pull at his leash. "Let me put this plywood down."

I was holding the pieces in front of me and the back steps were blocked from my view. When I put the wood down, though, I nearly jumped out of my skin. Sitting on the steps was what looked like a very dirty child. Woofer was barking like crazy, and I backed up a step just as the child looked up.

"It's me, Mrs. Hollowell," said Claire Moon. "I'm sorry, but I don't have anywhere else to go."

She looked, as Sister is fond of saying, like the wrath of God. Her face was streaked with mascara, the gray sheath she had worn the night before was torn and stained, and she was trying to cover her bare feet with the long skirt. "I'm sorry," she said again, and put her head down on her knees, sobbing.

"My God, Claire. What's happened?" I started toward her and nearly fell over Woofer's leash. "Wait a minute. Let me put him up." I pushed the reluctant dog inside his fence, sat down by Claire, and put my arm around her.

"I'm so cold," she whimpered.

"Are you hurt?"

"I'm just so tired and cold."

"Well, let's go in where it's warm. Do you feel like standing up?"

"Yes."

As I helped her to her feet, I could feel her whole body shaking with a hard chill. First things first, I thought. I would find out what happened later. Right now, I had to get her inside and get her warm.

I am a small woman. Fortunately, Claire was even smaller, probably five feet tall, but wraith thin. She leaned heavily on me as I got her to the den sofa and covered her with an afghan. I got the heating pad from the closet and put it under her feet, which were scratched and dirty.

"Think you can keep down some coffee?" I asked.

She nodded and closed her eyes. The lids were bluish against her black brows. She needed medical attention, I realized. We could be dealing with shock or hypothermia here.

"No doctor," she said, reading my hesitation. "Please, no doctor. I'll be okay when I get some coffee."

"I think you need some help, Claire." I reached over and smoothed her bangs back from her forehead.

"Please, Mrs. Hollowell." Tears rolled from her closed eyes. "Please. I'm already feeling better."

The quivering of her body told me she was lying, but upsetting her more wasn't going to help.

"I'll get the coffee," I said.

She sighed deeply. "Thank you."

When I got back, a matter of only a minute or two, she was asleep. For a second, it frightened me. She lay just as I had left her, on her back with the afghan covering her. Her mouth was slightly open, and tears still ran down her cheeks, but she was breathing quietly and the shaking had lessened.

"Claire?" I said softly, wondering if this was a natural sleep.

She mumbled, and turned into a semifetal position.

"You okay?"

"Don't do it," she said.

"Do what, Claire?"

She mumbled again, and put her hand under her cheek. I sat down and looked at her. Her breathing gradually deepened, and I realized this was the sleep of deep exhaustion. The best thing I could do was let her rest. While I watched, her black hair slid down over her hand. Claire Moon, I thought. Beautiful Claire Moon. Are you still Claire Needham in your dreams?

I tiptoed from the room and called Sister to tell her I couldn't bring the twins to see Santa.

"Claire Moon?" she said, when I explained. "What's wrong with her?"

"Cold and exhausted. How she got this way, I don't know."

"You didn't ask her? My Lord, Patricia Anne."

"I didn't get a chance. I thought for a few minutes I was going to have to call 911 or take her to the emergency room."

"Does she know about Mercy?"

"I have no idea."

Sister made a sound of disgust. "I can't believe that. I'll call you from the mall. Okay? Maybe by that time you'll know something."

"I'm taking the phone off the hook."

"Fine. You do that, Miss INF."

"What?" I said. "What?" But Sister was gone. I was about to dial her again when I remembered INF stood for intuitive, introverted, feeling, three personality traits that Mary Alice wouldn't be caught dead with.

I finished the cup of coffee I had fixed for Claire and called Bonnie Blue. Her brother, James, answered and said she had already left for work, that the shop was opening early during December. I asked him if he had heard about Mercy Armistead's death, and he said Thurman had called him.

"Pretty shook up," he said. "I'm going over there this morning."

"Did they know she had a heart problem?"

"Old Thurman's the one with heart problems," James said. "That's why he had to quit the NFL. Sort of ironic, isn't it?"

I agreed that it was and then remembered to tell James that I had found several pieces of plywood for Abe.

"He'll be tickled," he said.

I left the phone off the hook and went to check on Claire. She hadn't moved, so I tiptoed around the kitchen fixing cereal and toast, which I carried into the bedroom to eat.

The thought had occurred to me that Claire was distraught over Mercy's death. She had glowed the night before when she was talking about working at the gallery, and when Mercy was making her catty remarks about the Outsider artists, I was the one who had snapped back, not Claire. She had been nothing but admiring of Mercy and of Mercy's work. But how had Claire ended up on my back steps? Where was her car? Her shoes? And what about that "no place else to go" bit? She had an apartment somewhere, and a husband, presumably, since she wasn't Claire Needham anymore, but Claire Moon.

When I am upset, I lose my appetite. I tried to eat, but the cereal tasted like paper. I put the bowl down, went to the bookcase, and got out the yearbooks that Claire was in. It was startling to see her as a pale teenager with dark blond hair parted in the middle and hanging limply beside her face. No wonder I hadn't recognized her the night before. Only her eyes seemed the same, dark, with a slight oriental slant to them. A pretty girl, but one who would have faded into the crowd. Beside her picture, where honors and activities were listed, was "Art Club." That was all. Though she had been in my Advanced Placement English classes, she had not participated in debate or the literary magazine or the drama club, things that usually go hand in hand.

She had lived with foster parents. I remembered that. But had she gone to college? I had no idea, and I could have kicked myself. So many students. So many lives. I closed the books and wondered, for perhaps the millionth time, if these students had learned anything in my classes that was helping them in their lives. Had Frost made wrong choices easier to live with? Or Crane shown the true face of bravery? Had Agee taught them to deal with loss?

"For God's sake, Mouse."

Mary Alice's voice scared me so, I jumped straight up and the books went flying, landing on the floor with a thump.

"Damn it, Sister!" I hissed. "I'll bet that woke Claire up."

"I'll go see." She disappeared from the doorway but was back in a moment. "Nope."

I was picking up the books and willing my heart to slow down. "Where did you come from?"

"Home. Where do you think?"

"I mean, how did you get here so quickly?"

"I'm not dressed." Mary Alice opened her raincoat to show a short pink nightgown and a lot of Mary Alice. "Good thing I came, too. You were getting ready to have one of your existential snits, weren't you?"

"You wouldn't know an existential snit if one hit you on the head. And have you got on underpants?"

"Of course, Patricia Anne. You think I want Mama to roll over in her grave? Speaking of which, you really should lock your back door."

"What?" Trying to follow Mary Alice's thought processes is not easy.

"Anyone could come in."

I agreed that they could, indeed.

"Anyway," Mary Alice said, plumping herself onto the

bed, "I got the scoop on Mercy's death to tell you, and I wanted to check on Claire."

"You're so kind, Mrs. Claus." But I sat down to listen.

"Bonnie Blue told me and James told her and Thurman told him, so this is straight. Okay?"

I nodded.

"The last people left the gallery about eleven o'clock, and Thurman said he was going to follow Mercy home, not that that's a bad neighborhood or anything, but he didn't want her locking up and driving across town by herself. So he helped her straighten up some and went to his car thinking she was coming right out behind him. Only she didn't."

"Where was Claire?"

"James Butler took her home earlier. Mercy stayed to talk to some customers."

"I wonder if she knows Mercy's dead."

Sister shrugged. "Do you want to hear this?"

I did.

"Well, when Mercy didn't come right out, he thought she'd gotten a phone call or gone to the bathroom. Finally he went to check on her and she was lying on the floor by the door clutching her chest."

"On the floor by the door."

Mary Alice clutched her ample chest to demonstrate. "A heart attack. He called 911 and Bonnie Blue says they used the paddles and everything, but it was too late."

"And no history of heart problems."

"None," Mary Alice said. We were silent for a moment, both of us, I'm sure, picturing the seemingly healthy red-haired woman we had seen the night before circulating around her gallery, full of life.

"So, what about Claire?" Mary Alice asked.

"What do you mean, what about Claire? You saw her when you came through the den."

"I thought maybe you found out why she showed up on your doorstep."

I shook my head. "She seems to be resting quietly," I

said. "I'm not going to bother her. Whatever her problem is, it'll come out in due time."

"Hmm," Sister said. "Maybe she has fever."

"Maybe she does," I said, "but you're not going in there poking at her to see. She needs the sleep."

"Well, you must admit it's strange that you haven't seen her in years and she shows up like this."

"She saw me last night. I was on her mind."

"Maybe her husband abuses her," Mary Alice said.

I shivered, remembering how frail Claire had felt when I helped her into the house. "God, I hope not. She's had too much of that in her lifetime."

"Any at all is too much," Mary Alice said.

For once I agreed with my sister completely. "I'll find out when she wakes up," I said. "She may just be in a state of shock at Mercy's death."

"Let me know. We don't have to be at the mall until two o'clock, but I've made an appointment with Delta at Delta Hairlines for eleven."

"You haven't. You're not having your hair dyed black!"

"I told Delta I wanted her opinion."

"Ask for a second one."

"You ought to go with me, Patricia Anne. Get something done to yours."

I ran my hand through my curly gray hair. "Forget it."

Mary Alice got up from the bed and slipped her feet into white huaraches.

"Are those winter white?" I asked.

"They were the first ones I found, Miss Smart-ass!"

I followed her down the hall and into the den. We stood for a moment looking down at the sleeping Claire, who was again lying on her back.

"You think she's okay?" Mary Alice whispered.

Claire's eyes opened suddenly, widely, and she stared at us.

"The police," she said. "Oh, God. We have to call the police. Right now."

Four

Claire sat straight up and covered her face with both hands.

"Ohhh," she moaned, rocking back and forth.

"Claire," I said, "Claire." I sat on the edge of the sofa and put my arm around her, trying to soothe her. "You've just had a bad dream."

"Nooo." It was a loud breath. "Call the police."

"But why, Claire?"

Mary Alice, who had jumped a foot when Claire opened her eyes, reached for the phone on the end table. I slapped at her hand.

"What are you doing?"

"She said call the police."

I glared at Mary Alice. "Will you wait just a minute? I'm sure Claire was just having a nightmare. Weren't you, Claire?"

Claire pulled her knees up, wrapped her arms around them, and buried her face in the afghan.

"I wish I could bend like that," Sister whispered.

"Shut up," I mouthed.

"Someone tried to kill me last night." Claire's words were muffled.

"What?" Mary Alice and I both asked.

Claire lifted her head. "Tried to kill me. Last night. Somebody."

"Who?"

Claire shrugged and put her face back into the afghan.

"See?" Mary Alice said. "That's why she wanted the police."

"Claire, are you sure?" I asked.

"In my apartment. When I came in. They had a knife. I ran and I ran and I'm so scared." She whimpered like a hurt animal.

Mary Alice reached for the phone; I didn't stop her. I sat beside the terrified Claire, patted her, assured her everything would be all right. The girl's shoulders were rigid with fear. Tears came to my eyes when one of her hands came up slowly to cover mine.

"They'll be here in a few minutes," Sister said. She sat down in Fred's recliner and we looked at each other. Sisters for sixty years, we didn't need words for our conversation.

"What is going on here?" she asked with a motion of her head.

"I have no idea," I shrugged silently.

Mary Alice looked at Claire, who was still slumped over but was holding my hand.

"I'm worried," Sister said by pressing a finger to her lips.

"Me, too," I nodded.

"Claire," Mary Alice said, leaning forward. "Do you want a Valium?"

Claire nodded yes.

"I don't think that's such a good idea," I said. "She may be in shock."

"She needs something to calm her down."

"You got a Valium?"

"No, but you do. There's some in your medicine cabinet left from the Skoot 'n' Boot when you got shook up."

"Shook up? You call a fractured skull and God knows what else 'shook up'? And what were you doing in my medicine cabinet?"

"Looking for aspirin, of course."

"You know I keep the aspirin in the kitchen cabinet."

"Aspirin should be in the bathroom." Mary Alice pushed herself out of the recliner. "I'll get you a Valium, Claire."

Time was I would have stuck out my foot when Sister walked by. The urge was still there, but knowing Mary Alice, she would fall on *me* and break *my* hip. I refrained.

"I'll get you something to drink," I told Claire. "You want coffee or Coke?"

She nodded, so the decision was mine. I went into the kitchen and put a lot of ice into a glass. The coffee was decaf, but the Coke had caffeine. Maybe it would offset the Valium's effects some.

While I was pouring the Coke, Mary Alice came into the kitchen. "What is this?" she asked, holding out her palm with a pink tablet in it. "Valiums have holes in the middle. Have you been mixing up your medicines again?"

"It's generic. And I never mix up my medicines."

"You do, too. You remember that time I took what was supposed to be penicillin and it was muscle relaxant that made me sick as a dog because you had it in the wrong bottle. Remember?"

"Mary Alice," I said, "didn't that teach you a lesson about taking other people's medicine?"

"It taught me I can't trust you to keep them in the right bottle."

I got a napkin for the glass. "That's Valium, but I don't think it's such a smart idea giving her one."

"It'll make her feel better."

"I think she needs to go to the doctor." But I followed Sister back to the den, where Claire was still hunched over like a question mark.

"Here, Claire." Mary Alice handed her the pink tablet and I gave her the Coke. Except for that first glance upward, it was the first time Sister had seen Claire's dirty, mascara-streaked face. "Oh, you poor thing," she said. "Mouse, go get us a warm washrag." She picked up part of the afghan that was sliding from the sofa and straightened it. "Wouldn't that feel good, Claire? Your face and hands wiped with a warm washrag? Go get us one, Mouse.''

"You know where they are," I said. I couldn't resist it. Mary Alice turned and looked at me, and I headed for the linen closet. I wasn't gone a minute, but when I got back, Sister was quizzing Claire about her attacker. Was it a man or a woman? What kind of knife was it? What did they say? Claire's answers were little head shakes.

"For heaven's sake, Sister," I said. "The police will ask all those questions."

And they did. In about two minutes, the doorbell rang. For a moment I thought it was Bonnie Blue. The woman standing there was as large as Bonnie Blue, and her skin was as dark. But I realized my mistake immediately. This woman was much younger, maybe thirty, and dressed in a police uniform.

"Mrs. Crane?" she said. "I'm Bo Mitchell. You have a problem?''

Bo Mitchell had the most beautiful smile I have ever seen. Fred and I had poured thousands of dollars into our children's mouths trying to achieve this effect and had missed by a mile.

I explained that I was Mrs. Hollowell and that Mrs. Crane was my sister and that a friend of ours had been threatened or attacked the night before, I wasn't sure which, and was right here on my den sofa.

"May I come in?" Bo Mitchell asked.

"Of course." I realized I had been babbling like I do when I'm nervous. At least I wasn't rhyming like I do sometimes. "Right through here."

Claire was sitting up straight with her feet on the floor. She looked exactly like one of those big-eyed, dark-haired children with the sad expressions that you see painted on velvet. Sister had wiped the mascara and dirt from her face, and the pallor of her skin was startling.

"This is Officer Mitchell." I introduced Mary Alice and Claire.

"I thought you policemen always went in twos," Mary Alice said.

"Like Noah's Ark?" Bo Mitchell smiled her fantastic smile. "Not always. Depends."

"Can I get you some coffee or Coke?" I asked. Fred says if the Devil himself walked in, I would offer him refreshments. He's probably right.

"No, thank you." Officer Mitchell sat on the sofa beside Claire. "I assume the problem is yours, Ms. Moon?"

Claire nodded. "Somebody tried to kill me last night." Her voice was faint but steady. "They were in my apartment with a knife."

"Are you okay? Not hurt anywhere?"

"No. I would have been dead, though, if I'd put the night latch on."

"How's that?"

"If I'd had to stop to undo it. I heard the knife hit the door."

Mary Alice and I looked at each other. Officer Mitchell wrote something on a clipboard. "Okay," she said. "Let's get some basic information, Ms. Moon. Your address?"

"Seventeen twenty-nine Valley Trace."

"Husband?"

"He's dead. He was killed."

"Here?"

"In California. On the freeway."

I closed my eyes. I knew, from watching Haley suffer, the grief Claire had gone through.

"Your age?"

"Thirty."

"Occupation?"

"I work at an art gallery." Claire turned and faced Bo Mitchell. "Please, I'm so tired."

"I know you are and I'm sorry. This is just routine stuff we have to have, though, before we get to the problem."

Claire nodded and sighed.

"This art gallery," Officer Mitchell said, "I'll need its name."

"The Mercy Armistead Gallery."

Bo Mitchell looked up from her clipboard. "That's the one where the lady died last night?"

"Who died?" Claire's head came up.

"Mercy Armistead."

Claire looked at Mary Alice and me. "Mercy's dead?"

We nodded. "Claire," I began.

"Mercy's dead?" Her voice rose to a wail. "Oh, God. They got to Mercy." Claire stood up, her arms before her face as if warding off blows. And just as quickly as she stood, she fell. The policewoman, in a remarkably agile move, caught Claire and eased her down, saving her from hitting the floor. Sister and I rushed to help.

"Prop her feet up," Officer Mitchell said. Mary Alice grabbed pillows from the sofa and placed them under Claire's feet. I knelt beside Mary Alice and rubbed Claire's hands, which felt like ice. Her eyes were half open but the pupils weren't visible. I touched her carotid artery to see if I could feel a pulse. I could. A faint one.

Bo Mitchell reached for the phone. "Need some help here," was all I heard her say. I couldn't have agreed with her more.

The paramedics came first, accompanied by a fire truck and all of my neighbors, who had probably been watching since the police car pulled up. I didn't mind this; it wasn't idle curiosity. We are a neighborhood of older residents who have been acquaintances and friends for much of our lives. After they were assured that all was well with Fred and me, that a visiting young woman had become ill, they left. It's good to have people like that around.

Bo Mitchell led the paramedics into the den, where Mary Alice was kneeling beside a still-unconscious Claire.

"Wait a minute, wait a minute. I'm getting out of the way!" I heard Sister say.

"Can we help you up, lady?" one of the men asked.

"No. I'm fine." Sister backed away on her knees to Fred's recliner, turned, clutched the chair arms, and pulled herself up. For a moment, it could have been the chair down or Sister up. The gods smiled on Sister. She came to the door where I stood and rubbed her knees and straightened her raincoat. I had forgotten until then that she wasn't dressed.

We tried to stay out of the way and still see what was going on. Blood pressure and heart monitors were brought out.

"You need to tell them you gave her a Valium," I whispered.

"She decided not to take it," Mary Alice whispered back.

"Well, thank goodness for that. You could have killed her."

Mary Alice looked at the busy scene before us and at the still figure in the center. "I'll be back in a minute."

"Where are you going?"

Mary Alice held up the pink tablet. "To take the Valium."

One of the paramedics, with "Rogers" embroidered on his shirt pocket, came over to me. "This your daughter, ma'am?"

"She's a friend."

"Well, we're going to call an ambulance. Her blood pressure is jumping up and down like a yo-yo and her heartbeat's erratic. She's beginning to come around, and we can stabilize her pretty good, but she needs checking out."

"Could a shock have caused this?"

"You mean like an emotional shock?" The young man scratched his head. "I suppose so, but in a healthy person, the body usually sends out stress signals and then calms down. You know what I mean?"

I nodded that I did.

"This lady's signals are stuck."

I loved his simplistic explanation. Why bother with such terms as *adrenaline* and *arrhythmia*. This lady's stress signals were stuck.

"Who's her doctor?" he asked.

"I have no idea."

"Anybody you can call?"

I realized there wasn't.

"Where do you want the ambulance to take her?"

I didn't know what to say. Fred and I have insured ourselves to the hilt for medical emergencies. Had Claire? Probably not, at thirty and working as an assistant in an art gallery. I felt terrible about it, but I couldn't take on the medical bills of someone I hardly knew.

"Morgan?" the man asked, reading my thoughts, I was sure. Morgan is a charity hospital, an adequate hospital, but charity, nonetheless.

"Take her to Memorial," Mary Alice said, coming up beside me. "I'll be responsible."

It's times like this I forgive her for everything.

The ambulance arrived with much flashing of lights and wailing of sirens. The neighbors came out on their porches to watch Claire be lifted in.

"You can ride with her if you want," the young attendant told me.

Claire had wakened some, and though she hadn't spoken, she clutched my hand all the way to the ambulance.

"I'll lock up for you," Mary Alice said. "Let me go home and get dressed and I'll come to the hospital."

Officer Mitchell and the attendant shoved me up into the ambulance. It was a most ungraceful entrance, and I was glad I was still wearing my sweats.

My life has been, fortunately, a fairly uneventful one. At sixty, I had never ridden in an ambulance before. By the time we reached the hospital, I had decided that not riding in an ambulance was how I had made sixty. The driver, who had had his license for maybe a week, was a maniac. There was no other way to describe him. He sailed through intersections, sped along the shoulders of roads, shot birds at people who were frantically trying to get out of his way. And all the time, he flashed the light and blew the siren. The young man who sat in the back with Claire and me seemed unconcerned. He would check gauges and then thumb through a *People* magazine. A toothpick flipped lazily from one corner of his mouth to the other.

"Does he always drive like this?" I asked him as we went around a dozen cars and down the median.

He looked up from his *People*, took the toothpick from

his mouth, and grinned. "He could win the Indy 500."

I thought it best not to look out of the window. "Is she all right?" I motioned toward Claire, who appeared to be sleeping.

The young man squinted at the gauges. "I think so."

No use pursuing this line of conversation.

Memorial Hospital is built on a mountainside, as most of the hospitals in Birmingham are. Which means that during a snowstorm we are cut off from emergency medical care. Emergency calls go out for people with four-wheel-drive vehicles, and the radio stations broadcast calls for help. Quite a few area babies have been born in four-wheel-drive vans.

The ambulance driver careened onto the incline that led to the emergency room, sped up it, and stopped abruptly at the emergency entrance. If the gurney Claire was on hadn't been strapped down, and if I hadn't been hanging on to it for dear life, I would have been the first one into the hospital.

"Shit!" I gasped.

The attendant grinned. "Sometimes," he said, opening the door for the emergency crew rushing from the hospital.

"Don't leave me," Claire said. "Please don't leave me."

"I won't."

And I didn't for about an hour. During that time a procession of doctors and nurses filed through the cubicle Claire was assigned, trying to get her medical history.

"Any history of diabetes?" they asked. Claire looked at them blankly. "Allergies? Heart disease? Hepatitis? Cancer? Lupus? Other inflammatory diseases?" The blank look.

Then each turned to me expecting enlightenment. I had accompanied her to the hospital. It was my duty to know these things.

"Sorry," I said, actually beginning to feel guilty.

Finally, a young woman who introduced herself as Dr. Langford called me into the hall and said they were admitting Claire for observation and psychiatric evaluation. Perhaps a neurological workup.

"Someone tried to kill her last night," I said.

"That's what I heard," the doctor said casually, waving

to someone down the hall. "We'll check on it."

"You do that, Sweetie."

The startled doctor met my schoolteacher gaze. To her credit, her face flushed. "We'll take good care of her"—she glanced down at the chart—"Mrs. Hollowell."

I patted her arm. "I know you will."

"You'll need to get her admitted."

"Can I speak to her first?"

"Of course." Dr. Langford and I both went back to Claire, who seemed to be sleeping again. An IV had been inserted into her arm.

"Glucose," the doctor explained. "She was dehydrated. And a mild tranquilizer."

No way I was going to tell Mary Alice about the tranquilizer.

"Claire," I said, taking her hand, "I'm just going to get you checked in. I'll be right back."

She squeezed my hand, but her eyes didn't open.

"You know," Dr. Langford whispered, "she looks like somebody out of *Gatsby*, doesn't she?"

There just might be hope for this young doctor after all.

Memorial Hospital is where Haley works in heart surgery. The odds were against my running into her. But as I walked through the door into the emergency room lobby, there she stood, dressed in her operating room greens and drinking a diet Coke.

"Haley!"

She turned, saw me, and froze. "Mama! What's wrong? Is it Daddy?"

"No, darling. We're fine."

"Aunt Sister?"

"She's fine. I'm here with somebody you don't even know."

Haley sat down weakly in one of the blue fiberglass chairs. "Lord," she said. "Scare me to death."

"I'm sorry."

"Who is it?" She crushed the can she was holding, a habit I hate, and threw it into a wastebasket.

"A girl named Claire Moon. A former student of mine. I saw her last night at the party Sister and I went to and then she showed up sick on my steps this morning. She said somebody tried to kill her last night."

"Is she hurt?"

"I suspect the doctors think it's mostly emotional. They're going to keep her for observation, though. Do some tests. I don't have any idea what's wrong with her, to tell the truth, or why she came to me." I sat down in the chair beside Haley. "What are you doing down here?"

"Waiting for a patient with a gunshot wound they're bringing in from Anniston. The bullet's touching his heart, so we're doing the surgery."

"Lucky man," I said.

"Lucky man."

"Come for supper tonight," I said. "Vegetable lasagna."

"You've got a customer."

An ambulance pulled up to the door. "That's probably me," Haley said, jumping up and rushing to the door. I watched her oversee the patient's removal, check his vitals. As they rushed by me, she wiggled her fingers.

"That's my daughter," I told an elderly woman who was sitting across from me knitting. She didn't answer, but that was okay.

I followed the signs to the admitting office, though I knew I was going to have to wait for Mary Alice. Neurological workups and psychiatric evaluations sounded like more than Fred and I had in our combined retirement funds. Sister surprised me, though, by coming in the front door of the lobby just as I came in the side. She still had on her raincoat, but red leggings said she was dressed for her Mrs. Santa stint at the mall.

"I'll have you know I missed my appointment at Delta Hairlines," she greeted me. "Delta rescheduled it, but she wasn't at all happy about it."

"Tough," I said.

"How's Claire?"

"They're admitting her for evaluation."

''Well, of course.'' Mary Alice looked around and sniffed.
''They've got us by the short hairs here, Mouse.''

I thought of the man Haley had just rushed through the
emergency room. ''Thank God,'' I said.

Getting Claire into the hospital was not an easy thing. We
spent several minutes dealing with bureaucracy. Finally a
social worker was called in—a ''Patient Advocate,'' her
badge said, an apropos title, given her job. Somehow she
worked things out so Claire was temporarily admitted, which
didn't sound very secure, until we were forthcoming with
information and insurance cards, etc.

''What et cetera?'' Mary Alice asked.

''Just et cetera.''

We took it, though the offer was almost withdrawn when
Mary Alice asked for a pin to prick her finger so she could
sign.

Soon as that was done, she dashed for Rosedale Mall and
I went to find out where they had taken Claire. She was in
Room 492. She had on a hospital gown and was sleeping
like a baby.

''Hey,'' said a woman sitting on the bed beyond the dividing curtains. ''You her mama?''

''No.'' I picked up Claire's hand and held it.

''She's a pretty one.''

''Yes. She is,'' I agreed.

''Very sick?''

''Don't think so.''

''Me neither. Just quit breathing every now and then.''

''Well, long as you start back.''

''God's truth.''

I looked at the sleeping girl. If the tranquilizers were going
to work like this, I could go home and come back tonight. I
went to the nurses' station and asked.

''She's fine,'' the woman in charge said. ''You just leave
your number and we'll call if she needs anything.''

''Maybe I'll bring her some gowns,'' I said.

''You do that, honey.'' She smiled and picked up a chart.

I was almost at the elevator when I realized I had no way

to get home. I didn't even have money for a cab. Or to call Fred. I was about to turn around and throw myself on the mercy of the nurses when the elevator opened and Officer Bo Mitchell stepped out.

"Ms. Hollowell," she said. "How's Ms. Moon?"

"She's sleeping. They're going to run some tests."

"She by herself?"

"There's a lady in the room with her. Another patient. Why?"

"She's telling the truth. Somebody's after her, all right." Bo Mitchell pointed to some chairs by the elevator, and we sat down. "I just came from her place and it's a mess. And a slice in the door a couple of inches deep where the knife hit it. Just like she said."

"My God!" I could feel my heart racing.

"Some of the boys are over there now, but I thought I better check on Ms. Moon."

"She's asleep," I said. Then the light dawned. "You're afraid whoever it is will come after her here?"

"We'll fix it so they can't," Bo Mitchell said. She got up and I followed her down the hall.

"Room 492," I said.

"I know."

We entered a room which had been quiet when I left and which was noisy and crowded now. The woman in the far bed was the center of attention of at least five various and sundry medical personnel. One of them saw us enter and smiled brightly. "She's fine," she said. "She just quit breathing."

In the bed nearest us, beautiful Claire slept.

Five

Bo Mitchell had Claire's name removed from all admittance records and had her transferred to a private room in the psychiatric section in the basement. Surprisingly, it was light and airy down there, with a large open atrium that seemed to be filled with natural sunlight where plants and even a couple of small trees flourished.

"They can watch her better here," Bo said. Judging from the number of personnel in the halls, I could tell she was right. "We do this sometimes when we aren't sure what's going on."

"It looks like an expensive hotel," I said.

"Hnnn." Bo Mitchell started toward the nurses' station.

"Hey, Bo Peep." A small, blond woman in a red nylon jumpsuit came up behind us. "You bringing us a customer?"

Bo Peep? I cut my eyes around at her.

"Hey, Connie. This is Mrs. Hollowell."

"I'm not the patient," I assured Connie. "Though of course, it would be all right if I were, wouldn't it? I mean, an illness is an illness. Right?"

"Right." Connie and Bo Peep spoke at the same time.

I could have kicked myself. I was protesting entirely too much. But how could these two young women who had been raised in the age of lithium and tranquilizers and antidepressants know the fear of mental illness that my generation had known? My grandfather's sister, Aunt Josephine, had "spells" when she would be unable to carry on with her everyday life. She would lie in the bed and cry, sometimes raging at her husband and children. And there was nothing anyone could do for her. Her spells, in fact, were looked upon as a weakness.

I still remember going with my grandfather, who was not an insensitive man, to see his sister as she lay facing the wall in her darkened bedroom. "Get up, Josie," he said, "and quit putting on. You've put us all through enough." This was just a few weeks before she slit her wrists.

I shivered, but Connie and Bo weren't paying any attention to me. They were talking about Claire.

"Good as done," Connie said.

"Thanks. We'll be checking."

The elevator opened and two orderlies pushed Claire's bed out.

"That her?" Connie asked.

Bo Mitchell nodded.

"Bring her in here, then." Connie motioned to a room directly in front of the nurses' station.

"Good," Bo said.

"Bug in a rug," Connie agreed.

After leaving my number at the desk in case Claire should awaken and want me, I asked Bo Mitchell if she could give me a lift home.

"Sure." Her car was parked right at the front door of the hospital in a No Parking zone. "A perk," she said, flashing those perfect teeth.

I realized that this was my second "first" for the day. The ambulance and now the police car. We rode along with squawks which made no sense to me blaring from the radio. Bo Mitchell seemed able to interpret, though. A couple of times she flipped a button and talked back. A lot of ten-fours and ninety-eights. It sounded exactly like a television show.

She turned to me. "Tell me about Claire Moon."

"Is your middle name Peep?"

She laughed. "Can you believe my mama did that? It's what everybody calls me, too, except down at the station. They said, 'Hey, girl. What kind of an image you gonna give us? Your name is Bo. Period.'"

She looked over at me. "When I came to your door what if I'd said, 'I'm Bo Peep Mitchell'?"

"I see what you mean."

"You'd have laughed like crazy." She swung up the interstate. "Now, tell me about Claire."

I told her all I knew about Claire as a teenager and how I had seen her the night before for the first time in years. I told her about her showing up on the steps and the condition she was in, and that that was all I knew. I hadn't even known where she lived or that she was widowed until she had answered the questions.

"You know anything about Mercy Armistead?"

"I never met her until last night. My sister had the invitation to the opening. Why?"

"Just wondered." Bo drummed her fingers against the steering wheel. It was too casual.

"She had a heart attack, didn't she?"

"That's what they say."

"But you're not sure."

"Hey, Mrs. Hollowell, I'm no doctor."

I thought about Claire's screaming "They got to Mercy!" and reminded Bo of it.

"I remember," she said.

"You think there could be anything to it? I mean, a woman in her thirties with no history of heart disease falls over dead and someone tries to kill her assistant on the same night. What do you think?"

"Don't know." We rode along the interstate for a mile or so in silence.

"Hey, Mrs. Hollowell?"

"Call me Patricia Anne."

"Patricia Anne, you want to get Claire some gowns? Her apartment's just off the next exit."

I thought about the policemen there. "Is it okay?"

"There's something I'd like you to see."

"Why?"

"See what you think of it."

I sighed. "Okay. But can you make personal phone calls on that thing?" I pointed to the squawking box. "My husband may have tried to call me."

"Here." Bo Peep reached into her pocket and pulled out a tiny cellular phone. "Use this." The phone was the size of a small calculator and almost as light. I decided at that moment what I wanted Fred to give me for Christmas.

He wasn't in, but I was so enamored of the phone I called my own number to see if I had gotten any messages. The library had a book I'd reserved, Bonnie Blue wanted me to call her, and Mary Alice said not to worry about Christmas.

"Everything okay?" Bo Mitchell said as I handed her the phone.

"My sister said not to worry about Christmas."

"That's nice."

"Not necessarily."

We had turned into an area of apartments that had been built right after World War II. Attractive and well constructed, when they went condo about ten years before, they were snapped up by people who appreciated the high ceilings, the molding, the arched alcoves. Since then, the prices have skyrocketed. I was startled when Bo stopped in front of a corner unit that had a view of the whole valley.

"This is where Claire lives?" I asked.

"Yep."

We got out and started toward the door, where we had to step over yellow crime scene tape.

"These places are expensive," I said.

"Claire Moon owns it, too, lock, stock, and barrel." Bo Peep Mitchell fumbled in her pocket, found a key, and opened the white door. She stood back while I walked in. "Well, what do you think?"

It was like falling into a snowbank. Everything in the whole apartment was white, not flat white but glistening. The carpet, walls, furniture, even paintings and bric-a-brac were all white. I felt like reaching into my purse for my dark glasses.

"What do you think?" Bo Peep asked again.

"It's white. I thought it was going to be messed up."

"Look carefully."

This time I saw slashes in the sofa where white stuffing was spilling and shards of glass shining on the white hearth. The more I looked, the more damage I saw.

"Here's where the knife hit." Bo Mitchell closed the front door and a dark gash shone in all that whiteness like a blood-stain. "Probably a butcher knife."

I shivered. "This is what you wanted me to see?"

"Upstairs."

These apartments all had three small bedrooms upstairs when they were first built. Many of the residents have combined the two smaller rooms into a large master bedroom. I saw immediately that was what Claire, or the people she bought the unit from, had done. Everything was white up there, too, and was made even more blinding by a large sky-light that centered a rectangle of December sun on a king-sized bed. Above the bed, the word *whore* was sprayed with red paint. The paint had dripped like blood.

"Oh, my," I said, closing my eyes.

"In here is what I want you to see," Bo said. I followed her into the small guest bedroom. By comparison, it was much darker than the adjacent room. My eyes had to adjust to the change.

"What do you think?" Bo asked.

"About what? I can't see a thing."

"Close your eyes a minute."

I did, and when I opened them, I was no longer immersed in whiteness. The walls were covered in graffiti done in bold, primary colors. Obscene words were written across the wall. Streaks of color crossed and crisscrossed in long swaths as if the vandal had delighted in aiming the spray can at the white walls.

"My God," I said.

"Just look." Bo Mitchell turned on an overhead light and

the extent of the damage sprang out at me. The reddest of red poured down the walls. What seemed to be an exploding sun rained fire over the whole scene.

"My God!" I exclaimed, fighting nausea.

"But look here."

I knelt down and looked at the corner where Bo Peep Mitchell was pointing. There, in a small rectangular area, probably ten inches by twelve, was a pastoral scene. In the softest of pastels, a red-haired woman sat in a meadow painting three pictures of a dark-haired subject. The painter's back was to us, so what we saw were the portraits on three easels.

"What is this?" I asked Bo. "You got a flashlight?"

She handed me one and I shined it against the painting with one hand and held my bifocals away with the other so the bottom part would magnify the pictures.

"All three of the pictures are of a woman with hair like Claire's," I said. "But they don't have any features."

Bo Peep sat down beside me on the floor. "Let me see your glasses."

She held them away from her and studied the painting.

"Mercy Armistead was redheaded," I said.

Bo Peep handed me my glasses. "That's what I heard." She motioned at the wall above us. "What do you think?"

"What do you mean, what do I think? Quit asking me that, damn it. I'm not a psychiatrist." I grabbed the handle on the door, pulled myself up, and stomped into the other room. The whole morning had finally gotten to me. "Are you asking me if I think the average person paints stuff like that on walls?" I pointed to the word *whore*. "I hope not. But can I psychoanalyze it? No."

Bo Peep followed me into the master bedroom.

"And right now," I said, "I'm going to get a sick girl some clean nightgowns."

"Bet they're white," Bo Mitchell said.

They were.

When I got home, I was exhausted. I fixed myself a peanut butter and banana sandwich and a glass of milk and sat down to watch an old *Bewitched*. I was just finishing when the phone rang.

"What are you doing?" Mary Alice asked.

"Eating a sandwich, watching *Bewitched*."

"With the old Darren or the new one?"

"The old one."

"I still can't believe we accepted that like we did. Samantha changed husbands in midstream and we weren't supposed to notice?"

"Maybe that's what witches do."

Mary Alice was quiet for a moment while she decided whether or not to take this personally. She decided not to. "Did you get my message?" she asked.

"About Christmas?"

"You always get in such a tizzy that I thought this year we'd all go to Foxglove for dinner."

"Foxglove? That's a poison."

"It is not. It's a perfectly beautiful place. Bill and I had dinner there the other night."

"Mary Alice, nobody would name a restaurant Foxglove."

"Somebody would and somebody did. And I've rented the private dining room for us. Henry wanted to do the cooking, but I told him we were all going to relax at a restaurant this year."

Henry Lamont is her daughter Debbie's "main squeeze," a term Sister picked up from TV, I'm sure, since Debbie would never use it. He's a very nice young man who Sister believes to be the father of the twins, Fay and May, based solely on the fact that he once donated to the UAB sperm bank where they were conceived. He's also a gourmet cook and had probably been looking forward to trying out new recipes on us for Christmas.

"You can have your children on Christmas Eve and then we'll all have dinner at the restaurant on Christmas Day."

"At Foxglove."

"That's right. One o'clock suit you?"

"Of course." Best to agree.

"That's what time I told them. How's Claire?"

"They have her in the psych unit. She's sedated. I went over to her apartment with Bo Mitchell, the policewoman."

"Did you find her purse?"

"What?"

"With an insurance card."

"No." I hadn't thought to look, but I hated to admit that to the woman who was footing the bills. "She's got some awful stuff painted on her walls, though. Really terrible. I can't even describe it."

"That means it doesn't match your Norman Rockwell plates."

That ticked me off. I happen to love my Norman Rockwell plates.

"Well, she's got to have a wallet somewhere," Mary Alice continued. "There or at the gallery. I guess I better call that policewoman."

"You do that. I'd like to know what you think of a painting over at Claire's that seems totally at odds with the graffiti."

"Listen, Mouse, you may not believe this, but I've gotten to be a damn good art critic."

"I'll look forward to your critique of the work on Claire's wall," I said.

After Sister hung up, I looked up the number and called the hospital. They did not have a patient named Claire Moon. Sorry. Of course they didn't; I had forgotten Bo Mitchell's orders. I called her at the police station, happened to catch her, and got the number. Claire was fine, still sleeping, Connie, the nurse, assured me. I put down the phone and thought about the room at Claire's apartment with the frightening graffiti. And the stark whiteness of everything else. Poor little girl. Poor terrified little girl.

I dialed the Big, Bold, and Beautiful Shop, and Bonnie Blue answered. "I'm on my break," she explained. "Pulled off my shoes, which was a bad mistake. Wait a minute." I could hear her puffing and groaning. "No use," she said in a minute. "I'm going to have to work in my stocking feet. What can I do for you, Patricia Anne?"

"You called *me*."

"Oh. Yeah. Actually I wanted to tell you two things. One is that we got in a great silk jacket, unlined, off-white, and decorated with beige shells. Loose and flowing. Just looks like Mary Alice, and we've got a 24W. Want me to put it back for you to see? For Christmas?"

"Sounds great."

"And the second thing is they did an autopsy on Mercy. You know digitalis?"

"We're having Christmas dinner there."

"What? I'm talking about the medicine."

"I know what digitalis is. It strengthens the heart. All Mary Alice's husbands took it."

"Well, so did Mercy. Not like a prescription; nothing was wrong with her heart. But she took a whole bunch last night, apparently, and that's what killed her. Thurman called James and James called me. They're already questioning Thurman."

"They think somebody killed her?"

"I reckon."

"Good Lord!"

"Bonnie Blue!" I heard someone calling.

"Got to go. I'll put the jacket up for you. 'Bye."

"'Bye. Thanks." I hung up the phone and thought about what Bonnie Blue had just told me. Officer Mitchell had known all about Mercy when she came to the hospital and when she took me to see the wall at Claire's apartment. Or knew there were suspicions about Mercy's death.

I gathered up my plate, glass, and napkin and took them to the kitchen, where Claire's Coke glass was still in the sink. Poor frightened girl, I thought, wishing there was someone I could talk to about what had happened. Someone who remembered Claire like I did. And at that moment I knew who the person was, someone who had known Claire very well.

I glanced at the clock and made another phone call.

"Robert Alexander High," Lois Aderholt answered.

"Lois? It's Patricia Anne. How are you?"

"Fine, Patricia Anne. All we need to do is live through one more week and we'll be out for Christmas. How are you?"

"Fine. Lois, is Frances Zata there?"

"Probably. Let me ring her. Come see us, Patricia Anne."

"I may be out there in a little while."

"Good. See you soon."

I could hear the phone ringing in Frances's office and then Lois's voice came back on. "I'm going to page her, Patricia Anne."

"Thanks." I listened to taped Christmas carols while I waited.

Robert Alexander High is where I taught the last twenty-five years of my career. It was built without windows and with few inside walls. This was to promote flexibility, which would lead to individuality within a community environment. Or something like that. Whatever the educational words were that year. Bright carpets, posters, and bookcases welcomed us in and were supposed to make us so happy we didn't need to look outside, where, incidentally, there were beautiful woods and a small lake. Soft classical music was piped into the library, which was in the very center of the cocoon.

For some of us, it was perfect. We walked inside that brick rectangle and shed our cares at the door. For others, it was torment. I believe the phrase "buried alive" was bandied about. Teachers and students who felt this way were quickly and mercifully transferred.

Frances Zata was the guidance counselor who had been there from the beginning and who loved it as much as I did. When I decided to retire, she took me to lunch and tried to talk me out of it. "What will you do with your time?" she asked.

"Whatever I want to," I replied.

"Frances Zata here." In the background I could hear rattling as if silverware were being dropped into a drawer.

"What in the world are you doing?"

"Hi, Patricia Anne. I'm in Pod 3 with a cardboard box

some service organization sent out crammed full of Just Say
No pins. They're so bad the kids just might wear them. Wait
a minute.'' I heard what sounded like tape being torn.
"Okay, I'm back. How are you? Ready to come back?"

"Is a raise in the offing?"

"Smart-ass. That'll be the day. I hope you're calling about
lunch Saturday.''

"That would be great. I'd like to see you sooner, though.
This afternoon or in the morning.''

"Something wrong?"

"You remember Claire Needham?" I asked.

"Clarissey Mae? Sure, bless her heart. Why? She's okay,
isn't she?''

"It's a long story, and I need you to fill in some gaps for
me.''

"Well, the juvenile court records are confidential. But a
lot of the stuff was in the newspaper. Can you come in the
morning?''

"Say when."

"Nine?"

"Sure."

Frances sighed. "She's in trouble, isn't she? That poor
little girl. Those poor little children.''

My thoughts exactly.

Supper was interesting that night. Fred came bounding into
the kitchen with a grin on his face, a bottle of sparkling apple
juice, and a bouquet of daisies. Chances are he had been
planning all day to pick up where we left off that morning.

"Haley will be here in a minute," I said.

"How soon?"

"Soon."

"Real soon?"

"Any minute."

"Okay," he conceded. He leaned down to kiss me, and I
put the palm of my hand against his cheek, which was
scratchy and familiar.

"Stay awake," I said.

"No problem." He patted me on the behind and disappeared down the hall. "What kind of day did you have?" he called back.

"You wouldn't believe. I'll tell you when Haley gets here."

I checked the lasagna, which was beginning to bubble, and cut up the salad. The kitchen was beginning to smell like the tangy aroma of cheese melting in tomato sauce. A thoroughly satisfying smell for a December night.

Haley agreed. "Smells wonderful," she said, coming in and taking off her coat. She ran her hand through her dark red hair. "Wind's picking up out there." She gave me a hug and looked through the window of the oven. "Lord, that looks good."

"Straight out of the freezer," I said.

"I'm suitably impressed." Haley went to the refrigerator, took a beer out, and popped it open.

Which reminded me. "Go look on the den wall," I said.

It was a moment of serendipity. Haley got to the painting just as Fred came into the den behind her.

"Oh, my," she said. "Oh, my. Is it a real Abraham, Mama? It is, isn't it? Oh, my, look at that." She reached over and touched the hair. "I can't believe this. Where in the world did you get it? And what bank did you rob?"

I couldn't have planned it this well. Fred came up beside Haley and looked at Abe Butler's portrait with a puzzled look.

"Hey, Daddy." Haley hugged him. "You got this for Mama for Christmas, didn't you?"

"No," Fred said. "It has a pop-top opener you hang it up with."

"I know. Isn't it wonderful?" Haley touched Abe's hair again and laughed.

"Bonnie Blue gave it to me," I said. "Did I tell you Abraham Butler's her daddy? That's his real hair."

"No. This is unbelievable."

"I think I'll get a beer." Fred headed toward the kitchen.

"There are some celery and carrot sticks in the refrigerator," I said. "Bring them back with you. And some napkins."

"Look," Haley said. "Look at his tiny teeth, the way they just stop. And the feet."

"I like the cane."

We heard the clunk as Fred put the sticks and dip on the coffee table. "Here," he said, handing Haley and me both a paper towel. "Couldn't find any napkins."

Fred sat in his recliner and Haley and I sat on the sofa. The gas logs looked exactly like a real fire.

"This is nice," Haley said, leaning back.

"How did the gunshot wound go?" I asked.

"He should be all right. What about your lady? What was her name?"

"Claire Moon."

"That sounds like 'Clair de Lune.' " Haley hummed a few bars. "Da *dah* da, dadada."

"I don't know. They put her in the psychiatric unit and they're running tests."

Fred, who had picked up the evening newspaper, put it down. "Who's Claire Moon?"

"A former student of mine. I saw her at the gallery last night and she showed up here this morning sick."

"What's wrong with her?"

"Don't know. But when Bo Peep Mitchell told her Mercy Armistead was dead, she collapsed. We had to call the paramedics and take her to the hospital in an ambulance."

"Who's Bo Peep Mitchell?" Haley asked. "Who's Mercy Armistead?"

"I know who Mercy Armistead is," Fred said. "She's Thurman Beatty's wife, and they're questioning him about her murder. It's here in the paper."

"Who's Thurman Beatty?" Haley asked.

"Wait a minute." I held up my schoolteacher hand. "Just wait a minute."

Fred and Haley both looked at me expectantly.

"I'll start at the beginning."

And I did, taking time out only to get the lasagna out of

the oven. I started with the showing of the Outsiders at the Mercy Armistead Gallery and seeing Claire Moon, who used to be Claire Needham, who at one time had been Clarissey Mae Needham from a very abusive family. I described both Claire and Mercy and how Mercy had been irked because, among other things, she was having a bad hair day. And James Butler and Thurman Beatty, and how pitiful Claire was when she turned up this morning. I segued into Bo Peep Mitchell and the ambulance ride and ended with a description of the graffiti on Claire's wall and the fact that Mercy had died from digitalis poisoning.

"And that's all," I told the openmouthed Haley and Fred. "Now let's eat supper."

The phone rang just as we sat down at the table. I answered it.

"It's Fox Glen," Mary Alice said.

Six

I went out early the next morning to get the paper and was sitting at the kitchen table reading it when Fred came in.

"Anything new?" he asked, pouring a cup of coffee.

"About the Mercy Armistead murder? No. They let Thurman Beatty go after they questioned him."

"That Thurman Beatty is the finest young man ever played football at Alabama. You know that, Patricia Anne. All-American. Should have had the Heisman. No way he'd be mixed up in anything like this."

"Hmmm," I said. I handed Fred the paper, poured each of us some cereal, and sliced half a banana into each bowl. Rain gusted against the windows. Woofer wouldn't appreciate being dragged from his igloo for a walk this morning; I would let him sleep.

"Thank you for the daisies," I said. In a blue vase in the middle of the table, they were a bright spot on a gloomy morning.

"Any time." He grinned and turned the paper to the back page.

"I wonder why they call it 'foul play'," I said, looking at the headlines.

"What?"

" 'Foul play suspected in death of socialite,' " I read. "It's foul all right. But playful?"

"It's the baseball term."

"But why would they use it for murder?"

Fred shrugged. "Says here her grandfather was the late Amos Bedsole, the Bedsole Steel guy. They used to buy a lot of my scrap metal. Old man Bedsole died, didn't he?"

"The 'late' Amos Bedsole, Fred." I crunched a spoonful of cereal. "You know, that's something else doesn't make sense. When you're dead, why are you 'late'? You can't very well make it on time."

Fred put the paper down and looked at me. "What are you planning to do today?"

"I'm going out to the school to wish everyone a Merry Christmas and by the hospital to take Claire Moon some gowns. Maybe some shopping. Why?"

"It would be a good day for you to read a book in front of the fire and take it easy."

I nodded that it would. "Stay with me."

"Can't." We looked at each other. Be safe. Be safe.

"You want some more coffee?" I asked.

The thermometer on the Central Bank Building read 45 degrees when I drove by on my way to Alexander High. The cold rain had turned into a heavy drizzle that seemed to coat everything like oil. I hoped it would be over before the temperature took its expected nosedive. We didn't need any ice right before Christmas.

I turned into the parking lot and found a visitor's space empty. Vice Principal Chesley Maddox, whom the kids called Chesty Maggot (but way, way behind his back), ran a tight ship in the parking lot. A scrawny little man, he had the Dirty Harry look down so pat that even while the students were laughing about him, they were shaking in their boots. "Come on," he seemed to say. "Try parking in the teachers' or visitors' lot." They never took him up on it.

Frances Zata was on the phone, but she motioned me to a seat. Her office was bright and cheerful—no windows, of course, but posters from Tivoli Gardens and the British Museum and the famous "Earth Rise" livened the walls.

"Sorry," she said when she hung up. "Come give me a hug. God, I miss you."

Frances is my age, sixty, but she doesn't look it. She is what my grandmother called a "handsome" woman. She found her style, a very elegant one, early, and it has done well by her. Her dark blond hair is pulled back into a chignon which she varies sometimes with a French braid. She wears simple silk blouses, straight or A-line skirts, usually in beige or black, and low-heeled pumps. Her earrings are either pearls or gold loops. And only I know that several years ago she had a face-lift because she was mad about a younger man. One of those sex slave things Mary Alice talks about. The affair didn't work out, but the face-lift did. Frances looks great.

"You want some coffee?" she asked after we had inquired about each other's families. Frances has one son, a lawyer, a friend of my Alan.

I shook my head no.

She leaned back and took a manila envelope from a bookcase. "Here's the stuff about Claire Needham," she said. "I had to go to court for her, you know, so there's some extra stuff in there. Nothing privileged. That would be down at Juvenile Court." She handed me the files. "What's the matter with her, Patricia Anne?"

"She's in Memorial Hospital in the psych unit." I started telling Frances that I had not seen Claire for years until I went to the opening of Mercy Armistead's art gallery. She stopped me.

"The woman who was killed?"

I nodded.

"Whose mother was Betty Bedsole, the Miss Alabama?"

"According to Mary Alice. How do the two of you keep up with these things?"

"Whoa. Wait just a minute." Frances scooted around the desk and grabbed the file I had just opened. "Wait a minute, wait a minute," she said, flipping pages.

"What?"

"Ah ha! I knew it. I was looking through these just before you came in and that name sounded familiar. Look here, Patricia Anne." Frances stuck a page right in front of my face. I took it away from her and held it so my eyes would focus. "Right there." She pointed.

I saw the typed name of Liliane Bedsole first. Then I looked to the left. "Guardian."

"I don't understand," I said.

Frances sat on the edge of the desk, took the form back, and looked at it again. "I'm sorry. Get on with your story. The name just struck me."

"Liliane Bedsole was Claire's guardian? She's Mercy's aunt. Great-aunt."

Frances nodded. "I thought there might be some connection. According to the records, Liliane Bedsole read about the abuse case in the paper and was so upset about it, she petitioned the court for all three of them. Those little girls finally had some luck."

"I thought there was a brother."

Frances shook her head. "Claire and twin girls five years younger. Precious children. Can't remember their names."

"They're all precious," I murmured.

"They looked like something out of a concentration camp. The twins did. Claire had fared some better nutrition-wise. Probably because they sent her to school and she got lunch. The twins had never gone to school when Youth Services finally took them over."

"But Claire was sexually abused by her father."

"Yes." Frances slid from the desk and went around to sit in her chair. "You sit there in court, Patricia Anne, and you see these people who don't look like monsters and then you see what they've done to their children and it shakes you to the core."

"Where are they now? The parents."

"Both dead, I understand. The father got in a fight in jail and a fellow inmate killed him. The mother died of a drug overdose."

"And Liliane Bedsole took the children."

Frances leaned back and toyed with a pencil on her desk. "It took guts. Children aren't as resilient as we would like to think."

"Let me tell you about Claire," I said, "what's happened to her now." I went back to the meeting at the gallery, mentioning that Liliane Bedsole had been there. I told her how beautiful Claire looked, thin, but elegant. I told her how Claire had shown up on my steps claiming someone had tried to kill her, which had apparently been true, and that I had no idea why she had turned to me unless it was because she had seen me the night before.

"Security," Frances said.

I shrugged.

"Hey, it's true. Teachers underestimate their roles in their students' lives."

"Maybe." I continued the story, including Claire's collapse and the trip Bo Peep Mitchell and I had taken to Claire's apartment.

Frances was sitting forward now. As I described the pictures, her eyes got wider and wider.

"Good Lord!" she exclaimed as I finished with the knife slit in the door.

"What do you think it means?" I asked.

"I think it means she's in the right place in the psych unit. I hope they're doing a good job of watching her."

"I wonder where her sisters are."

"God knows. And probably Liliane Bedsole. They were sent to private school, I understand, when they were strong enough."

Frances had to go to a parent conference in the principal's office, so she left me with the file. "Let me know what happens, Patricia Anne. And lunch Saturday. Okay?"

"How about the Blue Moon Tea Room at Rosedale Mall?"

"Fine. You don't want to go somewhere closer?"

"It's worth the drive," I said. "I guarantee it."

After she left, I opened the files and began to read. According to her teachers, Claire had been quiet and obedient, accident-prone (I could imagine the bruises that had prompted this notation), with a tendency to daydream and sleep in class. The target of much bullying, she had been urged by one teacher to "stand up for herself and hit back." Several mentioned poor hygienic practices (translation: she needed a bath and clean clothes) and parent conferences that parents failed to show up for.

It was a perfect portrait of an abused or at least a neglected child. And Frances had said teachers were children's security? Tears came to my eyes, and I brushed them away.

I already knew from looking at the yearbook that Claire had not been involved in any extracurricular programs except the Art Club. Her grades improved after Liliane Bedsole was listed as her guardian, though, and on her ACT, she had scored a respectable 23.

I put the file on Frances's desk and locked the door behind me as I left. I wasn't sure what I'd been looking for, maybe just some understanding of the frightened girl who had come to me for refuge. And I wasn't sure what I'd found, except more questions. The connection to the Bedsole family brought up a big one. Wasn't it logical that whoever killed Mercy Armistead had also tried to kill Claire? And that brought up the biggest question of all. If so, why?

I waved good-bye to the ladies in the office and wished them a happy holiday.

"We miss you," they said together.

"And I miss you." It was true. I still wasn't a hundred percent sure that retiring at sixty had been a good idea.

The rain had settled in for the day, but it didn't seem to have turned any colder. I parked in the hospital parking deck and crossed the street through a glassed-in crossover. Below me an ambulance hurtled up the hill to the emergency room. Lord!

The psychiatric unit was as sunny and bright as it had been the day before, which ruled out natural sunlight as the source of light in their atrium. I started toward the nurses' station to see if Connie was on duty and to identify myself if she wasn't so I could get a permit to visit.

"Claire's gone," a voice said behind me. I turned and saw Connie, who was carrying a tray of medications. "Mrs. Hollowell, right?"

I nodded yes. "What do you mean she's gone?"

"Left. Took off sometime during the night."

"By herself?"

"Unless somebody was with her." I looked at Connie to see if she was serious. She was.

"I brought her some nightgowns," I said, holding up a plastic Penney's bag.

"You want me to keep them?"

"They're for Claire."

"I didn't mean *me* keep them. I meant until she gets back."

"She's coming back?"

"Probably."

It was beginning to dawn on me that Nurse Connie was due for a transfer out of the psych ward. "Listen," I said, "tell me what happened."

"She was gone this morning when they took her her breakfast. That's all I know."

I was suddenly very anxious. "Did you call the police?"

"Oh, sure. Bo Peep's been here."

"What did she have to say about it?"

"She said, 'Well, hell, Connie. So much for the bug in the rug.' She said to tell you when you showed up to call her."

"Thank you."

"You're welcome."

I tried to remember if Connie had been this spacey the day before. There were a lot of medicines on that tray. Maybe she had been dipping into the Dalmane.

Officer Mitchell wasn't in, the woman said when I called. She would take my name (for a split second I thought she was going to say "and pray for me") and have her call me back. I gave her my home phone number. From the phone I was using in the main lobby, I could see how dreary the weather was. People hurried across the parking lot to the doors and then tried to figure out what to do with wet umbrellas. And Claire was out there somewhere, I thought. Confused and sick, with no coat or shoes. Damn, damn! I kicked the wall below the phone. For you, you imbeciles who let this happen! All I succeeded in doing was scuffing my shoe and hurting my toe.

My mood matched the weather by now. I had used the last of my quarters on the phone call, so I limped into the gift shop to buy some mints to get quarters for the parking deck. There was a change machine near the door, but a man was beating on the side of it, which didn't bode well. And on the door of the gift shop was a hand-printed sign that said NO CHANGE WITHOUT PURCHASE. Tacky, tacky!

I dropped three quarters into the meter at the exit of the parking deck and the barrier arm began to rise slowly. I scooted through as soon as I thought it was high enough. I have a fear, which I was crazy enough to confess to Mary Alice, that the arm is going to come down, *clunk*, right in the middle of my car as I'm driving through. And did she reassure me that would never happen? No. She swore she heard of someone who had been decapitated by one of those arms. She was probably lying, but I'm always relieved when I get through safely.

I turned left and headed toward home. I was still trying to absorb the knowledge of Claire's disappearance. She had been sedated, not heavily, but certainly enough to impair her judgment. She had no money with her, no coat, no shoes. She was hooked up to an IV. Had she been so out of it she walked out of the hospital into a stormy, freezing night? I didn't want to think of the alternative, that someone, possibly the knife wielder, had abducted her, carried her out. It would be possible. She was so small, so fragile. Why on God's green earth hadn't they watched her better!

All the way home, I had my fingers crossed that maybe, just maybe, Claire had managed to get back to my house. She hadn't. Woofer rushed out of his igloo to greet me and then rushed back inside. No fool, he. I checked the phone

messages and there weren't any, which always depresses me.
I dialed Mary Alice.

"Crane residence," a bright young voice answered.

"May I speak to Mrs. Crane, please. This is her sister."

"I'm sorry. Mrs. Crane isn't here at the moment. This is
Tiffany with Magic Maids. May I take a message?"

"Just tell her I called."

"I'll do that. Bye-bye, now."

"Bye-bye, now." I hung up the phone and stared at it for
a minute. Tiffany with Magic Maids? A Tiffany scrubbing
toilets? A Tiffany getting rich. And more power to her. It
was time housecleaning was recognized as the respectable
hard work it is. But a Tiffany?

My own house desperately needed a Magic Maid Tiffany.
I pulled on some jeans and got to work. I changed the bed
and put a tub of clothes on to wash. I swished disinfectant
around the toilets and got out the vacuum. I was just about
to plug it in when the phone rang.

"Mrs. Hollowell? Officer Mitchell here. You called?"

"Can it, Bo Peep," I said. "I know you lost Claire
Moon."

"You've been to the hospital."

"And talked to Connie. What the hell's going on?"

"Don't know."

"You knew yesterday that Mercy Armistead had been
murdered, didn't you? And you figured the same person was
after Claire."

"It's possible."

"What do you mean, it's possible?" The light dawned.
"Somebody's there with you and you can't talk. Right?"

"Right."

A second light came on. "The police took Claire from the
hospital, didn't they? Put her in a safer place."

"That's negative."

"Then where could she be? She's sick, Bo Peep."

"We understand that."

"I'm beginning to wonder. Look, call me back when you
don't have to talk like a robot." I hung up the phone,

plugged the vacuum in, and gave the carpet a vicious cleaning. Tiffany the Magic Maid would have approved. I dusted,
put the clothes into the dryer, and considered addressing a
few Christmas cards. But I wasn't in the mood for that. I
turned on the Weather Channel and saw the temperature had
dropped to 38. Cookies, I decided. I would make the fruit
drop cookies the boys always demanded for Christmas. They
would stay fine in the freezer.

I glanced out of the kitchen door, hoping, I suppose, that
Claire would be sitting on the steps. She wasn't, of course.
I fixed a cup of spiced tea and set to work on the cookies.
As soon as I got out the plastic cartons of fruit I could feel
my mood improving. The colors of candied fruits are awe
inspiring, no colors that exist in nature. The red and yellow
are close, but the green! A work of art!

I reached for my biggest mixing bowl so I could double
the recipe. My family won't eat fruitcake, but the fruit drop
cookies with the same ingredients disappear like magic. It
was quite possible, doing them this far ahead, that I would
have to make another batch before Christmas.

There have been no great cooks in our family, so I have
nothing to live up to, which is nice. Mama could fry great
chicken, and her cornbread dressing, which made an appearance only at Thanksgiving and Christmas, was why Fred said
he married me. She had no recipe, but I had watched her so
much, I thought I knew how to make it. I didn't. The first
Thanksgiving after she died was one of those standout mo-
ments when you realize somebody is really gone. We grieved
all day wanting the smell of the dressing cooking. Wanting
Mama. With Grandmama, it was the sweet potato pie with
meringue. None of us ever got that right, either. Other than
those specialties, they fed their families adequately and that
was fine.

The fruit drop cookie recipe has been in the family for as
long as I can remember. I take the card out each year and
follow the instructions written in Mama's precise handwriting. The last sentence says, "It is best to make this with a
friend because of the stirring." More fun than a Cuisinart,

certainly, but that was what would have to suffice today. I took a sip of tea, turned the radio to the Golden Oldies, and started chopping dates, cherries, pineapple, and pecans.

I hummed along with Doris Day while I creamed butter and added vanilla, lemon, and orange extract. Good baking music, Doris. Why aren't you still making records? In went the cinnamon, nutmeg, cloves, and sugar. The flour. Into the mixing bowl with the chopped fruit. Stir, friend Cuisinart.

I dumped the first batch into the big mixing bowl and began another. The local news update came on and was nothing but the murder of the internationally renowned artist, Mercy Armistead; the questioning of her All-American husband, Thurman Beatty; and the arrival in town of the former Miss America, Betty Bedsole, the mother of the renowned international artist, Mercy Armistead, wife of All-American Thurman Beatty, son-in-law of the beautiful former Miss America Betty Bedsole, etc., etc.

"Dear God." I reached over and turned the volume down until I was sure the music was back on again. Mercy Armistead was young, beautiful, and talented and should have had a whole lifetime ahead of her. However renowned she was, and that was questionable, was beside the point. And her family deserved the right to grieve in privacy regardless of who they were. A right which it looked like the press was going to deny.

I turned the oven on preheat to 325 degrees and dropped the dough by teaspoonfuls onto cookie sheets. I set the timer, fixed another cup of tea, and went into the den to read. I had every intention of rereading *King Lear* for my Great Books study group. But I couldn't resist the new Tony Hillerman that was on the coffee table. I knew what happened to King Lear anyway.

Twenty-five minutes later, the oven timer roused me from the Navajo Nation. I put the book down reluctantly and went to take the cookies out. They looked great, just slightly crispy on the edges. Who would bake Christmas cookies for Lieutenant Joe Leaphorn out there on the reservation, I wondered, now that his beloved Emma was dead?

The ring of the front doorbell startled me back into the real world and almost made me drop the sheet of cookies. A glance out of the window told me the rain had not slackened and that the afternoon was darkening. A UPS package, I thought, or maybe Bo Peep Mitchell. I wiped my hands on a dishcloth and went to see.

"Mrs. Hollowell?"

At first I didn't recognize the woman standing there, understandable since I'd only seen her once, at the gallery opening.

"I'm Liliane Bedsole. May I come in?"

I was startled. "Of course." I opened the door.

"I'm wet," she said, hesitating. She had on a red hooded raincoat that looked straight out of a fairy tale but was more likely straight from some exclusive designer. In her hand was a red-and-white-striped umbrella that dripped onto the porch.

"There's an umbrella stand right here," I said. "Come on in."

She closed the umbrella and stepped inside. "What a beautiful piece of furniture," she said, admiring the hall tree as I placed the wet umbrella into it.

"It was my grandmother's," I said. "May I take your coat?"

She slid the Red Ridinghood coat and hood off and I got a good look at her for the first time. Her face had a drawn look, not the drawn look of multiple face-lifts but the look of worry and lack of sleep. Her eyes were red-rimmed as if she had been crying recently. She looked old and totally exhausted. Against a black turtleneck sweater, her skin was splotchy and her hair, which had once probably been a strawberry blond, was definitely orange.

"I know you're wondering why I'm here," she said.

"You can tell me in the den," I said. "I'm having some spiced tea. Would you like some?"

She sighed. "That would be wonderful."

I led her into the den, where she sank onto the sofa. "It smells so good in here," she said.

"I'm making fruit drop cookies for Christmas."

"Oh, don't let me stop you."

"I'm at a good stopping place," I said.

Liliane Bedsole nodded. I went into the kitchen, turned the kettle on for tea, and took the spatula from the drawer. Each cookie popped up perfectly. I tasted one. Delicious. I put several on a plate to carry to the den.

"What a wonderful Abe."

I turned to see Liliane Bedsole standing in front of my picture.

"His daughter gave it to me," I said.

"Look at that hair. I saw it from the sofa and told myself it couldn't be, but it is. It's incredible."

"Thank you." I wished Fred could hear this. I poured the tea, put the cups and the cookies on a tray, and took them into the den.

"How nice." Liliane Bedsole came back and sat on the sofa. She picked up a cookie and looked at it. "My mother used to make these," she said.

I sat down beside her. "An old Southern recipe."

"Yes." She took a bite of cookie and so did I. She took a sip of tea and so did I. She looked up at the rain running down the skylight.

And I blurted out, "You're looking for Claire, aren't you?"

"Yes."

"I have no idea where she is."

Liliane sighed. "Claire's my foster daughter, you know. I was hoping you might have heard from her. I know she came here yesterday and that you took her to the hospital."

"Ms. Bedsole," I said, "I have no idea why Claire came here. I taught her ten or fifteen years ago and hadn't seen her again until night before last at the gallery." I put my cookie down. "I was sorry to hear about your niece's death."

Liliane Bedsole studied her tea as if she were reading fortunes. "Thank you. I still find it hard to believe that Mercy's gone." She was silent for a moment. Then, "Tell me about

Claire. The policewoman I talked to said she was in a state of collapse.''

I wished I could tell her what the paramedic had told me: Claire's stress signals were stuck. That described her condition perfectly. But Liliane deserved more. I told her the whole story except the graffiti on Claire's walls. Let Bo Peep Mitchell fill her in on that. I just mentioned vandalism.

Liliane Bedsole listened quietly and without a question. When I finished, she leaned over and put her teacup on the table. ''What do you think about her condition, Mrs. Hollowell?''

''Not good,'' I said. Another person asking me what I thought? Suddenly, I was angry. ''You're the one should know about her condition, Ms. Bedsole. She's your foster daughter.''

Liliane Bedsole turned and looked at me. ''She's my niece, Mrs. Hollowell.''

''I thought Mercy was your niece.''

''She is. Was. They both are. Were.''

''I don't understand.''

''Well, most of the people involved are gone, and in today's society things that used to be skeletons in the closet don't matter anymore.''

I looked at Liliane Bedsole and waited. I had no idea what she was talking about.

''Mrs. Hollowell, my brother, Amos Bedsole, ran off and married a girl he met when she was waiting tables at the Elite Cafe. He was eighteen. She was a pretty little thing. I only saw her once, the night Amos brought her home. Her father was a coal miner, not even American. Yugoslavian or something like that.

''Anyway''—Liliane sat forward—''the marriage was annulled almost as soon as they said 'I do.' Daddy probably paid them off, though I doubt that was what the girl was after. Amos went off to college and then he married Edna and they had Betty. Came into Daddy's business and eventually was running it. To tell you the truth, I'd all but forgotten the girl. Her name was Dania. Pretty little thing," she repeated.

Liliane was quiet for a moment, seeing a distant Dania. She took a deep breath and continued. "Then, sixteen, maybe seventeen years ago, Dania showed up in Amos's office. She was dying of cancer and told him they had a daughter. You can't imagine how Amos felt. He was a good man, Mrs. Hollowell, and would have been there for her if he had known. And then it turned out that Dania wasn't there about her daughter, but her granddaughters. She'd been living in Florida for years so she hadn't known the extent of the abuse in her daughter's marriage. She told Amos she had called the juvenile authorities when she saw the children and realized they needed help. They recommended counseling. Can you believe that? Starving, battered, and they recommended counseling." Liliane shook her head. "The abuse was even worse than Dania imagined. Amos always said it was a blessing that she died before she found out."

"What did Amos do?" I asked.

"Told Edna first. She was a good woman, Mrs. Hollowell. Then he got Youth Services out there before the day was over. You probably know the rest."

"What was the daughter's name?"

"Elizabeth. Amos had her hospitalized in a rehab center. Soon as she got out, she died of a drug overdose."

I fished in my pocket for a Kleenex. Damn. "Amos had two daughters named Elizabeth, then."

"Yes. Betty's name is Elizabeth."

I wiped my eyes. "Does Claire know? That she's Amos Bedsole's granddaughter?"

"She knows."

"And her sisters? The twins?"

Liliane smiled, the first happy look I had seen on her face. "Glynn and Lynn took off the day they graduated from high school. They're models in New York. You see them sometimes doing those twin commercials. They had counseling, of course, just like Claire did, but the doctors think that having each other protected them some from their environment. Their emotional environment, anyway. They were very malnourished."

"And you took them in for Amos."

"I took them in for me, Mrs. Hollowell, and now I need to find Claire. Mercy's death is just one more sorrow in her young lifetime."

"She said she was a widow."

Liliane nodded. "A terrible highway tragedy. She was devastated by his death."

Haley, I thought. Haley, you know.

The rain against the skylight suddenly began to make a clicking sound. We both looked up. "Sleet," I said.

"Oh, Lord, let me get home while I still can." Liliane Bedsole pushed herself up. Her black turtleneck sweater showed the curve of osteoporosis.

"If I hear anything I'll let you know," I said, helping her on with her raincoat.

"Claire must think a lot of you to come to you for help."

"I think I was just on her mind."

"I just wonder why she didn't come to me," Liliane said, pulling the hood over her orange hair.

I wondered the same thing, but didn't voice it. "Be careful," I said. "Go straight home."

Liliane took the umbrella. "I've lived here all my life. I know how to handle ice."

I looked at the red coat and the smooth face. This was one feisty little lady. "Be careful, anyway," I said.

I closed the door and went to the kitchen to finish the cookies and to think about all Liliane had told me. She was right about skeletons in the closet. Our social mores had certainly changed. I thought about the two daughters named Elizabeth, one the abused drug addict, the other a Miss America living in Hollywood with a movie mogul. Two sisters named Elizabeth and both of them might just have lost their daughters.

I stuck another batch of cookies into the oven and called Fred to tell him to bring home Chinese. Then I lit the fire and picked up my Hillerman book. I needed it. The Navajo Nation had never looked more inviting.

Seven

The sleet had turned back into rain by the time Fred got home. We ate our almond chicken and sweet-and-sour shrimp on cushions in front of the fire while I told him about Liliane's visit.

"And she thought the girl might try and get in touch with you?"

"Yes."

"How could anybody just walk out of a hospital like that?"

"Easily," I said, thinking of Nurse Connie. "The problem is Claire didn't have any clothes or money. How could she have gone anywhere?"

Fred got up and brought us both a cup of coffee. "What's Liliane Bedsole like?"

"Nice. Frail. Very worried."

"Sounds like she has good reason." He handed me a spoon and a package of Sweet'n Low. "Did Claire and her sisters inherit some of old Amos Bedsole's money? There was plenty of it."

"I suppose so. Claire has that expensive condo and she looks like a million bucks."

"Well, honey, it's not our problem, thank God," Fred said. "But I know you can't help worrying about the girl."

We were both silent, looking into the fire, when Fred suddenly said, "Damn!" and jumped so that he spilled part of his coffee.

I looked up, startled, and saw Mrs. Santa standing in our den door with the lights on her chest flashing merrily.

"Hey, y'all," she said.

"Mary Alice, for God's sake, can't you knock? We could have been doing anything in here." Fred mopped the coffee with his napkin.

"You wish." Mary Alice threw her coat over a chair and came over to the fireplace. "That smells good," she said, pointing to our plates. "What is it?"

"Sweet-and-sour shrimp. Almond chicken." I handed Fred my napkin.

"You got any left?"

"In the kitchen."

"I'm starving." Mary Alice headed toward the food.

Fred glared at me and I shrugged. "How'd you get in, anyway?" he called.

"Through the back door. Which is better? The shrimp or chicken?"

"Shrimp," I said.

"That woman's got the nerve of a bad tooth," Fred muttered.

I shrugged again. After forty years of living with Fred and Mary Alice's clashing, it takes a lot to get me upset.

"Any more soy sauce?" she called.

"No," Fred said.

"Look in the door of the refrigerator." I took a sip of my coffee. "This is good," I told Fred.

"Nobody keeps soy sauce in the refrigerator" came from the kitchen.

"Patricia Anne does."

I drank my coffee and stretched my feet toward the fire.

"Here we go." Mary Alice pulled a kitchen chair between the cushions Fred and I were on and sat down. "Y'all can't be comfortable down there," she said.

"We stay limber." Fred reached over and touched his toes

to prove the point. I tried to remember where the Ben-Gay was.

"Where's Santa?" I asked.

"Poker night." Mary Alice pointed her fork at her plate. "This is good."

"Glad you like it." Fred got up agilely (where *was* that Ben-Gay?) and announced he was going to go and watch the ball game.

"What ball game?" Sister asked.

"The Braves and Montreal."

I sipped my coffee.

"My, my," Mary Alice said. "Baseball season starts earlier and earlier each year, doesn't it?" She watched Fred disappear down the hall. "He's so smart-ass, Patricia Anne. I don't know how you put up with him. You didn't get egg rolls, did you?"

"We ate them."

"You ate a whole egg roll?"

"Yep."

"Will wonders never cease. Have they found Claire?"

"How did you know she was missing?"

"I saw Bonnie Blue at the mall."

"I wonder how she knew."

"Thurman told James and he told Bonnie Blue."

"I wonder how Thurman knew."

"Who knows?"

This was beginning to sound like an Abbott and Costello routine. I put my empty coffee cup on the hearth and told Mary Alice about my trip to the hospital and how Claire had either walked out or been abducted, that no one seemed to be very concerned. I also told her about Claire's being Amos Bedsole's granddaughter, Liliane Bedsole's foster daughter, and that Liliane had come visiting this afternoon.

"Great. Claire probably has hospital insurance then," Sister said.

"I'm sure she does. The question now seems to be whether she's alive or not. You remember how she said

'They got to Mercy?' and then she fainted? Wasn't that what she said?''

"Exactly the words."

"And if somebody killed Mercy and Claire knows who it was, they could have gotten to her, too."

"But why?"

"I don't know." I looked into the fire as if expecting an answer there.

"I know something you don't know," Mary Alice said. "I know how Mercy was killed."

"Digitalis," I said. "It gave her a heart attack."

"But I know how the murderer gave it to her. He deemosoed her."

"What?"

Mary Alice handed me her empty plate. "Here." I put it on the hearth beside my cup. "Deemosoed."

"What the hell is 'deemosoed' and can you make that shirt quit blinking? It's making me dizzy."

"No. Just don't look at it." Mary Alice paused.

"Well?"

"There's this stuff called DMSO, a clear liquid that when you rub it on the skin will carry stuff into your body. Mercy was deemosoed."

"I still don't know what you're talking about."

"Okay. Remember how Mercy's hair was all messed up before we got there and she was off trying to fix it."

"Sure I remember."

"Well, when they did the autopsy, they found DMSO— dimethyl something—and they went looking for it at the gallery and found it in the hair spritzer bottle. Full of digitalis."

I was sitting straight up by now. "You mean the digitalis got into her body in the hair spray?"

"Deemosoed."

"For God's sake, Sister. I'm sure there's not such a word!"

"Well, there ought to be."

I thought about this for a minute. "The DMSO acts as a carrier through the skin for medicines?"

Sister nodded yes.

"And so when Mercy sprayed her hair and it touched her scalp, she was getting a dose of digitalis."

"That's right. And it was in curling spritzer, so she probably scrunched it up with her hands and it got in there, too."

"That's diabolical. Who told you this?"

"Thurman told James and he told Bonnie Blue."

"Fred!" I hollered.

"What?"

"Come here a minute. It's important."

He came to the door. "What?"

"Have you ever heard of something called DMSO?"

"D'moso? No. What is it?"

"It's what killed Mercy Armistead," Mary Alice said. "It carries stuff through the skin."

"In her case digitalis," I added.

"I never heard of it," Fred said, and disappeared down the hall again.

"Could I make such a thing up?" Mary Alice yelled at him.

"Yes," he yelled back.

"Smart-ass," Sister muttered. "Hand me those plates, Mouse. I'm going to get some coffee."

"I'm going to call Haley," I said. "See if she's ever heard of it."

"I'm going to get some cookies, too. You need some help getting up?"

"No." I hopped up and felt muscles twanging like violin chords. Maybe the Ben-Gay was in the nightstand drawer. I limped to the phone and punched Haley's number.

"Hello?" she answered.

"Haley, have you ever heard of something called DMSO?"

"Don't think so, Mama. Let me call you back in a minute, though. I've got somebody on the other line."

I hung up and looked at the phone. "Does that hurt your feelings just a little bit?" I asked Mary Alice, who had come back into the den with a handful of cookies. "You know, when your children put you on hold or say they're busy and will call you back?''

"Of course not. Why should it?"

"I don't know. It just does."

"Takes more than that to hurt my feelings." Mary Alice handed me a cookie. "These are good." She turned on a lamp and sat down on the sofa. "So Claire is Mercy's cousin."

"Half cousin."

"How could you be a half cousin?"

"Well, they had different grandmothers."

"Still cousins."

Sister popped a whole cookie into her mouth. "Bet it didn't sit well with only child Miss America Betty Bedsole to find out she had three half nieces. Her picture's on the front page of tonight's paper, incidentally."

"Don't talk with your mouth full. Besides, if you can't be a half cousin, how can you be a half niece?" Fortunately, the phone rang at that moment.

"Mama? I'm sorry. That was Jed Reuse I was talking to. I'm going to the policemen's Christmas ball with him."

I covered the phone with my hand. "She's going to the policemen's ball with Jed Reuse," I told Sister.

"Whoop-de-do. Reckon policemen have big balls?"

"Mama?"

"I'm here, darling. So is your aunt Sister. She wants to know how big policemen's balls are."

"I'm surprised she doesn't know."

I relayed this to Mary Alice, who laughed.

"What we need to know," I told Haley, "is if you've heard of a substance called DMSO. Dimethyl something, Aunt Sister says."

"I can look it up. I've got a couple of pharmacology textbooks still around here somewhere. Why do you need to know?"

"Thurman Beatty told James Butler, who told Bonnie Blue, who told Mary Alice that they think that was the way Mercy Armistead was killed."

"I thought it was digoxin. Digitalis."

"This is the way they got it into her. This DMSO absorbs stuff through the skin."

"Wow. Let me see what I can find. I'll call you back in a few minutes."

"She's going to look it up," I told Sister.

We both propped our feet on the coffee table and took a section of the evening paper to read.

"Here's Betty Bedsole's picture," Sister said, showing me the front page. "She's still beautiful, isn't she?" The picture looked as if the photographer had called her name and snapped her as she turned. Beside her, holding her arm, was Ross Perry, the art critic who had stood out at the gallery opening in his bright red jacket. "It says her husband was too ill to come with her."

I took the paper and read the accompanying article. Mercy's funeral would be the next day at three o'clock at St. Paul's with burial in Elmwood. I shivered. "You know," I told Sister, "the only time I ever saw Mercy Armistead I snapped at her. And she was dying when I did it. Probably the reason she was acting like she was, the digitalis taking effect."

"Don't feel too guilty about it," Sister said. "Mercy pissed everybody off all the time. Digitalis or no digitalis."

"Don't talk about her like that, Mary Alice. She was young and beautiful and now she's dead."

"Probably because she pissed everybody off so bad."

I handed the paper back to her. "Read," I said.

"Well, it's true. You should have seen her at the museum meetings. That guy in the paper? That Ross Perry? She threw a can of diet Dr Pepper at him once. Mostly empty, but none of us could believe it."

"My Lord! What did he do?"

"Threw it back. The word *bitch* may have been mentioned."

"Heavens!"

"Yep. It's not going to be the same at the committee meetings without Mercy. I heard she and Thurman were having trouble, too.''

"You're just a font of information, aren't you? Where did you hear that?" I held up my hand before she could answer. "Never mind. I know. Thurman told James, who told Bonnie Blue, who told you."

"How did you know?"

I tapped the newspaper. "Read!"

Mary Alice stood up. "I'm going to get some more cookies."

The phone rang. "I've got it," Haley said when I answered. "It's dimethyl sulfoxide and Aunt Sister is right. It'll transport just about anything right through the skin. It would have worked with the digitalis. Take a few hours, maybe up to six unless she was drinking. Depending on how much they got in her, of course."

"It would work," I told Mary Alice.

"I told you it would." She sat down with another handful of cookies.

"But you would have to be a doctor or a pharmacist to have access to it, wouldn't you? That should make it easier to trace the person who did it.''

"It's not even a prescription drug," Haley said. "It's used a lot on horses with swollen knees. They rub it right on and apparently it acts as an antiinflammatory by itself, or they can add other medicines and it absorbs them right in. There's all kinds of warnings here about wearing rubber gloves so you don't get a dose of the medicine you're trying to give the animal. Principally for veterinary use, it says."

"Would you have to get it from a vet?"

"Not if it's not a prescription. You could get it at any farm supply store, I'll bet. Wait a minute. Let me make sure."

I could hear her murmuring, "Clear liquid or cream, extreme caution, transdermal route."

"She's reading about it," I told Mary Alice.

"Nope, Mama, no restrictions on it. This book is about five years old but anybody could buy it then. Probably still can. God, that's wild. And that's how Mercy was killed?''

"That's what Aunt Sister says."

"It's true," Mary Alice said, not even knowing what I was talking about.

"Mercy know any vets?"

"Mercy know any vets?" I asked Mary Alice.

"James Butler."

"What? Bonnie Blue's James is a vet?"

"Sure. What did you think he did?"

"I don't know. I thought he lived at home with his daddy and Bonnie Blue. Maybe worked in insurance."

"Don't be silly, Mouse. James Butler owns the new twenty-four-hour animal clinic out in Indian Trails."

"Pet Haven?"

"Something like that."

"Haley?" I said into the phone. "Did you hear all that?"

"I heard 'James Butler.' Who's he?"

"Bonnie Blue Butler's brother. Abe's son. And a damn vet."

"Got a house out in Shelby County looks like a country club," Mary Alice said.

"Got a house out in Shelby County looks like a country club," I repeated to Haley.

"Wife and a bunch of kids."

"Wife and a bunch of kids."

Mary Alice reached over and took the phone away from me. "Thank you, Haley, darling. Your mama made fruit drop cookies today. Come by and get some tomorrow." She nodded. "He's watching the Braves play Montreal." She smiled. "Yes, dear, I know. Night-night, now."

While Mary Alice was talking, sleet had begun clicking against the skylights again. I turned on the outside light and saw that the thermometer on the deck read 33.

"It's sleeting," I announced.

"Hmmm. What did Haley have to say about the DMSO?"

"It's used mainly by vets. On horses, but on other animals, too. It's an antiinflammatory. But the main thing is that you

can get medicine right to the spot where you want it. Trans-
dermally.''

''And you don't need a prescription.''

''Apparently anybody can buy it, but vets would be the
ones most familiar with it.''

''James Butler would know about it.''

''Of course.'' I looked over at my picture of Abe and
thought about the look on his face when the handsome James
had shown up at the gallery. Pure love and pride.

''The police know all this,'' Mary Alice said.

''Sure they do. They've probably already questioned
him.''

''It's sleeting,'' Fred said from the door. ''And it's sitting
right on freezing. Roads are going to be bad in just a few
minutes.''

''Thurman could have gotten it from James,'' Mary Alice
said, ignoring Fred.

''Or found out about it from James and bought it at a farm
store. And Thurman takes digitalis.''

''It may turn into snow,'' Fred said.

''I'll bet they're cold in Atlanta at the ball game.'' Mary
Alice bit into another cookie. ''These are good, Fred.''

''I'm glad you like them,'' he said, and went back down
the hall.

''You probably should go,'' I said. ''Your driveway will
be a sheet of ice in a little while.''

''I know it.'' Mary Alice stood up and brushed cookie
crumbs onto my newly vacuumed rug. ''You know what,
Patricia Anne? I wonder what they're going to do about the
gallery. All those folks have their stuff out there they were
planning on selling for Christmas and the police have it cor-
doned off.''

''You mean like Leota Wood's quilt 'The '60s' you were
getting me?''

''You wish. I was thinking of an Abe painting for Debbie,
though, and maybe some of that silver jewelry for Haley.
And I loved those dream-catchers that old lady had made.
I'd like one of them for myself. Hang it in my bedroom and

catch all the good dreams. Didn't you like them? That Indian look?''

I admitted that I had and made a mental note to tell Haley that a dream-catcher would be a good Christmas present for her aunt Sister. ''Maybe they'll let Thurman or somebody open up the gallery long enough for the artists to get their work out. It couldn't have happened at a worse time, could it?''

''Not a good one.'' Mary Alice reached for her coat and the lights on her chest quit blinking.

''How'd you do that?'' I asked.

''Just lucky.'' She stuck some cookies in her pockets as she went through the kitchen.

''Be careful driving,'' I said.

She stopped on the back steps and looked up at the outside light. ''Snow!'' she exclaimed.

I rushed out and saw she was telling the truth. Mixed with the sleet and rain were some snowflakes.

''Snow!'' we both squealed, sticking our tongues out to catch the flakes. ''Snow!''

''How terrible,'' Mary Alice said, turning in circles, holding out her hands.

''How awful. We'll be snowed in.'' I jumped down the steps.

''We don't have enough groceries. I need to make soup.''

''And stew. Lots of stew to heat on the fireplace.''

Snow. Snow that would bring the whole town to a halt. That would cause all kinds of problems. Snow. Terrible snow. Two old Southern women who had seen so little of the white stuff danced around the yard, celebrating the glorious Christmas gift. Woofer came out of his igloo to see what the excitement was about, barked once declaring us crazy, and went back inside.

''I better hurry. No joke.'' Sister headed toward her car and I darted back inside the warm kitchen.

''It's snowing!'' I yelled down the hall to Fred. ''Come look at it.''

Like it is to Mary Alice and me, the mention of snow is

galvanizing to Fred. Born and raised in south Alabama, he's seen even less than we have. We turned on the back lights and sat in the bay window to watch the flakes. The fact that we could have counted them didn't make it any less exciting.

"Tomorrow night, we're definitely putting up the Christmas tree," he announced. "And this weekend we'll finish our shopping. Why didn't we go the other night like we'd planned?"

"Haley came to supper."

"What did she say about that DMSO stuff?"

"It would have worked. Somebody could have put digitalis in it and it would have absorbed it into the body. Vets use it a lot. Like for horses' knees when they're swollen."

"I'll bet that's what Mort Adkins puts on his knuckles before we play golf. He's got a little bottle that looks like stuff you put in your eyes. Dropper and all. He won't tee off until he squeezes a drop or two on each knuckle."

"Could be." Mort Adkins is our vet and an avid golfer. So avid that his office hours are becoming more and more abbreviated. "You don't even have to have a prescription for it."

"Sounds dangerous to me."

"It can be. Obviously."

We sat admiring the snow and thinking.

"Bonnie Blue's brother, James, is a vet," I said. "Owns a twenty-four-hour clinic in Indian Trails."

"That's interesting. You know anything about him?"

"I didn't even know he was a vet until Sister told me. You can buy the stuff anywhere, though."

"But who would know about it?"

I shrugged. "Let's talk Christmas. Let's get a live tree this year."

"Absolutely not. Too dangerous. You remember how that tree flamed up at the Camellia Dance. It's a miracle the whole place didn't burn down."

"So I need to pull the old bottlebrush tree down again."

"Patricia Anne, a Christmas tree is like popcorn." This was a speech I had heard so much I mouthed the words with him. "The only difference is what you put on it."

"And the smell. Our tree smells like formaldehyde and mothballs."

"Get some of that spray. Hey"—Fred leaned so close to the window he frosted the glass—"you think it's getting harder out there? Look how that deck railing's shining."

"How about an evergreen wreath," I said. "We could hang it over the mantel and it would smell."

"We'll see."

I had already planned on getting one the next day, a big one I had spotted at the Green Thumb. One that cost a fortune.

"You're right," I agreed. "I think the snow's getting harder."

At two o'clock, I awoke to an unusual sound, Woofer barking. I got out of bed and grabbed my robe.

"What's the matter?" Fred mumbled. "You okay?"

"Woofer's barking." I put on my robe as I rushed down the hall. He was hurting, I thought. Sick.

I turned on the back light and saw him standing by the chain-link fence of his dog yard. I found my sneakers and opened the back door. The snow had stopped. In fact, a hazy moon was shining, too dim to see by. On the deck, however, there was a light white powdering.

"What's the matter, boy? You okay, my angel?" I hurried across the yard.

Woofer barked in delight at my appearance. He jumped up on the fence to greet me.

"Are you sick, baby boy?" He obviously wasn't. He ran around in a couple of circles and ended up in front of me with his red ball in his mouth. "You want to play?" I asked in amazement. "At two o'clock in the morning? Are you crazy?"

He nudged the ball toward me and I threw it once. "Enough," I said. "Go to bed. It's freezing."

Woofer brought the ball back to the fence and watched me go into the house. Fred was standing in the kitchen drinking Maalox from the bottle.

"Chinese," he explained. "Woofer okay?"

"He's fine. Wants to play. I can't believe it."

"He didn't have sweet-and-sour shrimp and egg rolls for supper," Fred said.

I reached over and got a swig myself. "But it was good."

Fred patted me on the behind. "I think I'll read a while."

He picked up the new *Time* and settled on the sofa. I knew about how much of that magazine would get read.

I went right back to sleep, too. Sometime later, I heard, or thought I heard, Woofer barking again. But I was dreaming too good a dream to be disturbed.

Eight

"**C**ome here, Patricia Anne. You've got to see this." Fred shook my shoulder.

"Did it snow deep?" I asked, turning over and awakening immediately. "Are we snowed in?"

"No. The sun's shining. But come here. There's something I want you to see."

"What?" I asked, reaching for my robe, but he had already gone down the hall. I padded barefooted behind him.

"Look," he said. He was standing at the bay window in the kitchen pointing at the deck.

"What?" I asked again.

"The footprints."

"I made those when I went out to see why Woofer was barking."

"You made these." He pointed to the left side of the deck, where three short steps led to the dog pen. "Somebody else made those." He pointed to the steeper steps that led to our driveway, the steps where Claire had sat waiting for me. Through the light dusting of snow was a perfect path of footprints that came up to the den and then over to the bay window. A second path led back down the steps, sometimes becoming one big or misshapen foot as the intruder stepped on his own tracks.

"That's why Woofer was barking," I said. "Somebody was out there when I went to see about him." I shivered.

Fred opened the kitchen door.

"Don't go out there," I said. "You'll mess them up. We've got to call the police."

"I've already called them. This snow isn't going to last long. I just want to look at the prints."

"You've already called the police?"

"They'll be here in a few minutes."

"I've got to go brush my teeth and comb my hair." I heard the snow give a crunchy sound as Fred stepped out of the door. I hurried into the bathroom, tended to the necessities, and pulled on my sweats. That sweet Woofer, I thought. Trying to protect us.

When I got back to the kitchen, Fred was still outside, kneeling beside the tracks closest to the window.

"Come in," I said, opening the door. "There's not a thing you can do out there except catch cold."

He crunched back to the door, almost falling on the ice. "Bastard," he said. "Right up here looking in on us."

I shivered again. "I'll fix us some coffee."

Fred pulled off his wet shoes and looked at them. "Small feet," he said.

"You're calling size twelve small?"

"The person on the porch. Some kind of running shoe with whorls on the bottom."

"The police will know." I poured water into the coffee-maker.

"I'm gonna get us a goddamn alarm system," he said. "Like Mary Alice's."

I didn't point out to him that Sister's alarm system had been effectively bypassed by a murderer a couple of months ago.

"Dopeheads. Damn thugs."

While he sat at the table and groused, I looked out of the bay window again. Was it possible the tracks were Claire's? That she had been trying to reach me? The thought was gone as soon as it entered my head. There was nothing here threatening to Claire. She would have knocked on the door or rung the doorbell, not skulked around looking in windows.

The doorbell rang and I jumped.

"The police," Fred said, and went to let them in.

"Good morning," Bo Peep Mitchell said brightly as she came into the kitchen behind Fred.

"Do you work all the time?" I asked ungraciously.

"Where duty calls."

Fred gave us a questioning look. "She's the one who lost Claire," I explained.

"Mea culpa." She turned to Fred. "What's the trouble, Mr. Hollowell?"

"Out here," Fred said, opening the kitchen door.

I poured a cup of coffee and watched them through the window. Bo Peep took out a small camera and snapped some pictures. Then she rolled out a measuring tape. The two of them squatted and bent and measured and even laughed at one point. I reached into the cabinet for the Cheerios. I was hungry.

"Whew," Fred said, stamping his feet on the floor I had mopped just the day before. "Cold."

"Whew," Bo Mitchell said, following his example.

"Y'all want some coffee?" I asked.

"That would be great."

I left my half-eaten bowl of Cheerios and poured them each a cup of coffee.

"Thanks," Bo said. She was sitting at the kitchen table filling out what looked like a triplicate form. I went back to my cereal.

"What did I say, Fred? About the heel?" Bo Mitchell chewed on her pen.

"There was a square pattern right in the middle."

"But it was worn on one side. You remember which one?"

"The inside."

"Aren't you supposed to take plaster casts of footprints?" I asked. Bo's methods seemed haphazard, to say the least. Not at all like TV cops.

"Snow's melting too fast. Don't have the stuff anyway." Bo put three teaspoonfuls of sugar in her coffee and stirred it. "Ahh," she said, tasting the resulting syrup.

"You hypoglycemic?" I asked.

"Just love sugar." She put the mug down and picked up her pen again. "Okay, tell me about the dog barking last night and if you heard anything else. What time was it?"

"About two o'clock," Fred said.

"And I went out to see about him," I said. "I was scared he was sick. He's old and never barks at night, especially when it's cold. But he was fine. Wanted to play."

"And you didn't see anything unusual?" Bo asked.

"I wasn't looking. I was worried about Woofer. I think I heard him barking later, too."

"I did, too," Fred added.

Bo Mitchell wrote this into her notes. "Any idea of the later time?" We both shook our heads. She drank some more of her decaffeinated syrup. "The dog was probably just excited. There was just one set of footprints up to the deck."

I took my cereal bowl to the sink. "Is it a man's or woman's footprints out there?"

"Can't tell. Could be some neighborhood teenager snooping around." Bo Peep shrugged.

That ruled out infants and toddlers. I glanced over at Fred, but he was looking at Officer Mitchell as if she had spoken pearls of wisdom. There's nothing like a uniform to impress a man, I thought. Especially at the breakfast table.

"Thanks." Bo Mitchell drained her coffee and stood up. "I'll get this on file. To tell you the truth, I don't expect anything will come of it. But I wouldn't worry if I were you. Lock up and close your blinds. You know. The usual stuff. I've got an idea it's just a neighborhood Peeping Tom and you wouldn't even have known it if we hadn't had the snow flurries. I'll check and see if there have been any more complaints."

"*Just* a Peeping Tom?" The idea of someone looking in on us appalled me.

"I'll see you to the door," Fred said.

I took the empty coffee mug Bo Mitchell was holding out to me. "Maybe it was Claire Moon," I said.

"It wasn't Claire." A look of worry flickered across her face for a second.

"She's dead, that's what you think, isn't it?"

"She'll show up," Bo Mitchell said, and followed Fred through the door.

But in what condition? I wondered, putting the dishes in the dishwasher.

It was my morning to tutor at the local junior high school. Math, of all things. At first, when they called me and asked me to help, I was hesitant. English, sure. But math? I confessed I had avoided it like the plague in school and that my checkbook never balanced. But surely I knew more than these failing kids did, the recruiter assured me. And besides, I was used to working with students.

I think it was the phrase "failing kids" that hooked me. I agreed to try it and it had turned out to be a wonderful experience. Not having been a math teacher, I wasn't hobbled with the vocabulary. Negative integers were the ones down in the hole and fractions should be turned on their heads to divide them. The kids and I got along fine.

This morning would be the last sessions before Christmas, so I took each kid some fruit drop cookies and an amazing calculator I had found at Radio Shack that was about the size of a credit card.

"Isn't that defeating the purpose?" Fred asked when I showed it to him.

"It's called 'getting the job done.' " I didn't feel at all guilty.

All the bulletin boards were decorated for the holidays. One unusual one had Santa shouting "Happy Hanukkah" as he and the reindeer sailed across the sky by the light of what could only be the Star of Bethlehem. A card stapled in the corner said this board had been decorated by Ms. Felix's homeroom and had won second place. I made myself a mental note to look up the first place winner before I left.

The kids were pleased with their calculators and cookies.

They were also full of plans for the holidays, plans that included much TV, Nintendo, and sleep.

"Hey, there's a whole world out there," I reminded Stevie Grayton, a sharp thirteen-year-old with a tough veneer.

"You're right, Mrs. Hollowell," he agreed. "I'll watch the Discovery Channel some. I promise."

The winning bulletin board was a traditional nativity scene, nice, but lacking the charm and confusion of the Jewish Santa. There were reindeer among the flocks of sheep, which was interesting. Ms. Felix's class had been gypped, though.

I was in an upbeat mood when I left the school, and decided to go pick up Mary Alice's jacket at the Big, Bold, and Beautiful Shop. It was time to do some serious getting ready for Christmas.

Bonnie Blue was busy with a customer when I walked in, so I wandered around looking and admiring. The accessories were particularly pretty. I held a pair of large gold earrings made like sunflowers against my ear and checked them out in a mirror.

"Too big," Sister said.

"I was just looking at them." I turned around and saw she was standing right behind me. "What are you doing here? Have you given up your career?"

"Getting something to wear to Mercy's funeral. One of the Magic Maids is filling in for me at the mall this afternoon."

"Tiffany?"

"I don't know. Why?"

"Mrs. Claus would not be named Tiffany. And when did you decide to go to the funeral?"

"Ross Perry called me. He thinks it would be nice for the museum board to go and sit together. He and I are having lunch beforehand. You can come if you want to. To lunch."

"I'm not invited to the funeral?"

"You hate funerals." Mary Alice took the sunflower earrings from my hand and held them against her ear. "These have possibilities," she said. "Come help me pick out a

dress. I wish I could find something that would do for today
and for the Camellia Club cocktail party next week.''

''You're looking for a cocktail dress to wear to a funeral?''

''Maybe a beige? I hate to wear black to funerals. It just
makes everything seem more depressing.''

''But black's hard to beat for cocktails.''

''True. Come on, let's see what we can find.''

I waved at Bonnie Blue as we crossed the room. She was
showing a woman how to tie a scarf so it would hang a
certain way.

''Here,'' Sister said. She had already picked out several
dresses that might do and had hung them on a dressing room
door. ''Tell me the truth now.''

The truth, and I told her, was that she should buy two
dresses. God knows she had the money.

''Don't be silly,'' she said.

We ended up choosing a black silk suit that could be
dressed up or down. A hot pink blouse for the cocktail party
and a beige silk for the funeral, and Sister was in business.

''I didn't want black,'' she said, but I could tell she was
pleased with how elegant the suit looked.

While she was trying on dresses, I bought the jacket. It
was as nice as Bonnie Blue had said.

''You heard anything from Claire?'' Bonnie Blue asked
while she gift wrapped the jacket.

''No. Have Thurman or James?''

''No.'' Bonnie Blue unfolded a big red ribbon and placed
it in the middle of the box. ''I'll tell you one thing, though,
Patricia Anne. Thurman Beatty's going to be one more upset
man if anything happens to Claire Moon.''

''Wait a minute. Who would he be more upset about? His
dead wife or Claire Moon?''

''Go figure. All I know is he thinks Claire is the cat's
pajamas. You know?'' Bonnie Blue slid the package into a
bag.

''How should I know? I never met any of these people
until the other night. Except Claire, of course. And, Bonnie

Blue, you're too young to know about cat's pajamas."

"One of my daddy's sayings."

I took the bag. "Thanks."

Sister came up to pay for her suit and the blouses. "Come go to lunch with Patricia Anne and I," she invited Bonnie Blue.

"Me," I corrected.

"Well, of course you're going," Sister assured me.

"Can't," Bonnie Blue said.

"We're meeting Ross Perry at the Green and White."

"Sorry. Too busy. But I tell you what you can do for me."

"What?"

"Ask that Mr. Perry when he's planning on paying Daddy for all those paintings."

"What paintings?" Sister wanted to know.

"It's a long story. I'll tell you later. Just ask him."

"I will." Sister took the suit from Bonnie Blue and we headed for the door. "Wonder what Ross is doing with Abe's paintings."

"Selling them for him?"

Mary Alice shrugged. I held the door for her and we exited onto the sidewalk.

"Have you heard that Thurman Beatty thinks Claire Moon is the cat's pajamas?" I asked her.

"Good God. Cat's pajamas? You've got to get out more, Patricia Anne."

"I don't have to. I have you."

That seemed to please her.

The Green and White is a vegetarian restaurant that is so expensive you could buy the farm the vegetables came from with a tab for three. They specialize in things I have never heard of. Granted, being an Alabama native, black-eyed peas, corn, okra, and cabbage, with an occasional rutabaga thrown in, are the veggies I'm most familiar with. But asparagus, broccoli, and even artichokes appear on my table regularly. I am even aware that there is more than one kind of lettuce. But at the Green and White I can't understand the menu. There have been times when *pasta* was the only word I recognized. The upbeat mood I had left the school with had faded in the Big, Bold, and Beautiful Shop. The Green and White succeeded in erasing it completely.

The owner, Andre, is a short, pudgy man who looks like he rushes out to McDonald's as soon as he locks the door. He raises his own herbs in hanging baskets that fill the windows. It's really a very pleasant place if you don't think about how much each mouthful costs.

He spotted Mary Alice as soon as we walked in and probably would have kissed her on her cheeks except he's a head shorter than she is. Instead, he held out his arms expansively, beamed, and exclaimed, "Mrs. Crane! Mrs. Crane!"

Mary Alice gave him an awkward half hug and introduced me. I've met him at least ten times but it has yet to register with him.

"Mr. Perry is here already," Andre said. "Allow me to show you the way."

Ross Perry was sitting about ten feet from us in plain view, but Andre showed us the way. Ross Perry tried to hop up, not very successfully, since he and Andre have the same weight problem. Sister and I appreciated the effort, though.

She introduced me to Ross Perry while Andre stood by, rubbing his hands together in pleasure.

"I noticed you at the gallery opening the other night, Mrs. Hollowell," Ross Perry said.

"Call me Patricia Anne."

"Wine! Wine!" Andre exclaimed. "A nice chablis?"

"I'd like iced tea," I said. Sorrow filled Andre's face. "I'm allergic to alcohol," I explained. "I could go into anaphylactic shock, die right here in convulsions."

"Chablis would be wonderful," Mary Alice said to Andre, who was backing away from the table.

"Why does it surprise me to see wine in a vegetarian restaurant?" I asked.

Mary Alice shrugged. "It's grapes."

"The nectar of the gods," Ross Perry said. His red nose and the broken capillaries in his cheeks indicated he had been sipping on the nectar frequently and for a long time. Today he was wearing a black suit with white stripes that looked like a costume for *Guys and Dolls*. The basket of herbs hanging across from us cast a shadow on his bald head that looked exactly like Gorbachev's birthmark, including the drip.

Andre came back with the wine and the tea and announced that one of today's specials was angel-hair pasta with a delightful tofu and cubonelle sauce sprinkled with sun-dried tomatoes, another—''

"That's what I'll have," I interrupted, having recognized two ingredients.

Andre pushed his bifocals down and glared at me. I pushed my bifocals down and returned the glare. The music to *High Noon* pulsed between us.

"Or you could make my day with a T-bone," I said.

Mary Alice kicked me. "What are the other specials, Andre?" she asked sweetly.

He held his hand to his chest as he recited them. Mary Alice and Ross Perry both said everything sounded so wonderful that Andre should choose for them. Pretty smart.

"What's the matter with you, Patricia Anne?" Mary Alice fussed as Andre bounced away.

"He's so show-offy. What's wrong with iced tea and black-eyed peas?"

"Who mentioned black-eyed peas?"

"Nobody. That's the problem."

"You want black-eyed peas?"

"What's wrong with them?"

"Ladies"—Ross Perry held up his wineglass—"I'm so glad you could join me for lunch today."

"I hoped it would be all right. I ran into my sister and she wanted to come so badly." Mary Alice turned to him and smiled at the same time she aimed another kick at me.

"Yes, indeed," I agreed, smiling. The kick had missed by a mile. We clinked glasses and exchanged pleasantries.

Before the food arrived, though, the conversation had worked its way around to Mercy's murder and Claire's disappearance. Ross knew about the DMSO that had been used to kill Mercy. "Diabolical!" he exclaimed. But he hadn't realized I was the one who had taken Claire to the hospital, that she had come to me. I told him the complete story.

He shook his head. "Claire's a sweet girl, so fragile. I've always pictured her as the Arthurian Lady of the Lake with a lily in her hand."

It was a pretty good simile, I thought; the alliteration could use a little work.

A pretty blond waitress brought our food and a small loaf of bread straight from the oven, crusty and steaming.

"Looks as good as black-eyed peas," Sister said.

We concentrated on the food for a few minutes. Whatever it was, it was delicious.

"I went by to see Liliane Bedsole last night," Ross said, reaching for the bread. "Anybody want more?" he asked. Sister and I shook our heads no. "Anyway"—he sliced a large piece and buttered it—"she's in pretty bad shape, understandable, given the fact that her niece has just been murdered and her foster daughter has disappeared."

"Was Betty Bedsole there?" Sister asked.

"No. She's got a suite at the Tutwiler. I went by to see her, too. Bless her heart. Completely devastated."

Mary Alice and I looked at each other. Oh, God. To lose a child. Both of us put our forks down.

"What about her husband? Mercy's father?" I asked.

"Had a stroke in Mexico, I understand. He's in his eighties and apparently it did him in. And the son is in China making a picture."

"Is anybody with her?" Mary Alice asked. The thought of a bereaved mother alone in a hotel room was as unsettling to her as it was to me.

"Her secretary and her companion." Ross Perry took a big bite of buttered bread that left his lips greasy. "The companion's really a nurse, you know. Betty just got out of the Betty Ford Clinic."

"A slightly dysfunctional family." I moved my foot quickly before Mary Alice could kick it.

Ross Perry wiped his mouth with Andre's oversized napkin. "Sad," he agreed. But there was a look in his eyes that belied his words. I remembered what Mary Alice had told me about Mercy's throwing a can of cola at him. That act was becoming more understandable by the minute.

Ross pushed his chair back. "If you ladies will excuse me a minute, I need to make a phone call."

"He's a doll," I said, watching him waddle across the floor.

"If you weren't so old, I'd swear you were having PMS," Mary Alice said.

"We had a Peeping Tom last night. I'm still upset about it."

"What happened?"

I told her about the footprints and Woofer barking.

"Probably some kid," she said. "Out playing in the snow."

"I hope so." I watched Ross Perry leaning against the wall as he talked on the phone. He was having an animated conversation. At one point, he took out a handkerchief and wiped his forehead and bald head. "I don't like that man." I motioned toward the phone.

"Don't let on. If he knew, he wouldn't sleep nights worrying about it."

"I'm sorry," he said, coming back to the table. "It was something I'd forgotten for my column."

"Quite all right." Mary Alice smiled. She spotted Andre and held up her wineglass. He came rushing over and gave her and Ross both a refill. At this rate, they wouldn't suffer much at Mercy's funeral.

"Some decaf coffee?" I asked Andre. He pursed his lips. "The food was delicious," I added. He nodded, which meant he was agreeing with me about the food or was going to bring me some coffee. I would have to wait and see.

"I know this will sound premature," Ross Perry said to Mary Alice, "but last night when I saw Liliane I think I realized for the first time how little she has in her life. I think the board of directors of the museum should consider asking her to take Mercy's place. What do you think?"

"It hasn't crossed my mind," Mary Alice said.

"Well, think about it. I believe it would mean a lot to her."

"I will," Mary Alice promised.

I couldn't believe this. "Better hurry," I said. "Mercy's been dead two whole days."

Mary Alice slammed her wineglass down. "Patricia Anne, you are crossing the pig tracks."

I excused myself and headed for the ladies' room. Granted, none of this was any of my business. Granted, I hadn't been in the mood for lunch and shouldn't have let Mary Alice talk me into it. And maybe I had been too smart-mouthed. But pig tracks! I didn't deserve that!

Our grandmother Alice, who lived in Montgomery, and from whom Mary Alice inherited her size, was a formidable disciplinarian. We were taught very early that there were three things the women in our family never were. First was tacky. Wearing patent leather shoes after five was an example of this. Then, there was common. This included smoking on the street and not writing thank-you notes within a week. Finally, there was common as pig tracks. God forbid. I was never accused of this by Grandmother, but Mary Alice was. Grandmother caught her cutting her toenails on the front porch, a common as pig tracks offense, and she was taken to the bus station and sent back to Birmingham immediately for Mama to deal with.

"Thank God your grandmother didn't live to see this," Mama said one day while we were watching the people on a talk show. "It would have killed her. These folks are commoner than pig tracks."

I combed my hair and put on some lipstick, reassuring the woman in the mirror that she was not as common as pig tracks. I was closing my purse when the door opened and Claire Moon walked in. I was so startled, I dropped my purse and the contents went everywhere.

"Claire!" But the moment I said it, I knew I was wrong. This woman was taller, and her eyes were a pale blue.

"I'm Glynn," she said. "Glynn Needham."

"And I'm Lynn," said the identical woman who had come

in behind her. "Here, we'll help you pick up your things."

"I thought you were your sister," I said weakly.

They both grinned.

"Not a bit alike," Glynn said.

Nine

"You're Mrs. Hollowell," Glynn said. "We recognized you when you came into the restaurant." She and her sister were both scrambling around picking up the contents of my purse, which consisted of old receipts, change, half pieces of gum, and used Kleenex as well as the usual wallet, checkbook, and lipstick.

"You want these?" Lynn held up two capsules which looked like some kind of antibiotics. They were covered in lint.

"I don't know what they are," I admitted. "Maybe from a sinus infection last spring."

"Then we toss them." She threw them into the wastebasket. "You need to get you a backpack, Mrs. Hollowell. See?" She turned so I could see brown leather that seemed to cover her whole back.

"I don't carry that much," I explained. I accepted the articles they had picked up and crammed them back into my purse. "Thanks. You really startled me, you know."

"We're sorry," they said in unison.

"You shouldn't have bounced in like that, Glynnie," Lynn said.

"It was your fault, Lynnie."

They stood on either side of me, arguing into the mirror.

It was a slightly surreal experience being sandwiched that way between identical twins.

Lynn caught my eye in the mirror. "We knew you at Alexander High. Knew who you were. We only went there one year and didn't take AP English like Claire did."

"She's smarter than we are," Glynn said.

I looked at the two beautiful young women who stood beside me. Their shiny black hair was cut in the same style as Claire's with heavy bangs and the longer sides that brushed their cheeks, emphasizing high cheekbones. Their skin was as pale. But the eyes were startlingly blue, accentuated by the light blue sweaters each wore over jeans.

"She's no prettier," I said.

They both smiled. "We work at it harder," Glynn said.

"Like every day," Lynn said.

"You got any idea where she is?" I asked.

"No idea."

"She'll show up."

That was what Bo Peep Mitchell had said. Either they knew something I didn't, or they were being mighty callous about Claire's disappearance. I looked from one to the other. "Did you follow me in here to tell me something?"

"Just hello," Glynn said.

"Hello," Lynn said.

That wasn't good enough. "How come I didn't see you in the dining room?"

"We were hiding from Ross Perry," Glynn said.

"In a booth. Behind a big basket of basil. We hate him."

I nodded. That was understandable. "You're here for Mercy's funeral?"

Lynn turned to Glynn. "The funeral. Of course. We should go to the funeral. Don't you think?"

"Who is doing the eulogy?" Glynn asked.

I snapped my purse closed and moved from between them. They slid together, turned, and looked at me. I've read the studies on identical twins and have even had some in my classes, but they never cease to amaze me. I was facing oneness here.

''Thank you for taking care of Claire,'' Glynn, or was it Lynn, said. Since they had turned from the mirror I was confused.

I nodded. ''I wish I could have done more.''

Glynn turned to her sister. ''Claire wouldn't want Mrs. Hollowell to be worried, would she, Lynnie?''

''Certainly not, Glynnie.''

''You know where she is, don't you?'' I said.

''Did we say that, Glynnie?''

''Of course not, Lynnie. Turn around.'' Glynn reached into Lynn's backpack and took out a comb and lipstick.

''Thank you,'' I said.

''For what?'' Lynn reached down and took the two anti-biotic capsules from the top of the wastebasket. ''Here. Stick these in Ross Perry's throat for us.''

''Or any other orifice,'' Glynn said.

They were both laughing as I left the rest room. Surely, I thought, I had gotten the message right. Claire was okay and her sisters knew where she was. On the other hand, what had they really said? That I was not to worry. That Claire wouldn't want me to worry. There was a lot of room there for misunderstanding.

Mary Alice and Ross Perry were having a halfhearted argument over who should pay the check as I walked up. Both were insisting on the honor.

''You invited me,'' I reminded Mary Alice. No way I was going to get drawn into this argument.

''I'll leave the tip,'' Ross said.

Andre bowed and waved us into the street. As I went through the door, I looked around to see if I saw the Needham twins. If they were hiding behind the basil baskets, they were doing a good job.

''I've got to rush home to get dressed,'' Mary Alice said.

Ross Perry nodded. ''And I've got a couple of things need doing. I'll meet you at Saint Paul's about a quarter to three.'' He shook my hand with a surprisingly firm grip. ''Patricia Anne, it was a pleasure meeting you.'' He smiled and walked off down the street, turning to give a small wave as he reached his car.

"What are you going to do?" Mary Alice asked me.

"Christmas shop. I think I'll look around here for a while. There are some interesting places. Did you see that shop called the Witchery? I'll bet I could find Freddie's Celia something in there."

"It's the Stitch Witchery, a fancy sewing shop."

"Oh. I thought maybe it was one of those New Age goddess places. Crystals and stuff."

"In Birmingham? Are you crazy? Stick to T. J. Maxx, Mouse."

"Well, it could have been," I called to Sister as she disappeared around the corner, laughing.

It was a beautiful afternoon, no sign of the snow flurries of the night before. The sky was a clear blue, and abundant sunshine had pushed the thermometer on the bank building to a balmy 60 degrees. I threw my heavy coat onto the backseat of the car and headed for the mall to do some serious shopping. Fred and I usually shopped for the boys' presents together and Fred bought mine (I'd point it out to him), but the rest was up to me.

I found a parking place fairly close to an entrance, dropped some money into the Salvation Army bucket, and bought a paper angel from the Humane Society. Three hours later, I emerged, dropped some more money into the Salvation Army bucket, and bought another angel from the Humane Society. Mary Alice says don't be silly, send them one check a year. But if I did, I'd still have to stop and put in money and buy the angels. I know I would. When the Santa ringing the bell looks particularly bedraggled or they've brought puppies from the Humane Society, I'm a goner.

The sun was getting low in the sky, and I was tired, but Woofer hadn't had his walk the day before or this morning. I rushed home, took a package of bean soup from the freezer, put on my sweats, and went to the dog yard. Woofer was delighted to see me. When I bragged on him for barking the night before, he rolled over on his back and wriggled with pleasure.

We set out at a brisk walk. We usually do, slowing down within a couple of blocks and, like the old couple we are, meandering home at leisure. More Christmas decorations had sprung up in the last two days. Some of my neighbors, I realized, could have been students of Ms. Felix. Her Jewish Santa bulletin board and the Holy Family in a sleigh on the next block had a certain tangential similarity.

While we walked, I thought of Lynn and Glynn Needham and their cryptic message. If it *was* a message. Claire wouldn't have wanted me to worry. I stopped for Woofer to investigate a crack in the sidewalk. I should have pinned them down more, I thought. I glanced at my watch. The funeral would have been over a couple of hours ago. I wondered if the girls had gone to it. They certainly hadn't seemed bothered by Mercy's death.

The Bedsole granddaughters: Mercy, whom nobody seemed to like and who had been murdered; Claire, the lost one, the abused one whom someone hated enough to try to kill; Lynn and Glynn, each a beautiful half of a whole.

"Amos," I said to the late afternoon, "you might should have kept your pants zipped."

Woofer thought I was talking to him and stopped, wagging his tail.

"Not you, buddy. We had you fixed."

Fred's car came into the driveway as Woofer and I turned onto our block. He saw us and waved. He was waiting with the newspaper in his hand when we got there.

"I'll put him up." Fred reached down and scratched Woofer's ears. "Come on, boy."

I watched them cross the yard, two gentle old men.

"Sorry, Amos," I said guiltily to the late afternoon. "Maybe some of us are just luckier."

Fred got a beer from the refrigerator and disappeared into the bathroom while I heated the iron skillet for corn bread. Bean soup and corn bread on a chilly winter night are hard to beat. After I put the bread in the oven, I called Mary Alice to see how the funeral went. The main thing I wanted to know was if the Needham girls had been there. I got her answering machine. Maybe she had gone to relieve Tiffany, the Magic Maid, at the mall.

I put the soup in a saucepan to thaw and turned the burner on low. I could have done this in the microwave, but the smell of bean soup is too good to miss. It would take the bread a while, anyway.

Fred came in freshly showered and in his terry cloth robe. "We going out tonight?" he asked, nuzzling my neck.

"Did you see the bed?"

"Couldn't. There were too many packages."

"Then let's spend the evening admiring all I bought and getting the decorations down."

"Suits me." He turned me and cupped me against him. "Umm," he said, kissing me lightly.

"Umm," I echoed.

"I swear this is a den of iniquity," Mary Alice said behind us. "Don't y'all ever quit?"

Neither Fred nor I moved. "Mary Alice," he said quietly, "go outside and knock on the door."

"Why?"

"Because it's the polite thing to do."

"I could see through the window, anyway."

"Mary Alice." Fred still had not raised his voice.

"Shit." I could hear the door open and close.

Fred shoved me aside and slammed the dead bolt lock on the door. He whirled around the kitchen and den, closing the blinds so quickly, they rattled in their casements.

"Now," he said, coming back and putting his arms back around me. "Where were we?"

"Not breathing quite as hard," I giggled.

"Mouse?" I could hear Mary Alice calling. "Mouse, that's not very nice."

"Don't answer her," Fred said.

"Mouse, I came to tell you something terrible."

"Ignore her."

"I don't want to hear anything terrible!" I yelled back.

"Mouse, Ross Perry is dead. Somebody shot him."

"Oh, shit," Fred said, releasing me. He went to unlock the door.

"May I come in?" Mary Alice asked politely. Fred shrugged and she stepped back inside the kitchen. "That really wasn't necessary, you know. I know when I'm not welcome."

"What do you mean, Ross is dead?" I asked.

"Dead. Shot. Somebody shot him."

"Who's Ross Perry?" Fred asked.

"Where?" I wanted to know.

"In the head."

"Where was *he*? Not where did the bullet go in."

"Down in Shelby County. He didn't come to the funeral and all of us were pretty pissed because our going together was his idea. But he must not have been there because he was dead."

"Good excuse," Fred said. "Who's Ross Perry?"

"A friend of Sister's," I explained. I turned the burner off under the soup and sat down at the kitchen table. "I don't understand." I turned to Fred. "We had lunch with him today at the Green and White."

"I'm sorry." He patted my shoulder. "Let me put on some clothes. I'll be right back."

Mary Alice pulled out a chair and sat down beside me. She still had on her elegant new black suit.

"That suit was a good buy," I said.

"Comfortable, too. I hate skirts you can't sit down in or cross your legs in. This one's just right."

"A Baby Bear skirt."

"What?"

"I'm just babbling. Tell me about Ross."

"All I know is he's dead. James Butler and his wife were on their way to the funeral and saw this car weaving down the road toward them. Then while they were watching it, it went off the road and down the embankment into Kelly Creek, about a thirty-foot drop. The car was upside-down in the creek when the Butlers got there. James's wife called 911 and James grabbed his vet's first aid stuff and climbed down the bank. He even managed to get Ross out of the car, God knows how, upside-down like it was and under water, and dragged him over to the bank. By that time, his wife—what's her name?''

I shrugged that I had no idea.

''Anyway, James's wife had crawled down the bank and they started trying to revive him. Ross wasn't breathing, but he'd been under the water for several minutes. James even had this oxygen pump he carries in his car and he tried that, but nothing. Mrs. James, whatever her name is, said they were working so hard on Ross, they didn't notice the blood pooling under his head. Looks like a doctor would have noticed that, doesn't it? It's an important symptom.''

I agreed that a doctor might wish to investigate a pool of blood under someone's head. ''But they were just assuming he had inhaled water. Makes sense.''

''True,'' Mary Alice agreed. ''It wouldn't have made any difference, anyway. He was dead as a doornail by the time they started trying to revive him.''

''Do they know who shot him?''

''James says there are deer hunters all over those woods, even where they are posted. He thinks that's what happened. The hunters don't realize how close they are to the road and they shoot. He says this time of the year he and his wife are scared to let their children go out to play.''

''My Lord!'' I thought about Ross turning and giving a wave as he got into his car, about the shadow on his bald head that looked like Gorbachev's birthmark. This man had sat across from me at lunch and now he was gone.

''Mary Alice,'' I said, ''the Crazies are catching up to us.''

''God's truth.''

We sat quietly for a few minutes, each immersed in our own thoughts. When Fred came in and wanted to know what had happened, I listened to the story again. This time I had some questions.

''How did you hear about it?'' I asked when Sister got through telling Fred.

"James was supposed to be a pallbearer. When he didn't show up, Thurman called and got him on his car phone."

"That was good news to get at a funeral," Fred said. He hit the palms of his hands against the table. "I hope they catch the son of a bitch that shot him and lock him up for good. Remember that little girl that got killed on I-65 last year? The same thing. Riding in the car with her mother. Damn! Peeping Toms right on our own porch in the middle of the night and folks getting shot just riding down the road." He stood up, stomped to the back door, walked out, and slammed it.

"My goodness!" Mary Alice exclaimed.

"He's just going to talk to Woofer," I said. "Things that happen by chance make him nervous. He's a cause-and-effect man."

"Is that like bread and potatoes?"

I chose to ignore this. "Why do you suppose Ross was in Shelby County? He said he had a couple of errands to run, but he was pushing it to get down there and back in time for the funeral."

"I have no idea." Mary Alice went to the refrigerator and got a beer. "You want something?"

"A Coke. There's one already opened. That'll be fine."

Mary Alice came back to the table and handed me the bottle of Coke. It had lost some of its fizz but still tasted good.

"Were the Needham twins at the funeral?" I asked.

"I don't know them."

"You couldn't miss them. They look just like Claire, only taller."

"I don't think so. At least I didn't see them. There was a good crowd there, though. Betty Bedsole made it through okay. I don't think I could, Patricia Anne."

"I don't think I could, either." We were quiet for a few minutes, each thinking her own thoughts. Mine were about Tom's funeral. The only thing that had gotten me through it was trying to help Haley. "What about Liliane?" I asked.

"She got through the funeral okay. I'm sure Ross's death

is going to be another blow, though. They were pretty good friends, I understand.''

"I still wonder what Ross was ⁀oing down in Shelby County. You think he could have been going to see James? Was he on the road to their house?''

"It's the road, apparently. But why would he have been going to see James? He knew he would see him at the funeral.'' Mary Alice put her beer down and stood up. "Who knows?'' She shrugged.

"You want some bean soup?'' I asked.

"Nope. I've lost my appetite.''

I looked at Mary Alice in alarm. I had never heard her say this before. "You feel okay?''

"I'm okay.'' She started toward the door and turned. "You know, Mouse, I just don't think I can get away with wearing this suit to another funeral in the same week. Plus the cocktail party. Do you?''

"Go home,'' I said.

Mary Alice reached into the cookie jar, got a handful of fruit drop cookies, and left.

Fred came back in as I was turning out the corn bread. "Looks good,'' he said. "Smells good.''

"Is good.'' I carried the two bowls of soup to the table and Fred followed with the plate of corn bread.

"We are going to watch *Wheel of Fortune* with our supper.'' I took the small TV from the counter and placed it in the middle of the table. "We'll talk after a while.''

"Fine,'' Fred said, bless his heart. We ate quietly while Vanna turned letters. "Richmond, Virginia! Richmond, Virginia!'' Fred prompted a contestant who landed on $5,000 and called out an *n*. "That's a hard one,'' he sympathized with the woman who was unable to come up with another consonant and who eventually saw $10,000 disappear from the screen in front of her. "They shouldn't have them that hard.'' The woman agreed; you could tell by her pinched smile as she clapped for the winning contestant. I felt myself beginning to relax.

By the time we watched *Jeopardy* and I had answered the

Final Jeopardy question correctly (Wells Fargo), I was ready to talk about Ross Perry and seeing the Needham twins.

"After we get the Christmas decorations down," Fred said.

"We can talk while we're doing that."

Fred held up his hand. "No, we can't, Patricia Anne. You'll be telling me something important and I'll say where's the nativity scene and you'll get mad and say I'm not paying attention. We'll get the decorations down first." He was right and I knew it. One of the advantages of a forty-year marriage.

He pulled the attic steps down and I followed him up. The last time I had been up there had been a few months before. I had been with Haley, who was looking at her old formals stored up there. It had been a painful, purging afternoon when Haley accepted the loss of Tom. Until then, she had been fiercely, angrily, holding on to him. We had never put the dresses up, I realized. They bloomed on the old rocker, the sewing machine, the trunk.

"What are these dresses doing out?" Fred asked.

"I think Haley's going to give them to the Goodwill." I began to pick them up and hang them back in the closet.

"Let's see. The tree first." Fred dragged a long box over to the steps.

"The lights and the new ornaments." He handed me a smaller box.

"And the old ornaments." This was the most precious box of all. He placed it gently beside the steps. "Now, where's the nativity scene?" We both laughed.

Within an hour the bottlebrush tree was assorted and assembled in the living room. When it was new, the metal prongs that went into the plastic trunk were color coded. Now we had to hold the limbs out and guess which went where, not too hard a job since the result should be a perfect triangle.

"Fine," Fred said. "Now the lights."

"I'm going to talk about Ross Perry now," I said. "You just do the lights."

Fred nodded and plugged the first string in. It worked, which I found encouraging. I started by telling him about meeting Ross at the gallery, that he was an art critic for the paper and a friend of Mercy's and Liliane's. I talked about the lunch we had had today with Mary Alice and how Ross had waved as he got into his car and how I hadn't particularly liked him or the Green and White and had acted common as pig tracks, so Mary Alice said, though I really didn't think it had been that bad. And in the ladies' room Claire's twin sisters had shown up and might have had a message for me that Claire was all right, though I wasn't sure, but they were as beautiful as she was.

A second and a third set of lights came on while I talked. Fred would stop me occasionally with a question.

"Do the twins live here?"

"Liliane Bedsole said they live in New York and model. They're pretty enough."

"So they were here for Mercy Armistead's funeral?" Fred plugged in a fourth set of lights, which didn't burn. "Damn."

"I guess so. These are strange people, Fred." I handed him a string of lights that worked.

"How so?"

It was hard to describe the twins, not their appearance, but the way they communicated with each other. "They're sort of wispy," I finally said.

"Wispy?" Fred disappeared behind the tree, pulling lights behind him.

"Like they're only real for each other." I knew I was not doing a good job of explaining the twins. "I'll bet they're the ones got Claire from the hospital, though. I don't know why they did it, but I'll bet they're the ones. Somebody had to have done it. Claire was too medicated to have slipped out by herself."

"But why?" Fred stood back and admired the tree before he began to twist another string of lights around it. "Tell me if I've got a blank spot."

"Down there on the left at nine o'clock."

"Okay." He filled in the space.

I handed him the last string. "I have no idea why anyone would abduct a sick person from a hospital," I said.

"Well"—Fred crawled around the tree with this string—"there could be several reasons. One is that the person is in danger."

"She was being watched."

"So carefully she just walked out."

I agreed he had a point.

"Another reason is the kidnapper can't afford to have the kidnappee talk to the police."

"True."

"Which would be why she was in danger." I was getting confused here.

"Exactly. So, if her sisters took Claire, was it because they were trying to protect her from someone else or trying to protect themselves?"

"They were trying to protect her." I thought of the twins, of their eerie resemblance to Claire. Their oneness had reached out to include their sister. It was the only way they could have survived the brutality of their childhood. I was suddenly sure of this. "They were protecting her," I repeated.

Fred stood up and looked at the tree. "There," he said. "You want me to run to the drugstore and get a couple of more strings of lights?"

"The tree looks fine." Glynn, Lynn, and Claire. Sisters. The knot of worry that had taken up residence in my belly when I first saw Claire huddled on my steps, and which had increased in size when I saw the obscenities painted on her walls, relaxed slightly. "Let's put the ornaments on," I said.

Ten

Ross Perry's death made the front page of the paper the next morning. Accompanying the story was a picture of him taken at least twenty years earlier when he had hair. The headline read BIZARRE ACCIDENT TAKES LIFE OF ART PATRON.

I took the paper into the breakfast room to finish reading the article. For once, Sister had gotten the details right. Dr. James Butler and his wife, Yvonne, had just left their home and entered County Road 17 when they noticed a car weaving down the road toward them. The lunge down the embankment, the upside-down car, and their efforts to rescue and revive an already dead Ross were just as Mary Alice had said.

Mr. Perry (the article continued), 54, a well-known art critic and author of two books of art criticism, served on the board of directors of the Museum of Art and was active in all phases of the Birmingham art scene. He was survived by a sister, Mrs. Delia Reynolds, of New Orleans, LA, and several nieces and nephews.

The story segued into the sheriff's speculation that a deer hunter was probably responsible for the death; quoted the local president of the NRA, who assured us that guns didn't kill people, people did; and ended with the fact that the Birmingham art community had lost two of its greatest supporters in the last few days with the deaths of Ross Perry and Mercy Armistead, who had also served on the museum board and whose death was still under investigation.

I put the paper down and poured some Cheerios into a bowl, spilling a few of them. There had to be some connection, I thought between Mercy's murder, Ross's death, which could very possibly have been murder, and Claire's disappearance. I spread the spilled Cheerios apart. Claire Cheerio, Ross Cheerio, and Mercy Cheerio I placed across the top. Obviously what they had in common was that someone was after each of them, assuming Ross's death had not been an accident. It was possible, of course, but what was he doing out on that country road headed away from Birmingham just before Mercy's funeral? I left his Cheerio at the top. Now, what else did they have in common?

Mercy and Claire had a grandfather and aunt in common. I pushed two Cheerios into place for Amos and Liliane Bedsole. And a mother and aunt. Betty Bedsole took her place. Cousins and sisters. Glynn and Lynn Cheerio joined the Bedsole crowd. But that left Ross Cheerio sitting over by himself. The Bedsole family was a mess and very possibly could have done each other in, but for some reason, I didn't believe so.

I took another handful of Cheerios. Mercy and Ross had the museum and love of art in common. Claire loved art. One Cheerio went down as a common denominator. Mercy and Claire might both have had Thurman Beatty. And then maybe not. Thurman could have thought Claire hung the moon and still admired her from a distance. A man could certainly be attracted to a woman and not act upon it. But to be on the safe side, I broke a Cheerio in half for Thurman and gave one piece to each woman. Ross Cheerio was left sitting by himself with one denominator, love of art. Not exactly a cause for murder. I thought about Bonnie Blue's saying Ross owed her father money for some paintings. Money. Now there was a cause for murder.

"What are you doing?" Fred asked.

"Playing a game." I brushed the Cheerios into my bowl. "You want some cereal?"

"After a while. Just some coffee now." He poured a cup and came to the table. The paper with Ross's picture was lying face up. Fred picked it up and glanced at the story.

"I don't believe it was a deer hunter," I said. "I think whoever killed Mercy killed Ross, too."

Fred looked at me over his bifocals and tapped the paper. "Stay out of this, Patricia Anne."

"I just made a statement."

"You let that nutty sister of yours drag you into all kinds of dangerous situations."

"Like a gallery opening and lunch at the Green and White."

"Exactly. Trouble follows that woman, Patricia Anne. Look at all those dead husbands. I can't believe three men were crazy enough to marry that woman."

"My Lord, Fred. You make Mary Alice sound like a black widow. Her husbands were old as Methuselah and died happily."

"Listen to what I say, Patricia Anne." He pointed a finger at me and disappeared behind the paper.

I shot him a bird.

"I saw that," he claimed.

"You did not." I poured milk on my cereal and reached over to turn on the small TV, which was still on the table. A local newscaster was giving the same story about Ross Perry that was in the paper. I was about to turn it off when she announced that former All-American Thurman Beatty was being held for questioning in the death of his wife, the internationally known artist Mercy Armistead. They showed a picture of Thurman, dressed in a dark suit, being escorted by three policemen into city jail.

"It looks like they picked him up right after the funeral," I said. "Look how dressed up he is."

"Who?" Fred asked, putting down the paper.

"Thurman Beatty. He's being held for questioning in his wife's death. Held. Sounds like they mean business."

"That's ridiculous. All-American. Heisman candidate." Fred turned the TV so he could see it, but they had already gone to commercial.

"It'll be in the paper if they did it yesterday," I said, picking up the Metro section that was still lying on the table. It was—on the front page, with a picture of Thurman in his Alabama uniform. This paper needed some up-to-date pictures.

It was a fairly lengthy article since it not only mentioned that Thurman was being held for questioning in the murder of his wife but also reviewed each of his more remarkable Alabama football games as well as individual plays and reiterated that he had been gypped of the Heisman. His professional career was also examined lengthily. But the two sentences I considered most important were hidden between the goal lines: the fact that he had retired from the NFL because of health problems and that he currently owned a farm in Shelby County, where he raised quarter horses. I knew about the heart problems, but I hadn't known about the horses. Given the circumstances of Mercy's death by DMSO, no wonder they were questioning him.

Fred was reading over my shoulder. I finished before he did and handed him the paper. Nope, I thought, thinking of my Cheerio people. If Thurman killed Mercy, then why did Claire run, and what about Ross? Unless Thurman had kidnapped Claire and Ross's death had really been an accident. I could feel the beginning of a headache between my eyes.

I put my cereal bowl in the dishwasher and poured Fred another cup of coffee.

"I'm having lunch today with Frances Zata," I said. "What are you going to do?"

Fred was still reading the article. "God! I'd forgotten that Tennessee game when he broke two guys' legs!"

I patted him on the head and left the kitchen. The smell of testosterone was getting to me.

Frances swept into the Blue Moon looking like a million bucks in a black skirt and a black-and-white herringbone jacket. With it she wore an emerald-green turtleneck sweater, a combination I would never have thought of but which was a knockout. I had on my red suit, which was seasonal. Its days were numbered, though. You can only shave wool gabardine around the pockets and down the sleeves just so much before it begins to get shiny. I have a gadget I bought at K mart that whisks along fabric, depilling. A wonderful invention. Mary Alice says I shave my clothes more than I do my legs. Which is almost true.

Frances never looks like her clothes have been depilled. Or need to be.

"Morning," she said, pulling her chair back and sliding into it gracefully.

"I'll bet you don't sweat, either," I grumbled.

"Of course not." She grinned. "I know why you wanted to have lunch here. I just walked through the mall and saw Mrs. Claus."

"I hope she saw you."

"I waved and yelled 'Hey, Mary Alice!' I love the T-shirt that lights up, but that's the worst wig I've ever seen. It looks like a road kill."

"It looks like a poodle the taxidermist hasn't finished." We both laughed. "Did she wave back?"

"She raised a finger slightly. Does that constitute a wave?"

"Oh, God!" I laughed so hard I had to wipe my eyes with my napkin.

"Hey, Mrs. Hollowell, Mrs. Zata." We both looked up to see a tall skinny girl holding the menus. "I'm Susie Connors. I graduated six years ago."

"Susie, of course, how are you?" Frances said. "And David?"

"He's just started work with TVA as an engineer and I'm in graduate school. I'm working here for the holidays."

"That's great," I said. Susie Connors? I was trying to place her and Frances was already inquiring about her family! At least Susie had given her name. Most former students greet us with "You don't know who I am, do you?" expecting us to say, "Sure we do" and being crushed when we don't.

"You ladies look mighty pretty today. You want the chicken salad and orange rolls?"

"Absolutely," Frances agreed. "And decaf coffee."

"Iced tea for me."

"You got it." Susie started away and turned back. "It's good seeing both of you."

"You, too," we chorused.

"Who's David?" I asked as Susie walked off.

"Her twin brother. You remember him, Patricia Anne. He's the one fell off the stage during *South Pacific*."

I remembered the incident vaguely. "Was he hurt?"

"Broke his ankle." Frances looked at me disapprovingly.

"There are too many of them, Frances," I said. "I can't keep them straight."

"It isn't easy," Frances admitted.

"Speaking of twins, I saw Lynn and Glynn Needham yesterday. They are drop-dead gorgeous. Followed me into the ladies' room at the Green and White to tell me, I think, that Claire's all right."

"They won't let you visit her? She's responding to treatment okay, isn't she?"

I don't know why I had assumed Frances knew all about Claire's disappearance. I told her the whole story, including Liliane Bedsole's trip to my house to ask for help in finding her.

"Wow," Frances said. "Where do you suppose she is?"

"And Mary Alice and I were having lunch with Ross Perry at the Green and White when I saw the twins. He left there and drove right to Shelby County, where he was killed."

"What's going on?"

"Damned if I know. It's scary." I moved my arms from the table so Susie could put down my plate of chicken salad.

Frances took an orange roll and buttered it slowly. "They say it was a deer hunter shot Ross Perry."

"Maybe it was. I've got my doubts. I think there's a connection between Mercy's death, Claire's disappearance, and Ross's death.''

"What kind of connection?"

"I don't know. Look." I pushed my salad plate aside and took several packets of Sweet'n Low and played the Cheerio game for Frances. She watched carefully as each packet was added or rearranged. I ended up with the same three—Mercy, Ross, and Claire—at the top, the Bedsoles bunched to one side, and Thurman behind the sugar bowl. At least I didn't have to explain the relationship between Amos and the Needham girls, since Frances had been at the court hearings. I tapped the Liliane packet. "She seemed worried to death."

"Ummm," Frances said, studying the packets.

"You see something?"

"No. This salad's great."

I pulled my plate back and began to eat. Frances plucked the Thurman packet from behind the sugar bowl. "He's out again. I heard it on the radio coming down here. Where shall I put him?"

"Break the packet and sprinkle each woman?"

"I don't think so." Frances propped him against the orange rolls. "Something's missing," she said.

"From the salad?"

"From this equation here." She pointed to the table dotted with Sweet'n Low packets. "There's some big connection here that we're missing, Patricia Anne."

"Maybe we don't want to know what it is," I said.

"True."

I gathered the packets together and put them back into the bowl. We were quiet for a few minutes while we ate.

"Maybe it's the gallery," Frances said.

I grinned. "We aren't going to be able to let this go, are we? And no, I don't think it's the gallery that's the connection. That would leave Ross out. Besides, Claire was just Mercy's assistant."

"Well, I hate that the police have the gallery closed. I was planning on doing some of my Christmas shopping there. I was so pleased when I saw Mercy was opening with a showing of Outsider art. Was it wonderful, Patricia Anne?"

"It was bright," I said, remembering the vibrancy of the paintings and quilts, how they had seemed to pulse with color.

"That's what's so wonderful about Outsider art. The boldness and the self-confidence."

"And they're Outsiders because they don't fit into any particular school of art?"

"Exactly. They're self-taught. That doesn't make them any less great, though, just less derivative. I've heard them called 'visionary' artists, too." Frances buttered another roll. "Mercy Armistead was smart enough to be tapping into the wellspring here in Alabama."

"I wonder why there are so many of them here."

"Patricia Anne, if there's one thing people in Alabama appreciate, it's eccentricity. You know that."

I nodded. It was true. I thought about my sister, down the mall with her electric T-shirt, red leggings, and road kill wig. I thought about my Abe painting with his own hair glued on. I thought about Vulcan, the Iron Man, mooning half the city. God, I loved this place.

"I've got an Abe painting," I told Frances, and described it to her.

"That's wonderful! I've got a Tolliver and a Clark and a Leota Wood quilt."

"I love her quilts, but they cost a fortune." A thought occurred to me. "Frances, at this rate those artists aren't going to be Outsiders long, are they?"

"They'll always be Outsiders, just rich ones."

But I wondered if such a thing were possible.

"Here you are!" We looked up at Mrs. Claus. "Imagine you just happening to show up here at Rosedale Mall, Frances."

Frances grinned. "I wouldn't have missed it."

Mary Alice sat down and pulled the flattened poodle from her head. "Patricia Anne, I need to ask you a favor. Will you be Mrs. Claus for a little while this afternoon so I can go check on Bubba? I told him I would come see about him after lunch.''

Bubba is Sister's enormous cat, totally devoid of any personality traits except sneakiness and laziness. And she adores him.

"No, I will not be Mrs. Claus. And what's wrong with Bubba?"

"Projectile vomiting." Mary Alice's arms shot out over our chicken salad to show us the extent of Bubba's digestive upheaval.

"Twice," she announced, repeating the gesture. Frances and I both jumped back. "I tried to get one of the Magic Maids to take my place, but they don't work on Saturday. And I called you and you were gone and I called Debbie and she's gone."

"He's really sick?"

The arms shot out across the table. "Twice."

"Okay," I agreed reluctantly.

"Oh, let me," Frances said. "I'd love to be Mrs. Claus."

We both turned and looked at her as if she had lost her mind. "I mean it," she said, grinning broadly. "I think it would be great fun."

"The kids pee on you occasionally," Mary Alice said, taking in Frances's elegant outfit.

"I've got a nylon wind suit in my car. I'll just slip it on."

"And your chest has to light up with 'Mrs. Claus.' ''

"I love that part!"

Mary Alice looked at me. I just shrugged.

"I'll go get the wind suit," Frances said, pushing back her chair and hurrying out.

"What is it with her?" Mary Alice asked, watching Frances leave.

"Beats me," I said. "Who knows what secret yearnings lie in people's hearts?"

When we left the mall, Frances was lighted and delighted. Even the road kill wig looked okay on her. I saw Santa looking over appreciatively. So did Sister.

"I'll be back in a little while," Mary Alice said.

"Take your time," Mr. and Mrs. Claus both answered.

"Wasn't that nice of Frances?" I said as we pushed through the Christmas shoppers. "Bill certainly seemed to appreciate it." I stepped aside quickly. One of the shoppers got kicked, I'm sure.

I had promised Sister I would follow her home to check on Bubba. If he needed to go to the vet, she had informed me, I would have to drive while she held him, though if there were a kind God in heaven, the problem would be minor and she wouldn't have to ride with me driving. Truthfully, she informed me, she was fervently praying for a hairball.

Mary Alice's house is on the crest of Red Mountain. It's a beautiful old English Tudor home that was built by her third husband's grandfather, who made his fortune in steel. I love the house and the view, which is the same one you get from Vulcan Park. Mary Alice has always wanted columns on it, though. Like Tara. She's had the most outstanding architects from Birmingham and Atlanta study the feasibility of an addition that would incorporate just a few large columns, preferably Ionic.

"Hell, I'd even settle for a Truman balcony," I heard her tell one reputable young architect who was thoroughly appalled.

"Architects drink a lot," she grumbled to me one day. "Offer them something and it's bourbon straight. Always several. They're so tight-ass, too. Lord, even Frank Lloyd Wright was eclectic."

I pulled into the circular driveway and stopped behind Sister's car. The front door is the one that is used most there because the kitchen steps are a half mile around in back.

"She needs to get her a smaller place," I told Fred one day after we had been there for a family gathering. "She just rattles around in all those rooms."

He cut his eyes around at me.

"I'm here," I yelled down the hall.

Sister appeared at the study door. "I can't find him." She

was about to cry. "I never should have gone off and left him."

"Well, he can't be far," I reassured her, though the thought of searching through that big house for Bubba was not a happy one. "He usually stays in the kitchen or in your bedroom, doesn't he?"

Sister nodded. "He's not in his usual spot, though, on the heating pad on the kitchen counter."

"Bubba has a heating pad on the counter?"

"Well, he's not a spring chicken anymore, Mouse."

"But that's a fire hazard!"

"It is not. It's set on low." She sighed. "Anyway, he's not there."

"Call him."

We went through the downstairs with Mary Alice calling "Bubba! Sweet angel! Tiny pussycat!" I made a detour through the kitchen and felt the heating pad. It was warm, all right.

"Here he is!" Mary Alice exclaimed.

I followed her voice into the dining room and saw Bubba under the table regarding us coolly.

"Are you all right, Mama's angel?" Mary Alice cooed. Mama's angel seemed fine. "Crawl under and get him, Mouse."

"You get him. Or better still, just leave him there."

"He's sick, Patricia Anne. He never comes in here unless something's wrong."

I looked at Bubba and he looked back at me. Maybe his eyes did seem a bit bleary.

"Your knees are in better shape than mine, Mouse."

"What's wrong with your knees?"

"Standing at the mall. Picking all those children up to see Santa Claus."

"Oh, for God's sake." I got down, crawled under the table, and dragged a protesting Bubba out. "Here." He weighed a ton. Mary Alice took him and cuddled him against her shoulder.

"Damn, Patricia Anne. You didn't have to be so rough!"

Bubba turned and stared at me as if he agreed. My knees cracked loudly as I got up.

"A shot of cortisone would help that," Mary Alice said. Bubba agreed.

Fortunately, just at that minute the doorbell rang.

"Probably the UPS man. I'm having to shop mainly out of catalogs this year."

"Are you getting Fred the Fruit of the Month again?"

"Of course." Mary Alice headed toward the front door with Bubba draped over her shoulder. I rubbed my knees and then followed. I love the mystery of packages.

"Mrs. Crane?" A handsome black man stood at the door. "I'm James Butler, and my sister, Bonnie Blue, asked me to bring this by for you." He held out what had to be the painting Bonnie Blue had promised.

"It's my Abe!" Mary Alice squealed. "Here, Patricia Anne." She handed Bubba to me and took the painting. "Does it have hair?"

James Butler smiled. "I don't know. Depends on Daddy's mood and how long since he's been to the barber."

Mary Alice tore the paper away. It was another self-portrait, very similar to mine, except a few brush strokes of white paint instead of real hair topped the head. But real glasses were affixed to the bridge of Abe's nose. "Oh, my," Sister said. "Would you look at that, Mouse."

It was a totally charming painting. You couldn't look at it without smiling. "It's wonderful," I said.

"Daddy does good stuff," James Butler agreed.

Mary Alice held the picture out admiring it. "Dr. Butler"—she nodded her head toward me—"this is my sister, Mrs. Hollowell."

"We met the other night at Mercy Armistead's," I added. James Butler nodded. "How are you, Mrs. Hollowell?"

"Tell him how your knees crack, Mouse. He's a doctor."

"He's a vet, Mary Alice."

"That's right! Hand him Bubba, Patricia Anne."

"Mary Alice!"

She reached out, put her hand on James Butler's arm, and

drew him into the hall. "Please come in, Dr. Butler. We have an emergency here with my cat and I'm sure you're the answer to my prayers. Things just seem to work out, don't they?"

"Yes, ma'am, they do." A puzzled James Butler looked around. "Is this the sick cat?" He looked at Bubba, who narrowed his eyes and looked back.

"This is Bubba. Where would you like to examine him?"

"How about on the heating pad on the kitchen counter?" I said.

"You really want me to look at him?"

"Of course. He's sick." Mary Alice led the way to the kitchen, carrying her painting like a shield before her. I followed with Bubba hanging over my shoulder, and James Butler brought up the rear.

"It started with projectile vomiting," Mary Alice explained over her shoulder. "Then when we got home, he wasn't on his heating pad."

"He sleeps on a heating pad?" James asked.

"Of course."

"On the kitchen counter," I added.

James reached over and rubbed Bubba's head. "Lucky cat."

"Do you need a flashlight or anything?" Mary Alice asked.

"Please."

While she went to get one, I put Bubba down on the counter and James began to press his hands skillfully down the cat's body, concentrating on the abdominal area. "Okay," he said. "I think he's running some fever, though. I wish I had a thermometer."

"Will a regular one do?"

"A rectal one would."

Mary Alice, who had come in with the flashlight, handed it to me and disappeared again. In a moment she was back with a thermometer.

We were quiet watching James work. All except Bubba. He began to purr loudly when the thermometer was inserted.

"Good boy," Mary Alice said, rubbing his head.

"He's got a pretty high temp," James said when he removed the thermometer. "His abdomen is soft, though. Has he been out anywhere where another animal could have bitten him?"

"Absolutely not."

"Well, you need to take him to your vet. I'm guessing it's a urinary tract infection, but it's just a guess without tests."

"You must be joking. Take him to Dr. Adkins? It's Saturday afternoon," Mary Alice said. "If his answering machine were honest, it would say he's teeing off on the fourth hole just about now."

"Well, we really don't want this cat to get dehydrated. I could take him to my clinic, but it's all the way down in Shelby County."

Bubba purred, yawned. Enjoyed the attention.

"That would be wonderful. You want us to follow you?"

James Butler shook his head. "I'm going to have to keep him overnight. Why don't you just call and check on him tomorrow? Chances are you can come get him. I'll put him on an IV tonight, though."

"Thank you. I'll go get his carrying case." Mary Alice disappeared again.

Afternoon sun poured into Sister's kitchen and over the strong dark hands kneading the fur at Bubba's neck. I put my hand over and touched James's. He looked up, startled.

"Do you know where Claire Moon is?" I asked.

"No," he said.

Why did I not believe him?

Eleven

The moment James Butler's car left the driveway carrying the indignant Bubba, Mary Alice sank to the steps, her hands pressed against her chest.

"I should have gone with him," she said. "What do we know about that James Butler?"

"He seemed competent," I assured her.

"Because he knew where to stick a thermometer? I tell you, Patricia Anne, cats' health care isn't what it used to be. Remember Mama's Sugar Pie?"

I was trying to figure out Sister's thought processes, a losing battle. Sugar Pie was a huge gray tabby who terrorized the neighborhood for twenty years, who was never sick a day in her life, and who sent all of us to the emergency room at least once for stitches or tetanus shots. Mama adored her.

"I should call and check on his references," Mary Alice said. "It's not too late to stop him."

"Who are you going to call? The Better Business Bureau? The Medical Society?"

"It's Saturday, Mouse. Bentbrook Golf Club would be more like it." She pushed herself up. "Or I could just follow them. At least I can check on the clinic and get a Christmas tree."

Mary Alice's synaptic path had eluded me again.

"Don't you want one?" she asked.

"A tree? We put ours up last night."

"Not that bottlebrush thing. It *smells*, Patricia Anne."

"But it won't catch on fire."

"Don't be too sure. And if it does, they'll have to evacuate the neighborhood because of toxic fumes. What is that thing made of, anyway?"

I shrugged. "Where are you going to get your tree?"

"At the Christmas tree farm in Harpersville. You could at least get a wreath or a swag for your mantel, Patricia Anne."

I hesitated. "What about Frances? You told her you would be back in a little while."

"And I will. We can run down to Shelby County, check on James Butler's clinic, and cut a Christmas tree in nothing flat."

At the moment, it seemed like a good thing to do. It was a beautiful December afternoon; a stroll through a Christmas tree farm would revive my spirits. Some greenery would be nice, too.

"I'll drive," Mary Alice said.

"Do you know how to get there?"

"I'll call for directions."

Five minutes later we were headed south, following James and Bubba.

The city of Birmingham is located in the last gasp of the Appalachians. Three gentle old mountains—Red Mountain, Shades Mountain, and Double Oak Mountain—run parallel east to west across the area. South of Double Oak Mountain, the land flattens suddenly and soon becomes the coastal plain, fertile and semitropical. The mountains, though, rich with coal, iron, and limestone, are the reason for Birmingham's existence. The city was, and still is, a steel city.

The population has spread toward the south, first up and over Red Mountain, then Shades Mountain, and now is marching up Double Oak as inexorably as a battalion of army ants. I hate to see the mountains denuded. Fortunately, the state has bought much of Double Oak and intends to keep it wild.

Shelby County begins between Shades Mountain and Double Oak. The northern part of the county is the fastest growing metropolitan area in the state as well as one of the wealthiest. Cross Double Oak, though, and you are in rural Alabama. Old barns lean against the wind and advertise SEE ROCK CITY with faded paint. Small farm ponds dot the landscape, and washing machines adorn front porches.

"The lady said we couldn't miss it," Mary Alice said, turning onto County Road 17. "It's a couple of miles past the cross garden."

"What's a cross garden?"

"I asked. She said we'd recognize it."

We did. We passed a house that was surrounded by hundreds of crosses of all sizes. Some were wood, some metal, some plain, some decorated with paint or pieces of colored glass. There were so many of them, they had spread out into the adjoining field.

"A cross garden," Mary Alice said. "Isn't that great?"

I nodded, remembering what Frances had said about us embracing eccentricity.

"Right along here must be where Ross Perry was killed," Mary Alice said in a few minutes. "We can probably see where he ran off."

"I don't want to," I said. We had entered a stretch of road that was heavily wooded. Down an embankment, I could see fast-running Kelly Creek glistening through the trees.

But we did. There was no mistaking the tracks that had been made. Cars, wreckers, and ambulances had knocked down saplings and left deep grooves in the bank.

Mary Alice slowed the car and looked at the scene.

"For God's sake," I said, ducking down. "There could be some more crazy hunters out here."

"I think he was shot," Mary Alice said.

"I *know* he was shot, Sister. What's wrong with you? That's what hunters do. Shoot."

"I mean I think somebody deliberately shot him."

"It's very possible. Now, get the hell out of here!"

Mary Alice stepped on the gas. "What did Ross have for lunch yesterday, Mouse?"

"God knows. Some kind of unrecognizable vegetables. Why?"

"People's last meals are always significant. Don't you think?"

I cut my eye around at her. "Is there some point to this?"

"I was just thinking. Was that the food Ross would have chosen if he had known it was his last meal?"

I rubbed my forehead, which was beginning to ache slightly. "He seemed to enjoy it," I said. "Drank a lot of wine."

"What would you like for your last meal, Patricia Anne? I read in *Cosmopolitan* or somewhere that that's a good psychological test."

"I doubt it was *Cosmo*, and death makes me lose my appetite." Fortunately, just then we saw the sign for Indian Trails Veterinary Clinic with an arrow pointing toward the left. Mary Alice turned onto a gravel road that ran a half mile across a flat field toward a house. The setting reminded me of the Texas of Southfork. That was the only resemblance, though. Two-storied and pale pink, the house had the columns Mary Alice had always wanted and not a tree to block the view.

"Turn left," I said. Mary Alice had been admiring the house so, she hadn't seen the small sign that simply said CLINIC with an arrow pointing down another gravel road. She slammed on the brakes and backed up.

The clinic proved to be a large building with stables attached. Beyond the parking area was a small lawn and walkway with a sign on it proclaiming INDIAN TRAILS EQUINE HOSPITAL.

"Bubba's in a horse hospital!" I exclaimed. "I thought you said this place was called Pet Haven."

Mary Alice got out of the car. "A vet's a vet, Mouse."

"That's like saying a doctor's a doctor."

"They are." She marched toward the door. "Are you coming?"

I got out and followed her into an empty waiting room. "No one's here," I said.

"Sure they are." Mary Alice opened the door that led, presumably, to the examining rooms. "Dr. Butler? James?" she called.

The front door opened behind us and James Butler walked in with Bubba in his carrying cage. "How did you beat me here?" he asked.

"You must have stopped somewhere," Mary Alice said accusingly. "And where's your help? Nobody's here."

James put Bubba's cage down. The All-American Football Star and the Old Southern Lady glared at each other. Eye to eye. The outcome was inevitable. "I had to get gas," Football Star muttered. "And Dr. Grable is here. Probably doing rounds."

"I'll help you get Bubba out," Mary Alice said.

While they were in the back, I wandered out to look the place over. I would have liked to have seen the stables, but I wasn't sure I should go back there. Sick animals, like humans, like to be left alone. Several Hereford cows were grazing in a pasture beyond a white fence. They seemed healthy enough. I walked over to the fence and looked at them.

"You wouldn't believe the cost of a good bull nowadays," a voice said behind me. I turned and saw Thurman Beatty. He came and stood by the fence. "What brings you here, Mrs. Hollowell?"

"My sister's sick cat."

"James is doctoring a cat?" Thurman smiled.

"Isn't that okay? A vet's a vet, isn't he?"

"Oh, sure. It's just that James is the best large animal vet in this part of the state. He'll have to make himself think little."

"Not with Mary Alice in there."

We were quiet for a few minutes, then spoke together.

"I was sorry—" "Thank you—"

Thurman grinned. "You first."

"I'm sorry about Mercy's death. About all of your troubles."

"Thanks. I still can't believe it. And the way it was done. That's why they keep coming back to me, you know. Because James and I have a couple of horses together and they figure I'd know about DMSO." He shook his head. "Weird."

"It's not common knowledge, is it?"

"More common than you'd realize." He took off his hat and wiped his forehead with his flannel shirtsleeve. "What I wanted to thank you for was taking care of Claire, of getting her to the hospital."

"I hope she's all right," I said. "I saw her sisters yesterday and they told me she is."

Thurman turned toward me, startled. "You saw Glynn and Lynn?"

"Yes. In the Green and White restaurant. My sister and I were having lunch with Ross Perry. They followed me into the ladies' room and said Claire was all right. Words to that effect."

"Did they say where they are staying?" Thurman clutched the fence rail.

"I assumed with Liliane Bedsole. They didn't say."

"Damn. Damn, damn, damn. Excuse me, Mrs. Hollowell, there's something I need to tend to. It was nice seeing you."

"You, too," I said to the back of his plaid flannel shirt as he hurried away. Now, what was that about? I wondered.

Mary Alice came out in a few minutes, followed by James. Bubba had stayed, I noticed.

"He'll be fine," James was assuring Sister. "Like I said, he's a little dehydrated and I'll put him on an IV and get him started on some antibiotics. Call me in the morning."

"Remember he only weighs sixteen pounds."

"I promise."

While we were standing there talking, Thurman Beatty came from the stables in a pickup, waved to us as he went by and headed out the gravel road.

"I wonder where he's going," James said.

I wondered the same thing. The question was answered as we left the clinic, though. Where we turned right on the gravel road to get back to the highway, Thurman had turned left toward the pink wedding cake house in the middle of the field. Reddish dust was still standing above the road, marking the path of his pickup. Maybe that was where Claire was. I hoped so.

"That is one more gorgeous house," Mary Alice said. "Big enough for the whole Butler clan."

"I think Abe and Bonnie Blue like it just where they are."

"True." Mary Alice turned onto the main road. "I think Bubba's okay, don't you? I feel better about him even if it is a horse hospital."

"Bubba can hold his own," I assured her. I didn't mention that Thurman Beatty had said James would have to "think little" to doctor a cat.

On our way back to Highway 280, we passed the place where Ross had been killed. I looked at the deep woods and thought that it would have been very possible for a deer hunter to have shot him. We passed the cross garden. While I was wondering how many crosses there were, a bent old man stepped from behind one of the larger ones. He was carrying a rifle and pointed it at us. I hit the floor; Mary Alice hit the brakes.

"What's wrong with you?" she said.

"Get out of here before he shoots us!"

"With a hole digger? For God's sake, Mouse!" She tapped the horn and waved at the man.

"It's a hole digger?" I extricated myself from the seat belt, raised up cautiously, and looked back. The man was waving with one hand and holding a hole digger in the other.

"Did you hurt yourself?" Mary Alice asked.

I rubbed my chest. "Let's just say I'll never pass the pencil test again." I was referring to the pencil-stuck-beneath-the-breast test. If the breast is firm and perky, the pencil will fall. Needless to say, only the very young or flat-chested will try it.

"You haven't passed the pencil test in forty years. What's the matter with you, anyway?" She headed down the road again.

"A couple of murders, Peeping Toms, kidnappings, trips in ambulances. Just a few things like that."

"Maybe you need to up your estrogen."

I hooked the seat belt again, closed my eyes, and said my mantra.

"What are you doing? Saying your mantra?" Sister asked.

I nodded.

"I think we got into that too late, don't you, Mouse? I mean, when you're our age it's too far in to the inner self. You know what I mean?"

In a strange way, I did.

"Warren Newman keeps wanting me to drag my inner child out and I said, 'Well, hell, Warren, you'd think you were talking about a Shirley Temple doll in a cedar chest.' And he said maybe he was, and then I remembered how you lost my Shirley Temple doll and told him all about it."

I sighed. Warren Newman is the psychiatrist Sister visits just enough to confuse us all.

"He asked if you had ever apologized about losing the Shirley Temple doll and I told him no."

"I'm sorry I lost your Shirley Temple doll, Mary Alice."

"I forgive you." She turned onto Highway 280 and headed toward Harpersville. "Don't you feel better? I do."

A mini traffic jam greeted us at the Christmas tree farm. The owner had decided to add to his income by providing mule-drawn wagon rides to the fields where the trees were planted. We each handed over two dollars and climbed on the wagon.

"This is wonderful," Sister said. "You should have dressed more appropriately, though, Mouse."

My red suit and heels weren't exactly tree-cutting, mule-riding clothes. "I was having lunch at the Blue Moon," I reminded her. "With Frances Zata. Have you forgotten her?"

"Of course not. I'm sure she's fine."

The mules lurched forward. "Here we go," everybody said.

The next hour was wonderful. Trying to spare my heels,

I tiptoed through the trees helping Mary Alice look for the perfect one.

"Here it is," she finally said. I inspected it and saw she was right. It was a tall fir that would look perfect in her living room.

"It's too pretty to cut," Mary Alice said. But that didn't stop her from calling over one of the helpers with an ax.

We rode back on the wagon and selected a couple of wreaths and swags. With the tree tied on top of the car, and the inside filled with greenery, we looked and smelled like Christmas. I tried not to think of the condition of my good navy shoes.

We passed the cutoff to Highway 17 on the way home. "There are some interesting things down that road," I remarked, thinking of the fairy-tale pink house and the cross garden.

"Leota Wood lives down there," Sister said.

"The quilt lady?"

Sister nodded. "I thought I might come out and do some Christmas shopping. Probably get a better price at her house."

"Who told you she lives there?"

"Bonnie Blue. Said she lived right down from James. You want to go down there now?"

"You've got to get back to the mall, and I need to get home."

"One day next week?"

"Great." I doubted I could afford any of Leota Wood's work, but it would be fun to look.

As we came over Double Oak Mountain, we saw clouds massing toward the northwest. The dark bank reminded me of the snow we had had a few nights before, of the footprints, and, for some reason, of Ross Perry.

"Tell me about Ross Perry," I asked Mary Alice.

"What do you want to know?"

"What do you know about him? The only time I ever talked to him was at the Green and White."

Mary Alice pursed her lips the way she does when she's

thinking. "He was knowledgeable," she said. "A good board member at the museum. Maybe gay." She paused. "Not that that bothered me, Mouse. You know that. The older I've gotten, the more I appreciate gay men. They're a lot more thoughtful."

I agreed. "Did he live with someone?"

"Not that I know of. He had a beautiful house in Forest Park and invited the museum board and their spouses out for a supper and pool party last summer. No one else seemed to be in residence." Mary Alice stopped at a light at the foot of the mountain. "Didn't seem to lack for money. Had some spectacular artwork." When the light changed and she stepped on the gas, we could hear the scratch of the Christmas tree on the roof of the car. "Damn," she said. "No telling how much that tree's going to cost me."

"Were Mercy and Thurman at the party?"

"The pool party? They were the only ones who went swimming. Mercy could pass the pencil test, Mouse."

"But she and Ross didn't get along."

"They sure didn't. That night she pushed him into the pool. Tried to act like it was an accident. But she tripped him deliberately. I saw it. And so apologetic. Bouncing around in that bikini."

"I hope he could swim."

"Mouse, he *walked* out of there, he was so mad. And trying not to act like it. It's a wonder he didn't have a stroke right then."

"Was Claire there?"

Mary Alice shook her head no. "The only person I remember being there who wasn't a board member or a husband or wife was Liliane Bedsole. Knew good and well what Mercy had done, too, but did a great job of smoothing things over. By the time Ross got back into dry clothes, she had us all just about smashed."

"The only job Ross had was with the paper?"

"Far as I know. He'd written a couple of books. Art books, not commercial. Not the kind you get rich on. He had money, though, probably family money."

"He was from New Orleans? I saw in the paper that's where his sister is."

"Yes, but I think he came to Birmingham right out of college."

The $64,000 question. "Did you like him?"

Mary Alice thought for a moment. "He was the kind of guy you didn't want to turn your back on."

"How so?"

"Damned if I know. A coldness, maybe. But I know this. If Mercy weren't already dead, the cops would be questioning her around the clock."

"I wonder why they disliked each other so."

"Maybe I can find out," Sister said. "Though if he was murdered, Mercy wasn't the only one had it in for him."

"There could have been a spurned lover."

"And there could have been a stupid deer hunter."

We were silent for a moment. The Saturday two-weeks-before-Christmas traffic was heavy along what's known as the 280 Corridor. Housing developments, strip malls, and shopping centers have made what used to be a two-lane mountain road a traffic engineer's nightmare. Many of the cars, like ours, had trees tied on the roof.

Mary Alice darted into the space between two cars in a lane that seemed to be moving faster. It wasn't. We went about ten feet and stopped. "Where are all these people going?" she complained.

The woman in the lane of traffic next to us seemed to be addressing Christmas cards. Holding a list of addresses with one hand, she propped envelopes on the steering wheel and wrote. It didn't look very comfortable or conducive to good penmanship, but I had to admire her efficient use of time. While we sat there, she addressed three.

"This is ridiculous." Mary Alice drummed her hands on the wheel. "Don't you think Christmas has gotten away from us, Mouse? Remember how we used to be grateful for a tangerine and some hard candy?"

"You're thinking of the Cratchitts, Sister. We could hardly get into the living room for all the stuff." It was true.

Mama had always made a big deal out of Christmas, and since we were the only grandchildren on both sides, we racked up with gifts.

"But I remember being grateful for a tangerine and hard candy, too. Especially the kind with the little flower on the side. Reckon they still make those?"

"I haven't seen any in a long time."

"What color flower was it? Pink or yellow?"

"The candy was pink with a white side and a yellow flower."

"I think some of the flowers were pink."

"How could you remember? You were too busy tearing into packages. Yours and part of mine, too."

Mary Alice sniffed. "You were always scared I was going to get more than you did."

"You usually did. You got yours and half of mine when Mama wasn't looking."

"Not true."

"True."

"You lost my Shirley Temple doll deliberately, didn't you? Because you didn't get one."

"I've already apologized for that."

We had moved up beside a car in which the woman driver was reading *Southern Living*. I liked the cover, which showed a cozy fireplace decorated for Christmas.

"I talked to Thurman Beatty for a minute back at the horse hospital where you left Bubba," I said, changing the subject.

"Did he say anything about Claire?"

"He seemed startled when I mentioned that I had seen Glynn and Lynn Needham. Upset. I think that's why he took off like he did."

"Because you saw Glynn and Lynn? Why would that upset him?"

We moved up beside a woman who was putting on mascara. "I guess he wants to find out what they know about Claire. Where she is. At first I thought maybe the twins had taken her from the hospital and then I thought no, it was Thurman, but the twins knew about it and knew she was okay. Now I'm thinking it was the twins again and Thurman didn't know anything about it." I paused. "Are you keeping up with this?"

"Sure. But there are bigger questions. Why did they take her and where is she? What do you really know about those twins, Patricia Anne?"

"Just that they are gorgeous and live in New York, and their aunt Liliane says they weren't as harmed by their abusive childhood as Claire was."

"Well, the way I see it," Sister declared, "whoever took Claire from the hospital was either doing it to protect her or to get rid of her."

"My God, Mary Alice!" I shivered.

"What? You know it's the truth."

"They did it to protect her."

"From the person who killed Mercy and maybe Ross?" Mary Alice changed lanes again, needlessly. In a moment the card-addressing woman pulled up beside us.

"I don't know. I don't know how I even got involved in this." I rubbed my forehead.

"Just like you got involved out at the Skoot 'n' Boot. You do that, Patricia Anne. Take things so personally."

I didn't remind Sister that the Skoot 'n' Boot, the country-western bar where I almost got killed, was her place. Nor did I remind her that I had attended the opening of the Mercy Armistead Gallery at her invitation. Instead, I rubbed my head harder and asked her if she had any aspirin.

"Sure," she said. "Look in the side of my purse. And there's some Coke in that can." She pointed to a Rubbermaid drink holder on the floor. "It might even have a little fizz left in it. I think I bought it yesterday."

It didn't, but I had to drink it to wash the aspirin down.

Mary Alice said Bill would help her get the tree off the top of the car, so I collected my swag and wreath and headed home. The clouds had moved farther across the sky, partially blocking the late-afternoon sun. As I drove along the valley, I could see Vulcan's rear end gleaming golden and bare in the late light. Not for the first time, I thought how startling a sight this must be to strangers approaching the city from the south.

When I opened the kitchen door, I smelled hot dogs.

"Hey," I called.

"Hey," Fred and Haley answered. I looked into the den and saw them, each eating a hot dog and drinking a Grapico. Haley was sitting on the sofa, her feet propped on the coffee table; Fred was relaxed in his recliner. An empty Sneaky Pete's sack was on the table.

"We're watching *It's a Wonderful Life* again," Fred said. "Your hot dogs are in the refrigerator."

"Did you get me a Grapico?"

"Of course."

I put the greenery on the hearth. "Where's your car, Haley?"

"Debbie borrowed it. Hers is broken. She dropped me off to show you the dress I bought for the Policemen's Ball."

"Good. Who went to Sneaky Pete's?"

"We both did."

"Smells wonderful." I slipped my worse-for-wear navy heels off, got my hot dogs with everything on them, and zapped them for a few seconds in the microwave.

"What's happening?" I asked, coming into the den with my hot dogs and Grapico.

"Jimmy Stewart and Donna Reed just got married," Haley said.

"Oh, good." I unbuttoned the waistband of my skirt and settled onto the sofa happily. I'm no purist. I like Ted Turner's colorizing. I also like Sneaky Pete's hot dogs. At that moment, I was a happy woman.

"And there are Goo Goo Clusters for dessert," Haley said.

Heaven.

Twelve

The next morning I put a load of washing on and took Woofer for his walk through a light drizzle, more like a heavy fog than rain. It was a pleasant walk, the slight moisture refreshing and cool against my face. It made my hair frizz, a problem I had learned to ignore years before. It also must have emphasized smells, since Woofer had to stop and investigate every tree, fence post, and bush along the way. I didn't hurry him. We were both enjoying ourselves.

When we got back, I called to see how Bubba was but got Mary Alice's answering machine. She had ordered a set of seasonal greetings from some catalog, so what I heard was "We cannot come to the phone now, won't you ple-ease leave a message" sung to a tinkly "We Wish You a Merry Christmas."

"I'm calling to check on Bubba. I hope he is feeling better," I sang back. "Just give me a ring when possible. I should be right here."

"What was that about?" Fred asked, standing in the door and yawning. "And how long have you been up?"

"Ages. You're a slugabed."

He came over to hug me. "You're wet."

"I've already taken Woofer for his walk. It's drizzling."

"Coffee." He shuffled over to the stove. Last Christmas

Freddie gave him some nice leather house shoes with lamb's wool lining. The trouble is that they are slides, appropriately named as far as Fred is concerned. He has never gotten the hang of keeping them on, tending not to pick his feet up so he won't step out of them. He has the same trouble with flip-flops, walking across the beach like a man in dire need of an application of Preparation H.

"Scrunch your toes," I tell him. It does no good.

"Paper."

I pointed. He shuffled into the den, carrying his coffee. I put the clothes into the dryer, poured myself another cup of coffee, and went to join him.

"Ross Perry made the front page again," he said, handing me that section.

"Well, he worked for the paper. They've got a personal interest." I sat down and read that the police still had no leads. James's and Yvonne's role in pulling him from Kelly Creek was rehashed. The only thing new was that the family said a memorial service would be announced at a later date.

"They must be burying him in New Orleans," I said.

"What?" Fred didn't look up from the Reviews and Comments section.

"They're having a memorial service later for Ross Perry. Mary Alice won't have to worry about wearing her new black suit three times the same week."

"Good."

"I wonder where she is this early on Sunday."

"Absolutely," Fred agreed.

"I broke both legs while I was walking Woofer."

"You're right." He flipped the section over to the back page and continued reading.

I sighed, put my section down, and went to take a shower.

"Amazing how well you can walk," Fred called after me. Smart-ass.

Fifteen minutes later, showered and shampooed, I came back into the den, where Fred had graduated to the Business and Money section of the paper. He has a small magnifying glass with a light on it that he uses to read the stock results.

He bought it the same day he bought some Wal-Mart stock, so it's his good luck charm. He wouldn't admit that it is, but I know this man. And I wouldn't dare tell him I use his magical magnifying glass to get ticks out of Woofer's ears.

"How are we doing?" I asked, pointing toward the paper.

"Wal-Mart's up."

"I've been thinking maybe we should diversify. Sell our thirty shares of Wal-Mart and invest it in something safe like utilities."

Fred clutched the paper to his heart. "Safe? My Lord, Patricia Anne, it was Sam Walton himself told me to buy Wal-Mart."

It was true. Fred had flown from Dallas with a nice old man who said he had invested everything he had in Wal-Mart.

"Everything?" Fred asked, worried about the old man.

"Just about. I think it's going to do okay."

Two weeks later, Fred, who had missed the man's name, was startled to see Sam Walton's picture on the cover of *Time*.

"It's a sign. A portent," Mary Alice said when he brought the magazine in to show us. "Sell the house and business and invest the money. Make Sam proud. Make America proud."

He bought thirty shares, which, for Fred, was a bundle.

"Utilities?" he gasped now. "Are you serious?"

"Just wondering if we want all our eggs in one basket." I went into the kitchen. "You want some cereal?"

"We got any bagels?"

"In the freezer."

"That's what I want."

"You know, Lender's might be a good stock."

But I had gone far enough.

"Shut up, Patricia Anne," I heard from the den.

It was a quiet morning. I wrapped Christmas presents and put them under the tree. I addressed Christmas cards. Several times I tried to get Mary Alice but was greeted with "We cannot come to the phone now, won't you ple-ease leave a message.'' I sang a couple of messages back, but it was too much trouble to leave one every time. Fred had disappeared into his basement workshop with the admonition that I was not to come down as he was working on my present. Since I had designed the plant stand he was working on, one to hang all my ferns on so they could be rolled outside when the winter weather was nice, I figured he just wanted to be by himself. Which suited me.

We had Patricia Anne's Cafeteria for lunch (everything left in the refrigerator), and Fred headed back to the basement. I collected my library books, a couple of which were overdue, and headed downtown to see a collection of Eudora Welty's photography.

The Birmingham Public Library system is an amazing network of over forty libraries. Usually I go to the nearest branch, but if I have time, or if something special is on display, I'll go to the main library. This consists of two buildings: the new, very modern structure that houses the materials that can be checked out; and the classical old building across the street with its three-story-high lobby decorated with murals depicting mythological scenes. The latter, which was the main library for fifty years, is now the research library. The two buildings are connected by a crosswalk over the street.

I love the new building with all the airiness and light, but the old one has a special place in my heart. This was where I had my first job. My title was Readers' Assistant, a fancy title which meant I had to go to the stacks dozens of times a day to find books for people. I also shelved books, filed catalog cards, and helped people look things up. The main perk was that I got to read the new books as soon as they came in. The main problem was permanent calluses on my feet from all the walking.

The libraries were, and are, used extensively, which seems to surprise people who are not from the South. ''You are so well read to be from Alabama,'' a woman told me once at a dinner party. I probably would have belted her one if Mary

Alice hadn't elbowed me and whispered, "Common as pig tracks, Mouse."

I found a parking place in the lot behind the new building, decided it wasn't raining enough for my umbrella, and darted toward the back entrance. This leads down a wide corridor open to a reading room on the right and lined with glass cabinets on the left. Eudora Welty's photography was on display in the cabinets. Several people were looking at the pictures and reading the captions, which were quotes from her books. I would look at them, I decided, on my way out.

The overdue books cost fifty cents, money well spent. I paid up and headed toward the new fiction. Current newspapers are kept in the same area, so several people were sitting in comfortable chairs reading them. The Ross Perry story had made the front page of the *Montgomery Advertiser*, too, I noticed. The newspaper was being read by a man who reminded me of Ross. Probably the way the light shone on his bald head.

So many questions, I thought.

"Lord!" I actually slapped the palm of my hand against my forehead. There were answers to a lot of my questions right here. I had been overlooking a perfect source of information. I turned and hurried toward the escalator. The research library was full of material about the Bedsoles. Ross Perry, too. All of his columns would be there. Even the record of the Needham trial. I couldn't believe I hadn't thought of this before. I almost gave a little skip as I entered the crossover.

I started with the Ross Perry columns since they didn't take any research. They usually appeared in the Friday section of the paper known as Marquee, which lists things to do for the weekend as well as an extended calendar of events for the month, lists new movies with a critique, TV shows, concerts, readings, and art exhibits. I took the tape of the newspaper for the year before, put it into the machine, and started scanning through the columns. Many of them I had read. Some exhibits got better reviews than others, but none were totally panned.

I skipped back five years and again scanned Ross's columns. The man could write. As an English teacher, I had to give him credit for that. As for his art criticism, I didn't know. That particular year everybody got rave reviews. It was either a remarkable year for Birmingham art, Ross Perry needed his glasses changed, or he had just found Prozac. I rewound the tape and inserted the one from ten years before.

And hit pay dirt! In the January fifteenth Marquee, Ross Perry had reviewed the opening of a new gallery in English Village. The gallery was attractive, three of the artists were fine, but the fourth artist, newcomer Mercy Armistead, had produced paintings that were dull, lifeless, amateurish. Obviously derivative, to name their derivation would be an insult to the originals. She, Mercy, ruined the whole show with her utter lack of talent.

After that, the review got worse.

"Wow," I said out loud. "Wow."

I located a librarian to find out how to copy the review. So ten years later, Mercy threw a can of Coke at him and pushed him into a pool. He had it coming. When Ross wrote this, Mercy was in her early twenties, just starting out. Regardless of how bad her work was then, and it probably wasn't bad if she had gone on to gain an international reputation, this was cruel and must have been devastating to her. I ran the tape forward but found no more reviews like this. Obviously, even ten years earlier, Ross had had it in for Mercy. I saw nothing that gave me a clue why.

I typed in the name "Bedsole, Betty," and retrieved the tape of newspapers for 1956, the year she was Miss America. There were pictures of her getting on the train for Atlantic City, holding a huge bouquet of flowers. There were pictures of her winning the swimsuit competition ("Strutting," Mama would have said) with rigid funnels for breasts and at least fifteen more pounds than any self-respecting Miss America would carry now. There were pictures of her winning the talent competition as Scarlett, clutching a carrot and swearing she would never go hungry again. "Not a dry eye in the house," the reporter noted.

"Very possible," I muttered. But I had to admit that Betty Bedsole had been beautiful, with long dark hair that she wore down for Scarlett and up for the swimsuit. Her smile was dazzling, and her eyes had the same slight slant that made Claire Moon's so spectacular.

There were pictures of her victorious arrival back in Birmingham, the crowd at Terminal Station and the flowers again. I was glancing at this page of the paper when something caught my eye. I switched to magnification and looked closely at the young man to whom she was handing a rose. It could be Ross Perry. I held the eraser end of my pencil over his head to cover his hair. But I still wasn't sure, and he wasn't identified in the story. I called the young librarian over to see how I could get a copy on magnification.

"I hope you're wearing comfortable shoes," I said.

"I am." She smiled. I looked down and saw army boots that must have weighed a ton. Still better than three-inch heels.

"She's the one whose daughter was murdered, isn't she?" the librarian said, pointing to the picture.

I nodded. "Betty Bedsole."

"Well, if you're doing research on her, there's a whole clipping file up in the Southern History Department. It would save you having to go through the papers."

"Thanks." Why hadn't I remembered that?

The girl nodded. "I think they're trying to get all the stuff copied, but right now, it's still in manila folders in file cabinets."

"That's great. Thanks." I put my two photocopied articles in my purse and headed up the steps.

The Southern History Department is an incredible resource for scholars. Partially funded by a wealthy Birmingham family, and ferociously guarded and added to for over forty years by a no-nonsense librarian aptly named Miss Boxx, it is a treasure trove for historians. The genealogy section alone brings people in by droves. Today, even this close to Christmas, was no exception.

I requested the Betty Bedsole clippings from the young

man at the desk. They were in my hands in about one minute.

"She would be proud of you," I told him, pointing to a portrait of Miss Boxx in which she glared down at the people taking advantage of her life's work. "Mess it up and you're dead meat," she seemed to be saying.

He smiled, genuinely pleased.

I found a place at a table and opened the folder. The clippings weren't in any order, which didn't matter. I wasn't sure what I was looking for, anyway.

The first one was from the fifties. It was a picture of Betty and her father, Amos, at the Camellia Ball. There were two other debutantes and their fathers in the picture, but all you saw was the Bedsoles. Almost as tall as her father and dressed in a strapless white sheath, eighteen-year-old Betty flirted with the camera. Or the photographer. Head slightly tilted, lips slightly parted, she seemed much more sophisticated than the other two girls in their frilly dresses who were dutifully saying "Cheese." Amos Bedsole, a handsome man in his early forties, smiled at his daughter instead of at the camera. His delight in her was so evident, it brought tears to my eyes.

The next clipping was of her marriage to Samuel Armistead. Underneath a picture of the wedding couple taken as they came down the steps of the Independent Presbyterian Church was the caption MISS AMERICA MARRIES. Betty was a traditional bride, bouffant everything. I scanned the story. Well-known movie producer. Ten bridesmaids. Blue dotted swiss dresses. Seated dinner. Birmingham Country Club.

The story was so long, it was continued on another page. I removed the gem clip and saw pictures taken at the dinner. One of them was of Ross Perry holding up a champagne glass, giving a toast. And this time, he was identified. It was the same man to whom she had given the rose as she boarded the train for Atlantic City.

"Hmm," I murmured. I glanced hurriedly through the rest of the clippings. The birth of her daughter, Mercy Louise, was announced. And the birth of her son, Andrew. For a while, Miss Boxx had clipped notices of Betty Bedsole's trips home. But not for long. Other people became more newsworthy. The last clipping was dated January 1969 when Betty had been a judge at the Miss America pageant and had posed with a Miss Alabama who didn't even make the top ten. Well, nobody could accuse Betty of showing partiality.

I rested my elbows on the table and stared up at grim Miss Boxx's portrait.

"So?" she said.

"I think Ross Perry was in love with Betty Bedsole and she dumped him and that's why he hated her daughter so."

"Mary Alice said he was gay."

"She said 'maybe' gay. Maybe he was 'bi.'"

"I like people who can make up their minds," Miss Boxx said. "'Bi' is so indecisive. You know what I mean?"

"I don't know anything. I don't even know what I'm doing here. None of this is any of my business."

"Business is as business does."

"What does that mean?"

"I have no idea." Miss Boxx pinched the bridge of her nose between her thumb and forefinger. "I hope you didn't have ten bridesmaids dressed in blue dotted swiss in your wedding."

"Just my sister, and she wore royal blue velvet."

"Ma'am. Ma'am." The young librarian tapped me on the shoulder.

"What?" I opened my eyes and raised my head from the table. Dear God, I had drooled on the clippings.

"We close at five on Sundays."

"What time is it?"

"Quarter till."

"Good Lord. Okay. Thanks." I got a Kleenex from my purse, wiped the drool from the clippings and the newsprint from my face.

"Sorry," I said, putting the damp folder on the librarian's desk. He was eyeing it with distaste as I left. I didn't dare look up at Miss Boxx.

I called Fred from the phone downstairs and told him I was running late. I didn't tell him I had just had an hour's nap and felt like hell, groggy and cross. Or that I had missed seeing the Eudora Welty photographs, the reason for my trip. I headed for the parking lot through the same light drizzle that had been falling all day. The coolness on my face made me feel better.

It was almost dark and the lights had been turned on in the parking lot. Several people were coming from the library, and one security guard was at the door and another at the exit from the parking lot. When I heard footsteps behind me, I didn't even turn, assuming it was a library patron like me who had stayed until the last minute.

I was wrong.

"Mrs. Hollowell had a good nap, didn't she, Lynnie?"

"She drooled on the folder, Glynnie."

I turned and saw the Needham twins had come up behind me. So close to me that I backed up.

"What are you doing here?" I asked.

"Research."

"Yes. Research."

"Well, I hope you found what you were looking for."

"We did," they said together.

"Good. Well, I'll see you later." I turned and started toward my car, but they were right beside me, one on each side. They hadn't said anything threatening or done anything to make me nervous, but I was not at all comfortable with them sandwiching me in this misty, half-empty parking lot, lighted and guarded though it was.

"Betty Bedsole is a slut," one of them said.

"She doesn't wear underpants," the other said.

"Oh? I'm sorry to hear that." That was a ridiculous answer, but what was I supposed to do? Argue with them? I kept walking toward the car, my keys in my hand.

"Mercy was a slut."

"She didn't wear underpants?" I ventured.

"See, Glynnie? Claire said Mrs. Hollowell was smart."

I slowed down. The drizzling rain that had emphasized smells for Woofer that morning was helping me out now.

Over the odor of exhaust from cars leaving the parking lot, I could clearly smell alcohol.

"Dania was a slut," one twin said.

The other laughed hysterically. "Dania. Did Liliane tell you about our grandmother? She was a slut."

I stopped, backed up, and looked at them. They were skunk drunk. Sloshed.

"Did you drive down here?" I asked.

"Our car is here."

"Our car is somewhere."

"Well, I don't think you should drive. I'll take you home. Just let me tell the security guard we're leaving your car. What kind is it?"

"A Mustang."

"No. It's a Mercedes."

"Slight difference," I said. I led them toward my car and unlocked the door. "Here, get in and I'll go explain to the man he's going to have a car here all night."

"Good for you, Mrs. Hollowell. Glynnie is drunk. I am the designated driver."

"And the designated driver is drunk, which is morally wrong," Glynn said. "Morally wrong."

"Get in. There's a towel back there on the floor. If you think you're going to throw up, use it."

By the time I got back from explaining to the guard, who didn't seem to understand at all and insisted there was no twenty-four-hour parking here, the twins were both asleep.

I poked the nearest one. "Where are you staying? Your aunt Liliane's?" My question was answered with a snore. "What am I supposed to do with you?" A snore.

Damn. I hit the steering wheel and accidentally blew the horn. The security guard walked toward us. I started the car, gave him a wave, and drove through the exit that had the arm propped up for all the late leavers. If it had slammed down on my car, I don't think either of the twins would have known the difference.

I drove them to my house. I would call Liliane from there

and she could come get them. Fortunately, neither of them used the towel on the way over the mountain.

"Who?" Fred said. "Who's in your car?"

"Claire Moon's sisters," I explained again. "They were drunk at the library and I couldn't let them drive home."

"Well, why didn't you take them home?"

"I don't know where their aunt Liliane lives, Fred. I'm going to look it up and tell her to come get them."

Fred pushed his glasses up and pinched his nose exactly like Miss Boxx had done in my dream. "I'm going out to get them," he said. "They can't stay in the car."

"Just throw a blanket over them," I said.

"No. I'm going to tell them to come in the house and have some coffee." He started toward the door. "I don't understand, Patricia Anne, why this particular family has latched on to you."

"They haven't latched on to me."

"Well, you could fool me."

By the time he was back without the twins, I had discovered that Liliane Bedsole had an unlisted number.

"Shit, shit!" I said to the recording.

The expression on Fred's face had softened. "They look like identical dolls," he said. "I decided not to wake them up."

"Identical drunks. Take a blanket out like I told you. I've got to find out how to call their aunt."

"It's not listed?"

"You got it."

"Maybe Mary Alice knows it."

"She wouldn't have any reason to."

"The social director of the world? Hah. Give her a call, Patricia Anne."

I did and got the same "We Wish You a Merry Christmas" message. "She's not there," I said to Fred as he came through the den with a blanket.

"Then try somebody else."

Easier said than done. I tried Bonnie Blue and got Abe,

who said she wasn't home and he didn't have the pictures so just get off his ass.

"What?" I asked. "What?"

"Leota?"

"It's Patricia Anne Hollowell, Mr. Butler."

The phone went dead.

"So much for Southern gentlemen," I muttered. I got the phone book and looked up Thurman Beatty. He was listed, but I got an answering machine with Mercy's voice telling me she couldn't come to the phone right now, leave a message.

"No kidding," I said, startled. The sound of her voice reminded me of the grim way she had died. It also reminded me of the way Thurman had rushed off from the clinic when I mentioned the twins. I hung up the phone.

"That was eerie," I told Fred, who came in from covering the twins. "Mercy's still on the answering machine at their apartment."

"You can't get hold of anybody?"

"I'm not sure that I should. You know?" The shock of hearing Mercy's voice had nudged me into caution. "I mean, how well do we know any of these people? Even the aunt."

Fred sat down in his recliner and looked at me in amazement. "You don't trust Thurman Beatty?"

"I don't *know* Thurman Beatty, Fred, and I don't know those girls out in the car. All I know is two people are dead and one is missing and they're all connected somehow. I say let's just let the twins sleep."

Fred nodded.

"Let me try one more time to get Bonnie Blue. She might be down at her brother's." I looked James Butler's number up, dialed it, and a small child answered who assured me she was two years old.

"Where is your daddy?" I asked slowly.

"I'm two years old."

"Is your mommy there?"

"I'm two."

I gave up on that one, told the child bye-bye, and hung up. "No luck."

"Don't worry about it. They're fine for the time being. Don't look real they're so pretty."

"Oh, they're real, all right. Wait until they wake up sick as dogs."

Fred smiled slightly, but for only a moment. Then he looked worried again. "You think they do this often?"

"What? Get drunk? I hope not. I don't know."

"They're so beautiful."

"You said that already. You want waffles for supper?"

"Sure." He pushed up from his chair. "I'm going to take another blanket out. They look so fragile."

I got the waffles and bacon from the freezer. The bacon is the cardboard kind old folks should eat because of cholesterol. I wrapped the strips in paper towels and slapped them into the microwave. "Nuke 'em," I said, hitting the start button. The waffles I put into the toaster. Some things, I had to admit, had gotten easier in the last sixty years.

The phone rang just as Fred came back in. He answered it and handed it to me. "It's Mary Alice."

"Where have you been all day?" I asked, wiping my hands on a paper towel.

"It's Christmas, Mouse. I was at parties. A brunch, a lunch, and an open house."

"My, aren't we popular."

"I assume from that tone of voice that you weren't invited anywhere today to celebrate the season."

"I went to the library."

"Whoop-de-doo."

"And picked up the Needham twins, drunk as coots. They're out in my car right now, passed out, and I don't know how to get in touch with their aunt Liliane."

"Are you serious?"

"Fred threw a blanket over them. They're dead to the world."

"What happened?"

"I'll tell you the whole story later. Just give me the phone number."

"I don't have Liliane Bedsole's phone number. Why should I have Liliane Bedsole's phone number? Why don't you look it up?"

"It's unlisted. And you have everybody's phone number."

"Call Thurman."

"I did. Mercy answered the phone."

"Mercy?"

"It's your fault."

"It is not!" We were both quiet for a moment. "What's my fault?" Mary Alice asked.

"That the twins are passed out in my car."

"I'll have to think about that one," Mary Alice said. "By the way, Bubba's feeling better. James said I could pick him up tomorrow. You want to go?"

"I'll have to think about it. I'll call you in the morning." I hung up the phone and turned to Fred. "It really is all her fault," I said.

"I know," he agreed.

Thirteen

Around ten o'clock, Fred and I went out, untangled the twins, and helped them walk on rubbery legs into our guest bedroom. They collapsed on the bed and went back to sleep immediately.

"Well, we couldn't leave them in the car all night, Patricia Anne," Fred said. "They'd catch pneumonia."

"I don't think so. They're well fortified against the cold." I looked down at Glynn and Lynn. They were lying on their sides facing away from each other. Their black hair curved against their cheeks just as Claire's had done when she lay on my sofa.

"I don't think I've ever seen such black hair," Fred said. "Looks like a crow."

"The name on the bottle is probably Raven."

"Patricia Anne!"

"Don't you Patricia Anne me. Their sister Claire's got the same black hair and eyelashes and she's a dishwater blonde. That's one reason I didn't recognize her."

"You're kidding." Fred leaned over the nearest twin and looked at her hair. "Are you sure?"

"I could have hair like that tomorrow."

Fred eyed me speculatively. "You could?"

"A quick trip to Delta Hairlines," I added.

He shook his head. "Nah. It wouldn't look the same."

I stomped into the hall.

"I meant it wouldn't be the same you, honey," Fred said, following me. "I love your gray hair, every curl."

By the time we were ready for bed, Fred had put his foot in his mouth so many times, he was sputtering. I almost felt sorry for him. Almost.

During the night, I heard one, or both, of the twins being violently sick in the guest bathroom.

"I'm glad we left the light on for them," I said. But Fred was sleeping. Worn out. I slipped from the bed and went down the hall. I could hear the shower beginning to run.

Their bed was empty, but the bathroom door was wide-open. One of them lay on the bath mat in a fetal position, the other was, apparently, in the shower.

"Are you all right?" Stupid question.

"We are not feeling well," said the twin on the mat. She opened her eyes, shaded them with her hand, and looked at me. "Mrs. Hollowell?"

"What? You want me to get you something? Some Alka-Seltzer?"

She slapped her hand against the shower door. "Glynnie, we are at Mrs. Hollowell's."

"Is that good?" A weak voice from the shower.

"I don't know. It's just where we are."

"It's fine," I said. "I'll get each of you a robe and see if I can find something to settle your stomachs."

By the time I got back with an old robe of mine and one of Fred's, Lynn had made it into the shower and Glynn sat on the edge of the bed wrapped in a towel, shivering.

I handed her the robes and went to the kitchen to fix some Alka-Seltzer. When I returned, both girls were sitting on the edge of the bed, still shivering in spite of the warm robes.

"Think you can keep this down?" I asked.

"We can or we can't," one of them said. They both took the glasses and drained them.

"Thank you," they said together.

"Try and go back to sleep."

"Lynnie was the designated driver," Glynn said.

"Shut up, Glynnie. You're always whining."

"Well, you were."

Sisters. If they felt like fussing, they would be okay. I told them good-night and went back to bed.

"You all right?" Fred murmured.

"I'm fine." I snuggled against him and put my cold feet against his leg.

"I love you," he said.

What a man.

I awoke to an empty bed and to the smell of coffee. Fred was going out of the back door as I walked into the kitchen.

"Don't do anything to your hair today, Patricia Anne. It looks great just like it is, gray and all."

I promised that I would not be a brunette when he got home.

"And get rid of those twins. Those folks aren't any of our business. They're just bad news."

"But so beautiful."

Fred's face softened. "Well, yes, they're that, all right." He didn't say anything else because I threw a spoon at him.

"Men can be such pains in the butt," Mary Alice said when I called her to tell her I wanted to go get a Christmas tree for the den regardless of what Fred said, that the one in the livingroom could stay, smelling of formaldehyde like it did, and be his. I would just close the door. So if she was going to go get Bubba, I wanted to go to Harpersville.

"Fred thinks the twins are beautiful," I added.

"Figures."

"I don't think they're going to be beautiful this morning, though, and I've got to take them home. I'll call you when I get back."

I peeked into the guest room and the sleeping twins didn't move. I got dressed and went out to walk Woofer. There was fog this morning settling in the valleys. This was the kind of weather I wanted my plant stand for, the one Fred was making me that would roll outside. My ferns would love it.

Lynn and Glynn were sitting at the kitchen table when I

got home. Each was holding a glass filled with a lot of ice and what appeared to be Coke against her forehead.

"Headache," one whispered. I opened the cabinet and handed them the bottle of aspirin. Each took three and looked at the tablets for a moment before gulping them down.

"Glynn?" I said. The twin in Fred's robe looked up with bloodshot eyes. "You need to call your aunt Liliane. She's probably worried to death about you."

"Why?"

"Because you didn't get home last night. That's why."

"You brought us here," Glynn said.

"I thought I could call your aunt Liliane to come get you, but her number's not listed. And God knows, you were in no condition to drive."

"Glynnie is always the designated driver," Lynn said, her forehead propped in her hands.

"Enough of this!" Both twins jumped. "Get up off your butt, one of you, and call Liliane. If she can't come get you, I'll take you home."

"We're not staying with Liliane," Lynn said. "We're staying at the Tutwiler."

"What?" The Tutwiler Hotel is catty-corner from the downtown library.

"We saw you cross the street and Glynnie said, 'Let's go see Mrs. Hollowell,' only we waited and waited and you didn't come out."

"We were in the bar." Glynn sighed. "For a long time."

"We even went looking for you and there you were, drooling on newspaper clippings about Betty Bedsole."

"So we went back to the bar to wait."

"For a long time."

I pulled a chair out and sat down at the table. The noise of the chair scraping made the twins cringe. "You mean you didn't have to drive anywhere? You're staying at the Tutwiler?"

"Did we say that, Glynnie?"

"Of course, Lynnie. It's true."

"So I made you get in my car because I didn't want you

driving and you were right where you were supposed to be.''
I began to grin. "I'll be damned. I kidnapped you."

Lynn snickered slightly and then pressed her fingers
against her forehead. "We won't press charges."

Glynnie also rubbed her forehead. "We just wish you
hadn't stayed in the library so long."

"Don't blame me for your drinking," I said.

"No. It was Betty's fault."

"We went in the bar to watch her leave and she looked
so sad."

"You *are* talking about Betty Bedsole, aren't you? The
woman you called a slut?"

Glynn looked at Lynn. "Did you tell Mrs. Hollowell Betty
was a slut?"

"Did I?" Lynn asked me.

"The lack of underwear was mentioned," I said.

Lynn nodded. "True. But she was very sad. We had a
drink because Betty looked so sad when she got in the taxi."

"I'd say you had quite a few drinks because Betty looked
so sad. I don't suppose it occurred to either of you that drinking is one of the reasons she looks so sad."

"Mrs. Hollowell will preach now, Lynnie."

The rolled-up newspaper was lying on the table, and I
would have loved to have swatted Glynn hard right on her
aching head. Instead, I got up, poured myself a cup of coffee,
and announced that I would take them back to the hotel in
fifteen minutes.

"You made her mad, Glynnie," I heard Lynn say as I
headed down the hall. "Claire will not like that."

It was almost an hour before we headed downtown. The
twins insisted on changing the guest room bed and cleaning
the bathroom. Whether it was remorse over making me angry
or over their binge, they wouldn't leave until everything was
spotless. When we left the house, sheets and towels were
chugging away in the washing machine and the physical effort of the cleaning seemed to have made the twins feel better. Before we went out of the back door, I had one of them
write down their aunt Liliane's phone number and address,

which I stuck up on the refrigerator. I almost asked why they weren't staying with her but decided it was none of my business.

It was a quiet ride back to the hotel. Glynn sat beside me but closed her eyes and seemed to be dozing. Lynn stretched out on the backseat. They both woke up, though, when I came to the corner of the library and slowed.

"We'll get out here," Glynn said. "Thank you, Mrs. Hollowell."

"Thank you, Mrs. Hollowell," Lynn echoed.

The light changed just as they got out, so they crossed the street in front of me. Wilted as they were, they turned the head of every man they passed. I wondered, idly, what possessing that kind of power would be like. Or if they would have the same impact away from each other. The person behind me blew his horn and I realized the light was green. I waved an apology and headed home.

It had been the twins who had spirited Claire from the hospital. I was more convinced of that than ever. Lynn's remark, "Claire will not like that," sounded as if they were in close touch. A taxi pulled up into the lane beside me, reminding me of what the twins had said about Betty Bedsole. How sad she looked. I thought about the picture of her as a debutante, eighteen, beautiful, with her adoring father looking down at her. Had Claire and the twins' mother also been beautiful? Probably. For a while. Before abuse and alcohol. Damn. Let the twins' getting drunk the night before be an isolated incident.

The sheets and towels had finished washing when I got home. I put them in the dryer and checked my messages. Bonnie Blue had called; she was on her way to work but would call later. That was it. No invitations to brunches, lunches, or open houses to celebrate the season.

"It's because you're so unsociable, Patricia Anne," Mary Alice said on the way to Harpersville. We were going to get the tree first and then pick Bubba up on the way home. "When have you had a dinner party?"

I tried to remember. "Last January?"

"There. You see? And that was just some couples from the neighborhood."

"Frances Zata came. You came."

"And the memory, pleasant as it is, is becoming dim. Why don't you do it again?"

"After Christmas. I can't afford Tiffany and the Magic Maids and caterers like you can."

"They're not necessary for a nice party."

"How come you always have them, then?"

"I said they weren't *necessary*. I didn't say they weren't wonderful."

We rode in silence for a few minutes. I was tired because of the interrupted sleep of the night before.

"What did the twins have to say?" Sister asked. She had laughed until she cried when I told her they were staying at the Tutwiler, that the whole night had been unnecessary.

"They know where Claire is."

"They say so?"

"Not exactly. They said they got drunk because they saw Betty Bedsole leaving and she looked sad."

"That's a new excuse."

"Their mother and their aunt are both alcoholics. I hope they remember that."

"They say anything about Mercy?"

"That she was a slut because she didn't wear underpants."

"What?"

"I swear."

"And these are the sophisticated New York models?"

"Go figure."

Mary Alice giggled. "Will Alec loved it when I didn't wear underpants."

I stuck my fingers in my ears. "I will not listen to this."

"Oh, for heaven's sake, Mouse," Mary Alice yelled. "You're such a prude!"

I removed my fingers. "I am not a prude. I just don't want to know things like that about poor dead Will Alec."

"You don't want to know that he was happy frequently?"

"Happy, yes. Kinky, no."

"Am I talking to the sister who stole *The Kinsey Report* from the library?"

"Am I talking to the sister who fought me for it?"

"Well, I kept wondering why you were squealing so much."

"Mama would have died, wouldn't she?"

"Don't be silly. She probably read it." Mary Alice passed a pickup that had a Christmas wreath attached to the back window. It was blinking like Mrs. Santa's shirt.

"I looked Betty Bedsole up at the library. Read some of Ross Perry's columns, too. He really lambasted Mercy when she had her first showing. Unmercifully. No pun intended. Anyway, in the clipping file on Betty, there he was at her debut and seeing her off to Atlantic City, too. You sure he was gay? Maybe he was madly in love with Betty and she dumped him. That would explain why he had the grudge against Mercy."

"Maybe he was. I don't know. Odds are it was Mercy's father he hated."

"Samuel Armistead? Why?"

"You remember the movie *Mer-men*?"

"No."

"Neither does anybody else." We passed another truck with a wreath. Something new. "Ross followed Betty to Hollywood, thinking he was going to be a big star. They say Samuel Armistead had promised to give him a hand up in a movie career. You know Ross always acted in plays around Birmingham. And was pretty good. I saw him do Scrooge and, I swear, if his wig hadn't kept slipping, I'd have cried."

I was confused. "What about *Merlin*?"

"Not *Mer-lin*. *Mer-men*. You know, men mermaids. Samuel Armistead got Ross a leading role in what is supposed to be the worst movie ever made. It's so bad, they still teach it in film courses and show it at film festivals. It was Ross's only movie." Mary Alice looked over at me. "I'm surprised you haven't heard this story."

I shook my head. "I had no idea he'd been in movies."

"Just the one."

"You ever see it?"

"As a matter of fact, I did. Mercy had a party for the museum board one night and showed it."

"Whoa."

"Yep. Old Ross had to sit there and watch himself flap around and say things like 'My tail is my prison.' Or something like that."

"I'm surprised he didn't leave."

"He stayed and tried to act like he thought it was funny. I'll give him credit for that. No telling what his blood pressure was, though. One of us should have had the guts to tell Mercy to turn the thing off, but we didn't."

"Sounds like a fun evening."

"A long one."

I thought about this new information for a few minutes. "You think Samuel Armistead was jealous of Ross?"

Mary Alice shrugged. "Who knows? He had a reputation for being the A-number-one son of a bitch in Hollywood. He might have just thought it was funny, doing Ross in like that."

"I wonder how Betty felt about it."

"I doubt that it mattered."

We passed the sign that said POLICE JURISDICTION, HARPERSVILLE. "God, we're lucky," I said.

"We're lucky, little sister," Mary Alice agreed. "All my husbands were wonderful. And sweet. Didn't you think so?"

"And rich. And old."

"Mature. I got three kids from them, remember."

"They were old."

"Not too old." Sister turned at the sign for the Christmas tree farm.

"Did you have a favorite?" I've always wanted to ask Sister this.

"Hmmm. Philip was the handsomest. The most intellectual, too. Remember how he used to read all the time? Will Alec was the most fun, but he didn't have a chin. Do you call that lantern-jawed? Seems like you do."

"I don't know."

"And Roger was probably the sweetest. A teddy bear."

"One of the originals."

But Mary Alice wasn't paying any attention to my remarks. She was busy comparing husbands. "Will Alec liked to dance, but Roger was more sensitive. He cried at movies. Philip liked to fly, but it made Will Alec sick."

Her litany, which continued, was better than a sleeping pill. By the time we turned into the Christmas tree farm, I was fighting to keep my eyes open.

"So I can't choose," she concluded, pulling into a parking space.

I opened the door and sat there, letting the cool, damp air revive me.

"Come on, Mouse," she urged.

"Maybe I shouldn't do this. Fred really has a thing against live trees."

"Tough titty" was my sister's comment.

I settled for a tree small enough to go in the bay window. Mary Alice chose another huge one.

"Weren't you ladies here yesterday?" asked the man who tied the trees on the car.

"We were so pleased we came back for more," Sister said. "You have very nice trees."

"We think highly of them." The man handed Sister one end of the rope to hold while he went around the car.

"We can tell," I said, making out a check. "Why didn't you tell me they cost a small fortune?" I fussed at Mary Alice when we got back in the car.

"Oh, for heaven's sake, Mouse. Spend your money so your children won't have to."

It sounded like it made sense.

We went by the cross garden, past the scene of Ross's accident, and past the entrance to the pink confection of a house and James Butler's veterinary clinic.

"Where are you going?" I asked.

"Bonnie Blue said Leota Wood lives down this road. I'd

really like to see some more of her work. You know how my girls love quilts. You mind?''

I didn't mind at all. I thought Leota Wood's ''story'' quilts were beautiful. ''You think it's okay, just dropping in?''

''She'll tell us if it's not. I've got an idea she'll be happy to sell without giving a gallery its forty percent.''

The trees closed in on us again after we passed James Butler's property. We were running parallel to the creek that Ross's car had plunged into. Wisps of fog still hung above the water since the sunshine we had been promised had not materialized.

''This place should be covered in Spanish moss,'' I said. ''This is definitely a Spanish moss place.''

''It would be if it were south of Montgomery.''

''And popcorn trees would be everywhere. Fred still misses them.''

There is a line straight across the state of Alabama called, simply, ''The Spanish Moss Line.'' It is such a clear demarcation, you can see it when you drive down I-65 and approach the Alabama River just outside Montgomery, where trees are suddenly laden with Spanish moss. Chinese tallow trees, popcorn trees, tend to stray slightly outside the line, but not far. It has to do with the slight variance in temperature and distance from the Gulf. But it's startling how obvious the line is.

''Start looking for her mailbox,'' Mary Alice said. ''Bonnie Blue said it wasn't far.''

''This is nothing but trees.'' But as soon as I said it, we came around a curve and saw a dirt road on the left. A mailbox, painted with bluebirds, had ''Wood'' on it.

Mary Alice turned onto the dirt road, which was full of ruts and mud holes. The Christmas trees scratched the roof as she tried to miss the deepest holes.

''My God,'' she said. ''These people must have a Jeep.''

''Or a truck.'' I was clutching both my seat belt and the door handle.

''I don't think we can make it,'' Sister said.

''Well, you sure can't back up.''

"What's underneath a car that can get smashed?"

"I think we're going to find out."

Fortunately, the house was close, in a small clearing that we didn't see until we were right on it. It was a log cabin that looked as if it had been added onto several times. A porch, with small logs supporting the roof, ran the width of the house. Several big caned rockers were lined up along the porch.

"Is that a real log cabin?" Mary Alice asked.

"Sure it is."

"I mean, like an Abraham Lincoln log cabin, not one you buy in a kit."

"Looks like it. Looks like an Abraham Lincoln dog on the porch, too." The ugliest dog I had ever seen, gray and white striped with a huge head, had raised up from behind one of the chairs. Not happy to see us. Hackles up, teeth bared.

"Is that a dog?" Sister asked.

"What else could it be?"

Just then the front door opened and a tiny black lady with white hair came out and waved. I let the window down a little. I had no doubt that the dog could hurtle across the swept yard and into our car window with one leap. "Y'all wait a minute," she called. "Let me put Rover up."

"She must be kidding," Mary Alice said. "Rover? That dog's an Attila."

"Look at him."

Rover had rolled over on his back and Leota Wood was scratching his belly. "Come on," we heard her say. He hopped up and followed her inside.

Mary Alice watched. "I hope it's someplace with iron bars."

Leota Wood came back to the porch and motioned for us to come in. "Rover makes folks nervous," she said after we had introduced ourselves. "He's a sweetie, though."

"What breed is he?" Mary Alice asked.

"A coydog. Half coyote, half dog. Born to my hound Bessie. There's lots of coydogs around here. Mostly wild. Run in packs. You ought to hear them some nights. Rover's a sweetie, though," she repeated. "Y'all come on in. You want to see some quilts?"

We said that we did, and she ushered us into a quilt lover's dream. Log Cabin, Grandmother's Fan, Heaven and Earth, Storm at Sea. They seemed to cover every surface, glowing with color as if they had captured the sun.

"Oh, my," I gasped. For once Mary Alice was speechless.

"They're right pretty, don't you think?" Leota Wood folded her arms across her chest and rocked back and forth slightly as if daring us to differ.

"They're absolutely wonderful." Mary Alice found her voice.

Leota Wood smiled. "My daughter did some of these. I do mostly the story quilts now. I help her with the colors, though. I swear that girl thinks brown and black are fancy and I tell her, I say, 'Look, Doreen, folks like bright quilts. Get that old dirty brown out of there.' And she does, mostly. Still sticks some in sometimes." She walked over to a television in the corner and turned off *The Price Is Right*. Bob Barker's smile faded like a Cheshire cat's. "Y'all look around. You want some coffee? I was just fixing some."

We said that would be nice and she opened a door that led into a small kitchen. "I wonder where Rover is," Mary Alice murmured nervously.

"He's in the bedroom," Mrs. Wood called.

Mary Alice and I looked at each other in astonishment. "How could she have heard that?" Sister mouthed.

In the kitchen, Leota Wood laughed. "I didn't hear you. I just know what you said. Everybody says the same thing. Worrying about that sweet animal. He won't bother you. Y'all look around."

I had already been captured by a quilt in the Heaven and Earth pattern. A deceptively simple pattern, consisting of alternating light and dark triangles in every color, it seemed to change as I took it from the back of a chair and unfolded it. An occasional placement of two dark or two light triangles together gave the impression of mountains slicing into the sky.

"That's one of Doreen's," Mrs. Wood said, coming back with a tray of coffee and cookies and seeing what I was admiring. "Mercy Armistead was going to put it in her gallery. Said she'd call it 'Space-Time' or something like that and sell it for a lot of money." She put the tray down on the coffee table and invited us to sit down.

"This is very nice of you, Mrs. Wood," Mary Alice said. "We weren't sure whether we should just drop in like this."

"Lord, yes, honey. And call me Leota. I'm used to having folks come by. It's the way I used to sell all my quilts. Then they came up with this 'Outsider' thing and claimed I was a primitive artist. I told that Ross Perry, I said, 'Listen here, Ross Perry, okay, so I live outside the big city, but I'm damned if I'm primitive. I got an inside bathroom and a satellite dish.' I said, 'Primitive? Do primitive folks take *People* magazine?' " Leota Wood shoved a plate of cookies at Mary Alice.

"I'm sure he meant it as a compliment," Mary Alice said, helping herself to a couple of old fashioned teacakes, each with a pecan half placed precisely in the middle.

"I reckon. Anyway, he liked my quilts, all right. Bought a lot of them."

"I can understand why," I said. "They should be in museums."

"Can't make any money there, honey," Leota said. "I guess since Ross and Mercy are both dead I'll have to hit the craft shows again." She offered me the cookies and I took one. It tasted just like the ones Grandmama used to make.

"These are wonderful," I said.

"It's the almond extract. Almond, not vanilla." Leota Wood sat back in her chair. "You know, I can't believe Mercy and Ross are both gone. Wham. Just like that." She slapped the arm of her chair to show what she meant.

"And somebody tried to kill Claire Moon," I said. "Probably the same person."

"Do, Jesus! That sweet child?" A shocked Leota put her coffee cup down.

"You didn't know?" Mary Alice seemed about to launch into a detailed description of Claire's plight.

"She's all right," I interrupted quickly. I didn't add "I hope," which would have been closer to the truth.

"But somebody tried to kill her?" Leota Wood's face, which had had a coppery glow to it when we came in, seemed ashen.

"Looks that way."

Leota folded her hands and brought them to her chin. The fingers were in the "Here's the church, here's the steeple" position. The "steeple" pushed against her lips. She was silent for a moment, thinking. Then she turned her hands over ("here's all the people") and said, "Y'all gonna buy any quilts?"

We were. Mary Alice bought three, one for each of her girls and one for Haley. I bought the Heaven and Earth. Less money my children would have to worry about.

With the bright quilts inside the car and the Christmas trees tied on the top, we looked festive as we pulled up to the clinic to pick up Bubba. James Butler was just coming around the side of the building, waved, and walked over. He was smiling brightly.

"Claire has shown up," he said. "She's okay and Thurman has gone to check on her."

"I'll bet I know where he's gone," I said. "To the Tutwiler Hotel."

"I'll be damned," James said. "How did you know that?"

"Would you believe a wild guess?"

"With you ladies, I'd believe anything. Y'all come on in and tell me about it. Bubba's chomping at the bit."

"Chomping at the bit?" Mary Alice murmured.

I laughed. "Well, what do you expect when you take your cat to a horse hospital?" We got out and followed James into the clinic.

Fourteen

"**H**ow come Thurman Beatty was still married to Mercy if he was so in love with Claire Moon?'' Mary Alice asked as we made our way home through the Christmas traffic on Highway 280. Bubba's carrying box was on the front seat between us, and, between yowls, he would snake his leg out of the holes, claws unsheathed.

"Maybe Bonnie Blue's wrong about Thurman. Maybe he's just a nice man, worried about a lady in distress,'' I said, dodging Bubba's paw. "This cat is dangerous.''

"He just wants some attention because he's sick.''

"I'd hate to see him mad.''

"He's a good boy, yes he is.'' Mary Alice patted the top of Bubba's box and jerked her hand back as Bubba made a swipe. She wasn't quite fast enough. "Shit!''

"He's a good boy, yes he is. Maybe he's a coycat.'' I watched her sucking her wrist.

"Shut up, Patricia Anne, and get me a Kleenex out of my purse. I mean,'' she continued after she had wrapped the tissue around the scratch, "supposing Bonnie Blue is right. People don't have to stay together nowadays unless they want to. If you were in love with someone else, would you want to stay with Fred?''

"I'd take him with me.''

"You probably would." She put on her right turn signal.
"Where are you going?"

"Jake's. I'm starving."

"What about Bubba? Or are you getting something to go?"

"He can go in. Nobody will know he's there." Bubba howled his answer to that lie.

Jake's Joint has the best barbecue in the whole state. In the South. Jake doesn't fool around with all that other stuff like slaw and beans and Brunswick stew. He serves barbecue, period. With white bread. And there are always crowds of people waiting to commit gastronomical suicide. Ask any of them if they know they are shortening their lives by hunkering down over a rack of ribs that requires a loaf of white bread and dozens of paper napkins to soak up the fat and they'll just grin, their mouths encircled with either red or yellow barbecue sauce. For here is the cosmic question Jake has presented us with: red or yellow sauce; the red being more traditional, the yellow a mustardy, spicier sauce. Families have split over which is better. Baptists tend to order red, Unitarians yellow. A routine question asked Alabama political candidates is "Red or yellow?" It's a good question, but being Alabama political candidates, they all say the good old traditional red sauce. Occasionally a maverick will admit to liking both.

A notice on the door proclaimed that shirts and shoes must be worn and that no pets were allowed.

"Signs like that are so tacky," Mary Alice said. "Makes us all look like a bunch of hicks. Like we'd go to a restaurant without shirts and shoes." She sailed through the door carrying Bubba.

For once, Jake's wasn't too crowded. A couple were leaving a booth in the corner and Mary Alice made a dive for it, putting Bubba's carrying case beside her on the seat.

"Maybe you better put him on the floor," I suggested.

"He's too upset."

Bubba did, indeed, sound upset. His yowls blended in with the other loud noises, though. Acoustics have never been at the top of Jake's priority list. Not only does a jukebox play nonstop country music—at the moment it was Hank Jr.—but the waitresses scream each order toward the back. When the order is filled, this is announced loudly as it is slapped on a high counter for the waitresses to pick up.

"Hey, ladies," said a skinny woman in a short maroon uniform with "Mavis" on the pocket. She had a damp rag in her hand which she swiped across the table. "What you want?" If she saw Bubba, she chose to ignore it.

"Small order of ribs with red," Mary Alice said. "Sweetened ice tea."

"The same," I said.

Mavis gave us a disgusted look over the order pad poised in her hand. The damp gray rag dangled from her fingers. "Why don't y'all order a large and half it? Get the same amount, maybe a little more, and save yourselves a dollar and a half. Enough to get a fried pie. Peach today."

"Can we get yellow sauce on half?" Mary Alice asked.

"No." Mavis was not one to argue with. "Large, red!" she screamed toward the back. Bubba screamed, too, but his voice was drowned out.

When Mary Alice and I were growing up, our father told us never to eat at a restaurant with dirty windows. He said the condition of the windows told more about the restaurant than any health inspection score.

"Look at the window." I pointed.

Mary Alice took a napkin, reached across Bubba, and wiped a small circle on the glass. "The sun's come out."

"I mean, look how dirty it is. Remember what Daddy always said."

"It's not dirt. It's barbecue sauce."

I looked around nervously. "Do you see their score posted anywhere?"

"For heaven's sake, Mouse. The food doesn't stay here long enough for any bacteria to grow in it."

She had a point. Nevertheless, salmonella was not on my wish list for Christmas. I spotted the cleanliness scorecard posted above the cash register, slid from the booth, and worked my way through the crowd waiting to pick up orders and pay—"98" it proclaimed in black Magic Marker.

Mavis was putting our tea down when I got back to the booth. Big Mason jars served as glasses. "Y'all want lemon?"

We nodded that we did. She reached around to the booth next to us and handed us a saucer with small wedges of lemon on it.

"Well?" Mary Alice asked me, squeezing a piece of lemon into her jar.

"Ninety-eight," I admitted. "Somebody's on the take."

"You are so picky, Patricia Anne. You ever hear of anybody getting sick at Jake's?"

"I guess not." I reached for some lemon. "I just don't need food poisoning on top of everything that's happened the last few days."

"Well, you have been borrowing trouble, that's for sure. Dragging those Needhams in off the street. Lord!" Mary Alice shook her head. I thumped a piece of squeezed lemon at her, hitting her on the arm.

"Is it safe to put this down?" Mavis asked, standing over us with a platter of ribs.

"Sorry." I unpeeled my arms from the sticky table.

"That's okay. I got a girlfriend I throw stuff at all the time." Mavis put the ribs and a stack of white bread on the table.

"She's my sister, not my friend," I said, nodding toward Mary Alice.

"Got one of them, too. Y'all want anything else?"

We said that we didn't, that it looked wonderful. And it did. For the next few minutes we concentrated on eating. Mary Alice slipped a few choice morsels through the holes in Bubba's carrying case.

"I thought James Butler put him on a diet," I said.

"Starting tomorrow," Mary Alice said. "He needs to build his strength back up first."

"You know," I said, after the stack of bread and ribs had diminished considerably and I was feeling more kindly toward my sister, "Claire's back, and I'm relieved she's okay. Now I can wash my hands of the whole thing. Whoever killed Mercy or Ross or tried to kill Claire, that's for the police to find out. Right?"

"Right." Mary Alice put another crumpled napkin on top of the considerable pile on the table. "What's that police-woman's name who keeps wandering in?"

"Bo Mitchell?"

"That's it."

"Why?"

"I just wondered."

Mary Alice never "just wondered" anything in her life. "Why?" I asked again.

Mary Alice shrugged and reached for the last rib. "You want some peach pie?"

"Might as well." I stood up and waved for Mavis, who, miraculously, saw me and came to take our order. "Now, what about Bo Mitchell?" I asked when Mavis had left.

"If I called the police station, I'd want to know who to talk to."

This was getting more and more curious. "Why would you want to call the police station?"

"I think I know where Ross Perry was going the day he was shot."

"Where?"

"Leota Wood's."

"What makes you think that?"

"Well, when I had to go to the bathroom, I just happened to open the door and look in her back bedroom to see if there were any more quilts there, and, Mouse, it was stacked full with stuff from all the Outsider artists. I couldn't look but a minute, but I swear I saw some of Abe's paintings. And Lonnie Holcombe's and Ruby what's-her-name. There was a lot more stuff than at Mercy's gallery. Just piled in there."

I skipped over Mary Alice's just "happening" to open the bedroom door at Leota Wood's house and went right to "Why didn't you tell me?"

"I was thinking about it."

"And what did you decide?"

"That Ross and Leota are art thieves. They were stealing the Outsider art and selling it on the black market and Leota told Ross—remember that phone call he made at the restaurant?—that their connection, probably some big art Mafia man, had just called and told her that he was going to make a deal with them that afternoon and Ross rushed out there, only it was a ruse and they were hiding in the woods and shot him."

I looked at my sister, who nibbled the last bit of barbecue from the last rib. She added the bone to the pile on the platter, dipped a napkin into her water glass, and wiped her mouth and hands with the damp paper. She didn't look like a woman who had suddenly taken leave of her senses.

"Well?" she said.

"You were figuring this out while you were driving down Highway 280 in Christmas traffic?"

"It makes sense."

"You think this makes sense? A Mafia art connection shooting Ross Perry in the middle of Shelby County makes sense?"

Mavis slapped down two fried pies and two forks. "Coffee?"

We shook our heads no.

"Don't burn yourself," she warned automatically as she walked away. Unnecessarily, also. Smoke poured from the pies.

"Ross was on his way to Leota's. I feel it in my bones," Mary Alice said, picking up her fork. "They were up to something."

"Well, Bo Mitchell wouldn't have anything to do with it. This is Shelby County. You're going to have to call the sheriff and explain the feeling in your bones. He needs to be alerted about that art Mafia, anyway. God knows we don't need that element running around down here in the Shelby County woods."

Mary Alice plunged her fork into her pie. "Okay, you explain it, then."

"I can't. I'm not even going to try. My sister warned me a few minutes ago to quit borrowing trouble. I'll dump a little more meat in the stew, though. I called the Butlers' the other night and got Abe. He thought I was Leota and told me, and I quote, 'The pictures ain't ready. Git off my ass.' "

Mary Alice blew on a piece of hot peach pie, touched her tongue to it, and blew on it some more. "It means something, Mouse," she said between puffs.

Bubba screamed for more barbecue.

"Everything does," I said.

We had a terrible time getting my tree off Sister's car. At least getting Sister's back on. The man at the Christmas tree farm had tied them together. So when we loosened the rope in my driveway, both trees fell. We were struggling to get Sister's back on top when a florist delivery truck pulled up and a young man got out with the largest poinsettia I had ever seen. At least two dozen brilliant red flowers, splashed with white as if someone had dripped a paintbrush over them, glowed in the winter sun. The plant was in a brass container, so large it was awkward for the young man to carry.

"Hollowell?" he said.

"That's me."

He shifted the plant's weight slightly. "You better let me put this inside for you."

I rushed to open the front door and held it open while the man climbed the steps carefully and came into the hall.

"I'll put it where you want," he offered. "It's not heavy as it looks. Just bunglesome."

I had him put it in the bay window in the kitchen. It was so beautiful, I caught my breath.

"Who's it from?" Mary Alice asked. She had followed us into the kitchen.

I opened the card and read aloud: "Merry Christmas, Mrs. Hollowell, and thanks for kidnapping us. Glynn and Lynn." I teared up a little.

"Oh, come on, Mouse. No tuning up." Mary Alice turned

to the deliveryman. "You know, I'll bet this nice young man would help us put my tree on the car."

And he did. And left smiling happily because of the "little Christmas something" Mary Alice gave him for helping.

After she and the still-unhappy Bubba left, I dragged my tree around the back and went looking for the stand. It had been so long since we had had a live tree, I wasn't sure where we had put it last. But I lucked out. It was on a shelf in the basement right by several strings of big colored lights. I eyed them for a moment, then decided that would be pushing Fred with his fear of fire too far. I was going to have to make a trip to the Big B for some tiny lights.

"What have you done, Mama?"

I jumped. I had been concentrating so, I hadn't heard Haley come to the basement door.

She answered her own question. "You've bought a live tree and Papa's going to have a fit."

I came up the steps with the stand. "Most probably," I agreed. "How come you're not at work?"

"Not much elective surgery this close to Christmas."

"People *elect* to have heart surgery?"

"They can put it off. Sometimes."

I looked at tiny Haley. The thought of her routinely rummaging around in people's chests still boggles my mind. I have never wanted to know what's under my skin. Let sleeping guts lie, is my philosophy. A bad one, according to Haley, who drags me in for mammograms, Pap smears, and other various and sundry indignities. She needles her father into going, too, fortunately. Several years ago, he had an early-stage melanoma removed from his back that neither of us had paid any attention to.

"See?" Haley told her father when the lab report came back. "See? I told you so."

"What do you do," Fred asked me, "when your children start telling you 'I told you so'?"

"Say thank you." And I meant it. Now he and I check each other over like monkeys.

"It's a nice tree. Bigger than mine." Haley was holding

the tree up when I came up the basement steps. "You got any decorations for it?"

"I can probably find a few. Help me get it in the stand."

This is never an easy job, trying to get those screws in the trunk of the tree. I was grateful for Haley's help.

"I need to borrow your black evening bag," she said as we hauled the tree that had looked so small in the field up the back steps. "And Grandmama's cameo. And that gold hair thing of yours. You know, the butterflies. I've decided to wear my hair up for the Policeman's Ball, Mama, because I'm wearing a dress that looks, I swear, like a slip or a night-gown. In fact, I bought it in Rich's lingerie department, but the tag said it could be used as a dress so I'm taking them up on it."

"Sheriff Reuse is a lucky man," I said. It was wonderful hearing Haley babbling happily like this.

"Whoa," she said as we went through the kitchen. "Where did those gorgeous flowers come from?"

"The Needham twins, Lynn and Glynn. Claire Moon's sisters."

"Because you took Claire to the hospital? That was certainly thoughtful."

"No. Because I dragged them home last night."

We put the tree in the corner of the den while I explained to Haley that I had been afraid for the twins to drive and had brought them home from the very spot where they were staying. "And I was right," I finished. "They had Claire there with them. They were the ones who took her from the hospital."

"Have you seen her? Is she okay? And why did they take her?" Haley was down on her hands and knees trying to straighten the tree up. "How's that?"

I backed up and looked. "A fraction to the right. And no, I haven't seen her. James Butler said Thurman Beatty had gone to get her. We were out at his horse hospital getting Bubba."

"Aunt Sister's Bubba was in a horse hospital?"

"And held his own, I'm sure."

Haley backed away from the tree and stood up. "Is it still leaning?"

"Looks straight to me. Do you think I ought to move Abe's painting? The tree's not touching it, is it?"

"It's fine," Haley said.

The mention of the painting reminded me of the Mafia art connection lurking out at Leota Wood's house. I told Haley about Mary Alice's conclusions when she had seen the bedroom full of Outsider work. To my surprise, Haley didn't laugh.

"Mama, two people are dead and another had a close call, and the only connection among them is the gallery, the Outsider's work. Think about it. Aunt Sister may be on to something."

"The Mafia hanging out at Leota Wood's? Get serious, Haley."

"I am serious. Not the Mafia, but what do you know about Leota Wood?"

"That she's a nice old lady in her seventies who lives in a log cabin in the woods and who makes the most beautiful quilts I've ever seen in my life." I started to the kitchen. "Come on, I'll fix us some coffee, or would you rather have Coke?"

"Coke. I'll get it." Haley got two glasses down and pointed one toward me. "Suit you?"

"Sure. I need something to cool Jake's barbecue down."

"Red or yellow sauce?" Haley stuck the glasses under the ice dispenser.

"Red."

"Mama." Haley poured the Coke. "You ought to live dangerously sometimes."

"Eating at Jake's *is* dangerous." I sat down at the table. "And do you know they had a ninety-eight health department score?"

"Jake knows the right people." Haley joined me at the table.

"Maybe some of that art connection Mafia."

But Haley refused to take this lightly. "Tell me again about Leota Wood."

I did, including the coydog, Rover, and my phone call to Abe Butler when he thought I was Leota and told me to get off his ass. I also told her that it was possible Ross Perry had been on his way to Leota's since he was killed only a mile or so from her house, but that he could have been going to see anybody who lived along that road, including James Butler. "She's just a nice, talented old lady, Haley," I concluded. "There's a logical explanation for all that artwork being in her bedroom. You can bet on that. Probably wasn't as much as your aunt Sister said, anyway."

"She's a fence," Haley said, gazing into her glass as if it were a crystal ball. "All that stuff is stolen and when Ross called she told him she had one particular thing that he collected, knowing he would pay her a fortune for it."

"Then who stole all the stuff and fenced it with Leota and why did she shoot Ross Perry?"

Haley stirred the ice with her finger. "Claire Moon stole it."

"What?" My head was beginning to throb. "Why not her sisters?" I got up and took two aspirin from a bottle that was almost empty. "Or her aunt Liliane."

"The twins weren't here for Mercy's party, were they?"

I swallowed the aspirin. "I have no idea. Why?"

"To kill Mercy."

I had started a grocery list on a notepad that had "Keep on truckin'" printed across the top. Some company Fred did business with. I tore a couple of sheets from the back and handed them to Haley. "Here. Write me a short synopsis. I'm still confused about some points."

"So am I." Haley grinned good-naturedly. She stuck the paper in her pocket. "I'll let you know when I figure it out."

"Well, in the meantime, let's get the stuff you came for and see what we can find to go on this tree. And we need to talk about the boys. It's okay for Freddie and Celia to stay with you, isn't it? Like they did last Christmas?"

"Sure, Mama. I enjoy having them."

"Well, Aunt Sister said she would love to have them. The thought of Mary Alice and Celia together for a couple of days bothers me, though. No telling who would get hexed."

Haley laughed. "I'll change the sheets on the bed for them. Even mop the kitchen floor."

"The" bed. That bothered me, too. Damn it, why didn't folks get married like they used to?

"Mama?" The tone of Haley's voice changed. "Is it all right if Jed comes over for Christmas dinner? I haven't asked him yet, but I think he's still having a hard time with holidays. You know, since his wife's death."

"Of course, honey. Ask him." Sheriff Jed Reuse was not the man I would have picked for Haley. Not that there was anything wrong. He was just a rather formal man, very reserved, the opposite of what Haley's Tom had been. Which was probably my hang-up. A rowdy Christmas at our house should be interesting for him—and us, too.

Haley patted the pocket where she had put the sheets of paper. "I'll get him to help me with this," she said.

"Frankly, my dear, I think Celia might do a better job."

"Don't bet on it." There was a softness in Haley's voice that I welcomed back almost as much as I did her laughter.

Fifteen

"**W**here did that poinsettia come from?" Fred asked as he walked into the kitchen. "That's the prettiest one I've ever seen."

"The Needham twins." I was standing at the stove sautéeing mushrooms. Two small steaks waited to be popped on the grill and fresh asparagus was already placed in the microwave, thick parts to the center, forming an incredibly expensive wheel.

"That was nice," Fred said. He came over and nuzzled my neck. The steaks caught his eye. "What is this? You're actually allowing pieces of marbleized red meat into this kitchen?"

"The rice and asparagus don't have any fat. We can splurge occasionally." I thought about my lunch at Jake's Joint and realized *splurging* might not be the right word to describe my cholesterol intake today. *Going overboard* was more like it. Drowning in fat. I'd have to do better tomorrow. I reached around and patted Fred's behind. "Get a beer, why don't you? The paper's on the table."

"You bought a Christmas tree today, didn't you?"

"Yes, I did," I said defensively. "And don't think for a moment I'm trying to get you in a good humor about it with steak. I quit playing that game a long time ago."

"It's fine, honey." He gave me a hug and headed for the refrigerator.

"Fine? You've been saying for years you didn't want us to have a live tree and now it's fine?"

"Patricia Anne"—Fred popped a beer open—"there is a Christmas tree in our den, decorated and lighted. I can see it reflected in the picture there." He pointed toward a framed poster of a Georgia O'Keefe poppy that hangs next to the bay window. "Now, the way I see it, I have a choice. I can go into the den, sit in my chair, read the paper, and enjoy the tree. Or I can throw a fit and say, 'I'll not have that fire hazard in our house, Patricia Anne,' in which case we would have an unpleasant evening. I'm opting for the first. Let me know when you're ready and I'll put the steaks on the grill." He picked up the paper and disappeared into the den.

He drives me crazy when he's so sensible. Takes all the wind out of my sails.

We did have a nice evening, though. The steaks were delicious, and the Christmas tree, scantily decorated though it was, added to the brightness of the season. Even Fred's propping the fire extinguisher noticeably near the tree didn't dispel the magic.

Fred was dozing in his chair and I was dividing my attention between reading a new biography of Greta Garbo and watching *Christmas in Washington* when the phone rang.

"What are you doing?" Mary Alice asked.

"Reading about Greta Garbo. Finding out a lot more about her than I wanted to know."

"Fred like the tree?"

"As a matter of fact, he did."

"Oh." Mary Alice sounded disappointed. "Well, what I called for was to see if you wanted to have supper here tomorrow night. I know it's Fred's pinochle night."

"Sounds great."

"I'm going to see if Frances Zata can come. I owe her a thank-you for filling in for me at the mall. And Bonnie Blue. Reckon they play bridge?"

"As well as we do, I imagine." Neither of us plays worth

a hoot. I plod, trying to remember the rules, refusing to take chances, and Mary Alice makes up the rules as she goes along. And usually wins. Our mother, who was an expert bridge player and who tried for years to teach us, finally refused to let us fill in at any of her parties, swearing neither of us had a lick of card sense.

"We might play some bridge, then. You can still come if the others can't, though."

"Gee, thanks."

"Sure. Seven o'clock?"

"Okay. How's Bubba?"

"That angel's asleep right in the middle of my bed."

"Where's Bill, then?"

"Soaking in Epsom salts. That Santa costume's giving him a rash like you wouldn't believe. You ought to see it."

"I'll pass. You want me to bring some fruit drop cookies tomorrow night?"

"Sure. And Mouse?" Mary Alice hesitated.

"What?"

"Nothing. I have to go rub calamine on Bill."

"Have a good time," I said.

Fred had opened his eyes and was yawning widely. "Bill has a bad rash," I told him.

"That's understandable." He got up and stretched. "What are you reading?"

"A biography of Greta Garbo. You wouldn't believe some of the things she did."

"Turn off the tree and come show me."

I took him up on the invitation.

The next morning I got my silver flatware from the freezer and polished it. Fred laughs at my keeping it there and says it's the first place a thief would look. But in the pull-out drawer under the peaches and blueberries I put up last summer? I doubt it. Plus, it's wrapped in heavy freezer paper and has "Shrimp" written on the side. I feel pretty safe about it.

I washed my crystal and china and put the red tablecloth

through the gentle cycle since it smelled musty. While it was in the dryer, I started making out a combination grocery list and things-to-do list. "Bert—Mortal Combat," I wrote. I had been assured by his parents that this was what my ten-year-old grandson wanted. I nibbled on my pencil eraser. It sounded awfully violent. Should I check it out? I put a question mark by "Mortal Combat" knowing full well that I would buy it, but feeling better for questioning it. A ten-year-old boy should be getting Erector sets, the fancy kind with lots of motors so he could build ferris wheels and helicopters.

The doorbell rang and somehow I knew before I opened it who it would be. And it was. Claire Moon stood there smiling. Dressed in a black turtleneck and black pants, which I realized by now was the sisters' usual outfit, she was a dead ringer for Audrey Hepburn. She looked pale, but her eyes were clear; in her arms was a large pink poinsettia. I smiled and held the door open for her.

"Merry Christmas, Mrs. Hollowell. And thanks for everything." She handed me the plant.

"Come on in," I said. "Are you okay?"

"I'm fine." She followed me into the den, where I put the flower on the coffee table and turned to hug her.

"You had us worried to death," I said.

"I'm sorry."

"I know the twins were trying to protect you. At least now I know it. At the time we didn't know what had happened."

"I don't remember any of it."

"I'm not surprised. Why don't you sit down and I'll make us some coffee."

Claire sank down on the sofa. "That would be wonderful."

I went into the kitchen to start the coffee. "The flower's beautiful," I called. "Thank you."

"You're welcome. I'm glad I got the pink. I see you already have a red." Claire could see the bay window from the sofa.

"Your sisters sent that," I said.

"Glynn and Lynn?" She sounded surprised.

I turned on the percolator and came back to the door. "You didn't know I kidnapped them?"

Claire shook her head no. I sat down in Fred's chair and told her about the night the twins had spent with us. The whole episode was beginning to seem funny, and I expected to see Claire smiling about it, at least. Instead, she looked upset.

"Oh, Mrs. Hollowell, I'm so sorry. We've been nothing but worry to you."

"I was worried *for* you. Nothing that happened was your fault. Remember that, Claire."

"Then why do I feel like it was?"

"My niece says guilt is a 'chick' thing. She's a lawyer and says if she's got a female client who was hit by a car that ran up on the sidewalk, the woman will feel guilty because she was standing at that particular corner waiting for the light to change. You think a man would?"

Claire grinned. "I don't think all women would. Mercy wouldn't. She'd be up checking the driver's insurance." Her smile faded.

"My sister, Mary Alice, wouldn't either. She'd just say it was my fault she was on that corner and make *me* feel guilty. The crazy thing about it is I probably would."

Claire and I looked at each other and her grin came back.

"I'll get us some coffee," I said. I went into the kitchen and got mugs from the cabinet.

"Mrs. Hollowell?" Claire was standing in the den door. "You went to the hospital with me, didn't you? I meant it when I said I was having trouble remembering what happened, but it seems like you were there holding my hand."

I nodded. "I went with you. You were in shock and that can be pretty dangerous. The paramedic said your stress signals were stuck on go. Or something like that. You were really out of it." I put the coffee on the kitchen table and motioned for Claire to sit down. "Put a lot of sugar in it," I said. "For energy."

"I'm feeling okay. When I woke up, I was with Glynnie and Lynnie at the hotel. I didn't even know how much time had passed or how they got me out of the hospital. I made them promise to let you know I was all right and I went back to sleep. That's all I wanted to do—sleep."

I thought about the lunch at the Green and White, the twins' startling me. "They told me," I said. "But what about your aunt Liliane? She was so worried, she came here wanting to know if I knew anything. Made me promise to let her know if I heard anything."

Claire looked up from stirring her coffee. "Liliane came here?"

I nodded. "I didn't know anything to tell her at the time. In fact, even after the twins told me you were safe, I wasn't sure where you were."

Claire shrugged and sipped her coffee. She was holding the mug with both hands as if to warm them.

I asked the questions I had been wondering about. "Why aren't the twins staying with Liliane? And how did they know you were in the hospital?"

"Did Liliane tell you that Dania story? She usually does." I nodded, surprised.

"Well, it's a lot simpler than that. Liliane's our grandmother. She got pregnant when she was in college and had our mother. Everything was covered up, of course, and the baby was adopted by an employee of my grandfather's who was paid well for the favor, I'm sure. God knows where Liliane got that Dania story. From a soap probably."

"I believed it," I admitted, remembering my tears.

"It ticks Lynn and Glynn off. They take it personally, the fact that she won't come out and claim us. The twins and Liliane have always fought like cats and dogs. Always. About everything from the length of their skirts to their friends. The day they graduated from high school they swiped the money from Liliane's purse for one-way tickets to New York and took off."

"How do you feel about Liliane?" I asked.

Claire shrugged. "Maybe she did the best she could, given the time and circumstances."

"And the circumstances were certainly different fifty years ago."

"Yes. On the other hand, I can understand how the twins feel." Claire was quiet for a minute. "You asked how they found out I was in the hospital. You know, I didn't think to ask. But they're in Birmingham because Mercy sent them an invitation to the gallery opening. Of course, they got here a day late, but that's Glynn and Lynn for you. Typical." Claire ran her finger around the rim of her cup.

"Were the twins and Mercy good friends?"

"The twins and Mercy? Not particularly. I was surprised they came. They pop in every now and then, though, since I've been back in Birmingham. I'm always happy to see them. But they take it upon themselves to bedevil poor Liliane. Lynn and Glynn showed up at a fancy party last spring at the Botanical Gardens, picked her up about a foot off the floor, and gave her a big juicy smack on each cheek. They angled in so it looked like Liliane had red cat whiskers. They've always driven her crazy with stuff like that."

I could imagine Liliane Bedsole with her orange hair and her tight skin sporting red cat whiskers. "I wish I had seen it," I said truthfully.

"They act like mischievous kids sometimes seeking attention." Claire motioned to the purse she had hung over the arm of the chair. "That's Glynnie's purse I've borrowed, and I swear I'm scared to open any of the compartments, scared something will pop out like a jack-in-the-box."

"That's not such a bad trait," I said.

"No, it's not." Claire pushed her chair back and stood up. "I've got to get their rental car back before they wake up. I need to go over to my place and get some clothes and things. I'm going out to James and Yvonne Butler's to stay a few days."

"Is it okay, your going in the apartment?"

Claire, who had started for the hall, turned. "You think it wouldn't be?"

"Well, it's a crime scene." The rest of the sentence, "where somebody tried to kill you," hung in the air between us.

"You think I ought to check with that police lady? What's her name?"

"Bo Mitchell. And yes, I think you should. If she says it's okay, I'll go with you. I don't want you out there by yourself."

"It'll be okay. I know what to expect this time. And it's daylight."

"Just make the call," I said.

The twins' rental car was hardly large enough for Claire and me. "I hope you aren't planning on getting a bunch of stuff," I said as we pulled up to her town house.

"Just a few clothes. These are Glynn's." Claire parked in a space marked "Owner" and we got out. It had only been a few days since I had been there, but Christmas decorations had sprung up on the tiny lawns like mushrooms. "I can't believe it's almost Christmas," Claire said.

"Do you know about Mortal Combat?" I asked.

Claire turned and gave me a puzzled, almost frightened look.

"It's a TV game," I hastened to explain. "My ten-year-old grandson wants it for Christmas and I was worried about how violent it is."

"Give him one of those things that projects the night sky on his ceiling. All you have to do is put in the date and where you are."

"That's a wonderful idea, Claire." I meant it.

"My husband had one. He loved it."

It was the first time I had heard her mention her husband, and it surprised me. She reached forward and put the key in the lock. "Well, here goes." She stepped across the threshold.

The shock value was gone for me. The stuffing pouring

out of the sofa was just that. Cotton. Claire and I stopped
and looked around.

"Can I help you do something?" I asked.

"Recommend a good upholsterer." She stepped over to
the sofa and ran her hand over one of the cuts. "Why on
God's earth would anybody do this?"

"I don't know, Claire." And I didn't.

She came back to the door and ran her hand over the hole
the knife had sliced in the door. "Damn," she whispered.
"Damn."

"Are you all right?" I asked. "I can go upstairs and get
you some things. Just tell me what you want."

"I'm okay. I'm not going to pass out on you again, Mrs.
Hollowell."

She did seem to be okay. She backed away from the door
and eyed the knife mark. She walked toward it again, stood
by it, measuring it against her body. "There's something
wrong here," she said.

I agreed that there was a lot wrong.

"No. Wait a minute." Claire went up a couple of steps,
turned, and came back to the door. She held out her hand as
if she were reaching for the doorknob. She shook her head,
turned, and went back up the steps.

"What are you doing?" I asked.

"There's something wrong," she repeated, coming back
down the steps and reaching for the door again.

"You want to clue me in?" I asked after Claire had repeated this action several times.

"The knife slice is wrong. Look at it."

I went over to the door and looked at the cut. It was on
the left side of the door, and when I stepped close to it, I
realized a knife plunged at this angle would hit me in the
chest. "Lord!" I said, shuddering.

"But look." Claire went up the steps again. "Come up
here, Mrs. Hollowell."

I followed her, wondering what in the world she was doing.

"Okay," she said. "Get two or three steps above me."

She waited. "Now watch. I'm running down the steps and you're chasing me with a knife." She ran down the steps and lunged for the door, jerking it open. I stood on the steps and watched her.

She came back up the steps. "Now, this time you follow me and try to stab me."

"This gives me the creeps," I said.

"Please, Mrs. Hollowell. You'll see what I mean."

"What kind of knife was it? You remember?"

"A big one."

I raised my arm up. "Okay. But this better prove something."

"Just chase me and try to stab me. Okay? Here I go." Claire dashed down the steps and opened the door. I was still on the steps when she turned around.

"Let's try it again," I said. It was amazing the effect the imaginary knife was having on me. I felt like Lady Macbeth.

"You want me to chase you?" she asked.

"No. I'll do it. Come on back."

Down the steps we went. Claire jerked open the door and I jammed my fist into it.

"Shit," I said, waving my throbbing hand in the air.

"Where did you hit it?" Claire asked.

"On the door."

"I meant where did you hit the door?"

"I don't know. You got any ice?"

"In the refrigerator." Claire stood back and studied the door again. "I know what. I'll get a crayon. You can use that and we can tell exactly where you hit."

"I may have a broken hand." I looked to see if it was swelling. It was.

"I'll get the crayon," Claire said, darting toward the kitchen. She was beginning to remind me a lot of Mary Alice.

I was watching my hand puff up when Claire came back. "Okay, let's do it again. And this time hit the door with the crayon, Mrs. Hollowell."

"Run fast," I said.

This time I was right behind her when she opened the door. The crayon broke, but I protected my injured hand.

Claire stuck her head inside. "Where's the mark?"

"Right here. What are you trying to prove?"

"How far is the crayon mark from the knife slice?"

"A couple of feet to the right."

"And angled because the door was opening against it." Claire studied the red slash.

"So?"

"Mrs. Hollowell, I'm running. There's a man or a big woman behind me with a knife. What looked like a butcher knife. I jerk open the door and he lunges. Does the knife hit on the left side of the door or even in the middle?"

"It could," I said. "It would depend on how far he was from you."

"But it would splinter. The door was being slammed back, remember. The cut would have angled just like the crayon did. Now look at that knife cut."

I did. It looked deep, but it was straight with smooth edges.

"Someone stuck that knife straight in," Claire said.

"I don't understand," I said.

"I don't either." Claire sat on the steps and studied the door. I sat down beside her, cradling the hurt hand in the other. "Did you hurt your hand?" she asked.

I nodded. "Banged it into the door."

"I'll get you some ice," Claire said. She got up, still looking at the door. "You mind if we go through this one more time, though?" She picked the crayon up and held it out to me.

I shook my head. "This time you're the killer."

We got into position and I dashed down the steps, jerked the door open, and barreled right into Officer Bo Mitchell. *Bam* went the crayon against the door as Bo and I clutched each other, staggering, finally ending up in a sasanqua bush by the side of the stoop.

"Oh, God," Claire said. "Are y'all all right?" She helped me up first since I was on top. Bo Mitchell was lying down in the sasanqua on her back. White petals from the December-blooming shrub drifted onto her dark blue uniform.

"Y'all pull me out," she said. "I'm stuck."

Claire pulled and I pushed. Sasanquas, members of the camellia family, may look delicate, but they are dense bushes with strong limbs.

"What the hell!" Bo Mitchell said, coming to her feet.

"I'm sorry," I said. "Are you all right?"

"I think so. I expect that bush has bought it, though."

"I'm just glad that's where you landed," Claire said. "At least it cushioned you."

"Some cushion." Bo Mitchell looked at a long ugly scratch on her hand.

"Come on in. Let me put something on that," Claire said.

"I'd like some ice," I said. "For my hand."

We trooped into the foyer and toward the kitchen.

"What kind of game are you playing?" Bo Mitchell asked.

Claire and I looked at each other. "We don't think the knife mark in the door is right. The angle," she said.

"You're right," Bo agreed. "We noticed that right off. You got any Bactine?"

"Neosporin." Claire took the yellow tube from a drawer and handed it to Bo with a paper towel to wrap around her bleeding scratch. "Well, what do you think about it? The knife stab?"

Bo and I pulled out white ice-cream parlor chairs and sat at a glass-topped table.

"Somebody came at that door straight on," Bo said. "Not while the door was opening."

"That's what I think, too," Claire said. "What do you think it means?"

"Somebody was trying to kill the door?"

Claire brought me a dish towel and a bowl of ice. In the all-white kitchen, a huge asparagus fern was beginning to lose its needles because it hadn't been misted. This room had escaped the vandalism. "Y'all want some Pepsi?" Claire asked. "Diet."

"That would be nice," I said. I plunged my hand gingerly into the ice. It made it hurt worse. "I think I've broken my hand," I told Bo.

"Out in that bush? Couldn't have."

"I was hitting the door while Claire ran through it. I misjudged."

"I do that a lot." Bo studied her scratch.

"Here you go." Claire put glasses and napkins before us. Then she brought her own glass over and pulled out a chair.

She didn't beat around the bush. "Somebody tried to kill the door?" She looked straight at Bo.

"You got a better answer?" Bo downed about half of her Pepsi in one gulp. "Umm. That hits the spot."

"They were after me," Claire said. "I saw the knife, a big one. I heard it hit the door."

"It was a big one, all right. A butcher knife. We found it in that flower bush Mrs. Hollowell knocked me ass-over-end into."

"You found the knife?" Claire's voice was slightly shaky.

"Yep. You're not fixing to faint on us again, are you?"

"No, I'm fine."

"Well, drink some of that Pepsi. There's something else I've got to say."

Claire obediently drank. "What?" she asked.

"The only fingerprints on it were yours. It was the right knife, too. It's easy to check cuts in wood."

I looked at the two women and at the asparagus fern. "That plant's in bad shape," I said. "Where's your mister?"

"Under the sink." Claire took another drink of Pepsi. "You think I stabbed my own door?"

"Looks that way, doesn't it?"

I got up and headed for the sink.

"And maybe I ripped up all my furniture?" Claire motioned toward the hall.

I filled the mister with water.

"Could be," Bo said.

"But why on earth would I do that?"

Bo shrugged. "I thought maybe you could tell me. It

would be convenient, wouldn't it, if we thought the same person who killed your cousin Mercy was after you, too.''

I started spraying the fern with my left hand. Damn, I hoped I didn't have any broken bones.

''But that's crazy!'' Claire said.

''Sure is.''

I felt the soil around the plant. It needed watering as well as misting. I went to the cabinet, found a glass, filled it with water, and poured it over the plant.

''Am I going to need a lawyer?'' Claire asked.

''Honey, everybody needs a good lawyer if they can find one.'' Bo drank the rest of her Pepsi in one long swallow and pushed her chair back. ''I've got to go catch the bad guys,'' she said. ''You gonna be here?''

''I'll be out at Yvonne and James Butler's.''

''You know the number?''

Claire gave it to her and Bo wrote it in a small notebook.

''Thanks. Now I'm just gonna let myself out. Okay?''

I followed Bo down the hall, though. ''Are you saying Claire is a suspect in Mercy's murder?'' I asked.

''Mrs. Hollowell, I said what I said. You have a good day, now. I know a good orthopedic doctor you need one.''

''Thanks.''

When I got back to the kitchen, Claire was misting the asparagus fern. ''Damn,'' she said. ''Damn.''

My feelings exactly.

Sixteen

I sat down at the kitchen table and put my hand back in the bowl of ice. Pain shot up my arm. How the hell was I going to explain this to a doctor? Or to Fred? I could imagine the expression on his face when I told him I had been chasing Claire Moon with an imaginary knife and bashed my hand into a very solid door. His eyebrows would go up and his ears would flatten against his head like they do when he gets angry and amazed at the same time. Mary Alice calls it his pit bull look. She's seen it a lot and admires it, even tries to copy it—without success, since she can't wiggle her ears, which is the whole secret. Thank God. The two of them pit bulling at each other would not be good for the family's nerves.

I watched Claire misting and watering the plant I had just misted and watered. She got the Dustbuster and vacuumed up the needles. Then she wiped the white counter, put Bo Mitchell's glass in the dishwasher, and angled the venetian blind so the light was just right. In her black outfit, moving around the white kitchen, she was like a shadow someone had lost. I tried to remember in which children's story someone was looking for his lost shadow. *Peter Pan*?

"The thing is," she said, startling me, "I was the one who was alone at the gallery most of the afternoon before

Mercy was killed. I was the one with every opportunity to tamper with the hair spray. So let's face it, if nobody tried to kill me, if I staged all this"—she waved her hand toward the rest of the house—"that makes me the A-number-one suspect. Right?" She came over and pulled out a chair and sat down. "Right?"

"Maybe," I said. "Maybe not." I took my hand from the ice for a moment and checked the swelling. "Seems to me if Bo Mitchell were really suspicious, she'd have taken you in for questioning. I think she was just trolling."

"I think I ought to talk to a lawyer, though. What did you say your niece's name is?"

"Debbie Nachman. She's Mary Alice's daughter. And it probably would be a good idea to call her. Or some other lawyer."

Claire propped her elbows on the glass tabletop and cupped her chin in her palms. "I'm so tired," she said.

She looked it. Bo Mitchell's visit had brought back the lines between Claire's eyes as well as the dark circles underneath.

"Let me help you get your things," I offered. "And why don't you let one of the twins drive you down to the Butlers'?"

Claire shook her head. "I'm all right."

The phone rang and we both jumped. "The machine will get it," Claire said.

"Are you there, Claire?" It was one of the twins' voices. "If you are, please answer."

Claire shrugged, got up, and went to the phone. "Hey, Glynnie," she said.

I examined my swollen hand and listened to the one-sided conversation. No, she was not alone. Mrs. Hollowell was with her. And yes, she would have the rental car back soon, and sure, her car was fine, in the garage, and Glynnie was right. She hadn't been thinking.

"I should have brought one of the twins with me," she said, coming back to the table. "That way, I could have picked up my car. My mind was on a dozen other things."

I could have offered to drive her car to the hotel, but all I wanted to do was get home.

"You got any aspirin?" I asked.

"Sure." Claire reached into the cabinet and handed me a bottle. "You want some more Pepsi?"

I shook my head no and downed three aspirin while Claire sat back down.

"I really need to get home," I said.

"I'll go get my stuff." But the declaration wasn't followed by action. Instead, Claire leaned back and looked out of the window. "My husband was an artist, Mrs. Hollowell."

I had missed Claire's thought processes that had brought her to her husband, but it was part of her life I had wondered about, so I dipped my hand back into the ice and listened.

"He was a brilliant caricaturist. That's how I met him. We both had summer jobs at Disney World. His was drawing caricatures and mine was parading and working the concessions. We ended up in California when he got a job as an animator for Disney Studios. We really thought we had it made." Claire shrugged. "And then he died."

"What happened?"

"Three teenagers shot him on the freeway. They said he cut in front of them."

"My God!"

Claire turned and looked at me. "I had a total breakdown. If it hadn't been for Thurman and Mercy, I don't know what would have happened to me. They did everything, including making arrangements for me to be hospitalized for several months."

I reached over and touched her arm. "I'm so sorry."

"So am I, Mrs. Hollowell. And now Mercy's dead, and it looks like I've slipped a couple of cogs again, from the looks of this house and my ending up in the hospital in shock. You think the police aren't putting two and two together?"

"Not if they don't add up to four. Claire, there are millions of people who have had help for emotional problems, just like there are millions who have been treated for ulcers. Both are painful and both treatable. Give the police a little credit.

They're not going to charge you with a crime because you were once hospitalized for psychiatric treatment.''

Claire sighed. "You're right. It's just that things are finally getting to me. Like Mercy's death." She pushed her chair back. "I'll go get my things."

I took my hand from the ice, wrapped it in the dish towel, and followed her down the hall.

"This makes me sick," she said, pointing to the ripped furniture. "Did he get to the bedrooms, too?"

"Yes. He sprayed paint on the walls up there."

"That's what he was doing when I came in, wasn't it?"

"I don't know," I said.

"And he heard me come in," Claire continued. She paused at the bottom of the steps.

"I'll come upstairs with you," I said. "It's not very pretty."

In the master bedroom, the giant red "whore" above the bed was as shocking as it had been the first time I saw it. Part of the effect was caused by the fact that the paint had run, making it look as if it were written in blood that was still wet and dripping.

Claire clasped her hands to her mouth.

"Are you all right?" I asked.

Her answer was a dash to the bathroom.

I glanced around the room. "You will die" was written on a side wall in blue paint. It had been done in cursive with the "You" much larger than the other two words since, apparently, the painter realized he was going to run out of wall. The bottom loop of the "Y" was small and slanted toward the left. Some handwriting expert could do a lot with this, I thought. But surely Bo Mitchell and her cohorts had already thought of that.

The sounds coming from the bathroom didn't give me any hope that Claire would be out momentarily. I wandered into the other bedroom, remembering that there had been even more graffiti in there than in the master bedroom. In this room, the painter hadn't even bothered to write words. Slashes of red, blue, and green paint streaked across the wall, crisscrossing, looping. And then the small pastoral painting that the vandal had included in all of this madness. I got down on my knees, pushed my bifocals toward the end of my nose, and studied it again.

The light was better this time, so I could make out more details. A redheaded woman sat in a field painting three pictures, all of them the same, a dark-haired woman lying down. Holding something?

I needed more light. I looked into Claire's bedroom, but the bathroom door was still shut. Surely, though, there would be a flashlight in a kitchen drawer or in the garage.

There was. Claire's "junk" drawer was exactly the same as mine, the small one to the right of the sink. I picked up a yellow flashlight and checked to see if it worked. It did. As I closed the drawer, though, I saw exactly what I needed, a small lighted magnifying glass, exactly like the one Fred had, lying on top of the telephone book. So Claire was soon going to need reading glasses. Or already did.

I took both the flashlight and magnifying glass back upstairs.

"Feeling better?" I asked Claire, who was standing in the middle of her bedroom.

"I guess so. Did they do the same thing to the other room?"

"Yes."

"Dear Lord." She noticed the flashlight. "What are you doing?"

"Looking at something in here. You want to see it?"

"No, thanks. I just want to get out of here." She opened a drawer and took out some lingerie. "This won't take a minute."

"You need me, call." I went into the other room and knelt down to the picture again. Somehow I knew this was important. The slashes of paint and even the words had taken only a few minutes, but this small painting had taken time. And some skill. I turned on the flashlight and propped it against a small wicker table so it would shine directly on the picture. Then I turned on the magnifying glass.

It could only be Mercy who sat in the field painting the three canvases. She was turned toward the farthest left of the three paintings so her face was shown in profile. On each canvas she had painted Claire or one of the twins. The paintings were identical, though. Lying on a bier, a black-haired woman dressed in a white gown clasped a white flower in her hand. Were the women dead? I held the magnifying glass closer, but there were no features on the faces.

I studied the picture, thinking it had to mean something. But what? Was the silver beneath the figures Mercy was painting water? Were they on a river? And was that a castle in the background? The Mercy figure was dressed in a long, flowing blue robe, very royal.

Okay. I backed up and started over again. It was a picture of Mercy painting three pictures which seemed to be of Claire and the twins. Now, why would someone who had come in to tear the place up take the time to do this?

Okay again. It was a message. Mercy wanted the Needham girls dead. But Mercy, supposedly, was already dead, or dying, when this was painted. Wrong message. Or maybe Mercy had come out before the gallery opening and done this. It was possible but didn't make much sense.

"I'm ready," Claire called from the hall. "I'll wait for you outside. I've got to get some fresh air."

"I'm coming." I reached into my purse, found an envelope, and did a crude sketch of the painting on the back of it. Very crude. I also scribbled a few notes such as "white flower" so I wouldn't forget.

Claire was sitting on the steps when I came out. "What did you find in there?" she asked.

I told her about the picture and showed her my sketch. "It's lost a lot in the translation," I said. "Don't you want to come look at it?"

She shivered. "I've seen more than enough. Lots more."

"You're right. You need to get some rest. The police will work on this."

"I just hope they leave me alone. I don't have a thing to tell them." She locked the door and we started toward the car. "How's your hand?"

"The aspirin's making it feel better. I don't think anything's broken."

"Well, thank goodness for that." She tossed an overnight bag into the backseat.

"Claire?" I asked as she started the car. "When Officer Mitchell told us Mercy was dead, you said, 'They finally got to Mercy.' You remember that?"

"No, but I have a good idea what I was talking about. There are several people in Alabama who have made a very good living dealing in Outsider art. They buy it for nothing and take it to New York or Chicago. I know Mercy got several threatening calls. They were scared the artists would find out how much their work is really worth."

"Threatening?"

"Not enough to scare Mercy. She just told them to go to hell. It probably didn't amount to anything."

"Probably not." We rode along in silence for a few minutes. "Do you still have some of your husband's work?" I asked.

"I have a lot of it. Someday he'll have a showing at a gallery."

"What was his name?" I asked.

"Fred. His name was Fred."

"Fred," I said. "His name was Fred." Bonnie Blue, Frances Zata, Mary Alice, and I had just finished a wonderful chicken-and-tortellini salad, a take-out from Vincent's Market, I thought, until Mary Alice gave the credit to Henry Lamont, her semi-son-in-law, donor to the UAB sperm bank and therefore possible father of her granddaughters, and soon to be graduate of the Jefferson State Junior College School of Culinary Arts.

"And just shot in cold blood driving down the interstate." Frances shook her head. "I swear, that child's had more than her share."

Mary Alice got up, took the dinner plates, and brought in some tiny, flaky tarts and four small plates. "Raspberry," she said. "Help yourself. Now, who wants regular and who wants decaf?"

"Decaf," we chorused.

Bonnie Blue groaned as she bit into a tart. "Oh, my. These are so good they could make my feet stop hurting. Henry do these, too?"

"He did it all."

"You tell Debbie I said marry that boy tomorrow if not sooner." Bonnie Blue reached for another tart.

Sister's house looked beautiful. We were eating at a small table she had set up in the den, if you can call such a huge room a den. Through French doors that opened onto a terrace overlooking the whole city, we could see two lighted Christmas trees.

"What are you trying to do?" I asked when I came in and saw them. "Denude the Alabama forests?" She ignored me.

A fire was crackling in the fireplace and the mantel was draped with greenery. She had even set the table with her good Christmas china.

"Where's Santa?" I asked.

"In his workshop." She smiled sweetly.

"With Tiffany?" She stepped on my heel.

The evening was what a holiday celebration should be. Good friends, good food, beautiful surroundings. Interesting gossip.

But my hand was throbbing. The Ace bandage called for an explanation so the trip to Claire's town house was first on the agenda. It took a couple of glasses of wine—in my case, diet Coke—along with Norwegian crackers and a spicy pâté to get through the story.

Bonnie Blue was a wonderful listener. "Damn," she said when I told about the stuffing ripped out of the sofa. "Damn," she said at the "whore" above the bed and the gash in the door.

I raised my injured hand and showed how I had dashed at the door. "Damn," she said admiringly.

"Supper," Mary Alice said.

But Frances wasn't ready to let Claire's story go. "Tell me again about the small painting," she said as we headed for the table.

"A woman who looks like Mercy Armistead. Long curly red hair. She's painting three pictures. She's in a field or something. There's grass at her feet and she has on a blue robe. The women in the pictures have black hair and they're lying down dressed in white gowns, holding a white flower, probably a lily. They're lying on some kind of a platform or raft and there may be a castle in the background. I'll show you after supper. I've got a sketch in my purse."

"Damn," Bonnie Blue said.

"I think it's important. Anybody got any ideas?"

Three heads shaking no was my answer.

"Everybody finished their shopping?" Mary Alice asked brightly, passing the angel biscuits.

It was fifteen minutes later when Frances asked me about Claire's husband.

"James said it like to have killed her, his death," Bonnie Blue said.

"She told me today that Mercy and Thurman rescued her. Had her hospitalized."

Bonnie Blue nodded. "Bless her heart. She'd had enough to throw anybody into depression."

"She's lucky she had them to intervene," Frances said.

Mary Alice came in with the coffee. "What's the story with Thurman and Claire, Bonnie Blue? You said he's smitten with her. Did Mercy know it?"

Bonnie Blue reached for another tart. "Lord no, she didn't know it. Thurman knew which side his bread was buttered on. Which side the money was on, anyway. Mercy's daddy's on his last leg and rich as Croesus, and her mama's toddling on the brink. That Thurman's no fool. Besides, my sister-in-law Yvonne says it was as much Claire after Thurman as vice versa."

"Well, scratch Thurman's motives for killing Mercy," Sister said. "He lost out on her inheritance, didn't he?"

"Is his heart very bad?" I asked.

"James says someday he may have to have an aortic valve replaced, but he'll live to be an old man."

"Just not a rich one."

"Sure he will. He'll find somebody else with money," Frances said.

We all looked at her in surprise.

"Well, he will. I just hope Claire's not counting on him too much. She's been through enough." She slapped her napkin down in a way that precluded any more discussion. I tried to remember the details of Frances's divorce or of some subsequent affair, but they escaped me. There was a skunk in the woodpile somewhere, though.

"Y'all ready for bridge?" Mary Alice asked.

We played at the table where we had eaten supper. Bonnie Blue explained to us that she was just a country girl, not knowledgeable in the big-city game of bridge, and we should be patient with her, please. On the first hand, she opened with four no-trump, ended up with a bid of six hearts, and made seven.

"Should have chanced it," she said. "I'm just too careful."

That was the story of the bridge playing for the evening. When we were Bonnie Blue's partner, it was great. When we weren't, we were covering our butts.

My hand began to ache badly, and I went into the kitchen to get some more aspirin. Bubba was lying on the counter on his heating pad, and he looked up and yawned. "You feeling okay now?" I asked. He stretched and went back to sleep. I poured a glass of water and looked over the city, wishing every animal such comfort on this chilly night. For some reason, Leota Wood's coydog came to mind. I put the glass down and went back to the bridge table, where Bonnie Blue was laying down a five-club bid.

"Sister," I said, "you were going to ask Bonnie Blue about Leota Wood."

"What about her?" Bonnie Blue was writing another huge number on the score pad under "We."

Mary Alice picked up the cards to shuffle them. "Well, yesterday afternoon, Mouse and I went out to get Bubba, my cat. He was at your brother's clinic. Anyway, we went on down the road to Leota Wood's because we wanted to see her quilts and figured her prices might be better there than at a gallery. And they were. We bought several."

"I'm scared of that dog of hers," Bonnie Blue said.

"She came out and got him and shut him up," I turned to Frances. "He's a coydog. Did you know there was such a thing? A combination of coyote and dog?"

"Well"—Mary Alice rapped the deck of cards against the table—"she's got a whole room just crammed with Outsider art. I mean just crammed."

"Sister thinks she's a fence," I added. "She thinks Ross Perry was on his way out there when he was killed and that they're part of some kind of gang that's stealing art."

"Stealing's what she's doing, all right," Bonnie Blue agreed. "But it's not illegal. She goes down to somebody's house and says, 'I'll give you ten dollars for that painting or that old wooden horse you carved' knowing full well it'll sell for hundreds in some gallery. Waves the bill in front of them, and they're tickled to death. Say, 'Sure, Leota. I got lots more you can have.' Daddy's still selling her stuff. See, he can see that ten-dollar bill in his hand. He can take it in the liquor store and buy him a bottle." Bonnie Blue spread her hands out on the table. "Folks never had anything, that ten-dollar bird looks mighty good in their hand."

"So Ross Perry could have been buying the stuff from her and taking it somewhere to sell for a good price," Frances said.

"Most probably was. I doubt he was the only one, though."

"Claire said Mercy had received threatening phone calls from people who didn't want the artists to see what their work sold for in galleries," I said.

Bonnie Blue shook her head. "You tell some of these folks that you could get a thousand dollars for their work in

New York and they'd say, 'I'll just take the ten now, thank you, ma'am.' I know Daddy would.''

"What about the younger artists?" Mary Alice asked.

"Just as bad. See, what they're doing is fun. They don't take it seriously. Don't even think of it as art."

"Maybe that's the secret of its charm," Sister said.

"Most probably. Anyway, that's what all that stuff was doing in Miss Leota's house. You can bet on it. Somebody's getting ready to make a big Christmas haul.'' Bonnie Blue picked up the cards Frances had dealt. "Two spades,'' she said without even arranging her hand.

"Bonnie Blue," Mary Alice said, turning over the score pad and picking up the pencil, "give me the first six numbers you think of between one and forty-nine."

"Eight, fourteen, forty-three, twenty-nine, two, thirty-seven. Why?"

"Are you kidding? The Florida lottery's up to thirty-six million this week. Halves?"

Bonnie Blue grinned. "Halves."

We played for a couple of hours until Frances and Bonnie Blue said they had to call it a night since they had to work the next day.

"And you haven't shown us the sketch of the picture,'' Frances reminded me.

I got my purse and unfolded the sketch on the coffee table. I was amazed at how bad it was.

"What's that bump?" Sister asked, pointing toward one of the reclining figures.

"It's one of the women who looks like Claire that the woman who looks like Mercy is painting.''

"That's a person?''

"It was just to remind myself of some of the details.''

Frances and Bonnie Blue were slightly kinder.

"I wish I could see it," Frances said. "It sounds interesting.''

"Go back tomorrow and take a camera," Bonnie Blue suggested.

We walked out into a clear, crisp December night. In spite

of the lights of the city, the brightest stars were visible.

"There's Orion," Frances said, pointing to the three familiar stars almost directly overhead.

"I wonder," Bonnie Blue said, "about the Star of Bethlehem. Don't you? What it could have been?"

"Sure I wonder," I said. "It must have been something amazing for the Wise Men to follow it like they did."

Mary Alice had walked out to the driveway with us to pick up her paper. "Leaving their wives behind with the kids and dirty laundry," she added.

"Perchance, verily, to each wife was alloteth a Tiffany."

"Go home," she said, swatting me with the rolled-up evening paper.

We exited, laughing.

Fred was sound asleep when I got home, but I was cold and my hand ached. I put on my nightgown and robe in the bathroom and tiptoed down the hall to curl up on the sofa with the afghan. I read Tony Hillerman for a while, something usually guaranteed to keep me awake, but as soon as I began to get warm, the Navajo Nation drifted away.

Ross Perry came and sat at the end of the sofa. I could see the broken capillaries on his face and the shadow of the fern that reminded me of Gorbachev's birthmark. He leaned back and got comfortable. "Do you know what Claire has always reminded me of?" he asked. "The Lady of the Lake with a lily in her hand."

I came straight up. The dream had been so vivid, I could still feel his weight against my feet.

"Yuck!" I sat up and pulled the afghan around me.

"What's the matter?" Fred asked, standing in the door. "You okay?"

"I think I was just visited by Jacob Marley."

"Maybe it was something you ate."

"That's what Scrooge thought."

"Come to bed, honey. Is your hand hurting?"

I had broken down and told him how I had slammed the car door on it. His immediate sympathy made it hurt worse.

"It's okay. I'll be there in a few minutes."

"Don't get cold."

I sat hunched in the afghan for a few minutes and then got up and took the sketch from my purse. A white flower clasped in her hand. A lily. A white flowing gown.

The Lady of the Lake had been part of the King Arthur legend. But what was the story? She could look at the world only through mirrors? And then she saw Lancelot pass by and turned to look at him?

Tennyson. Tennyson had written a poem about her. I got up, still wrapped in the afghan, shuffled to the bookshelf and pulled down *Victorian Poetry*. It took me just a few minutes to discover that there were two ladies who died for love of Lancelot, had themselves decked out in white robes with lilies in their hands and set adrift toward Camelot. One was Elaine, whose rejection by Lancelot caused a galloping case of medieval anorexia. She was placed by her family on a bier on a barge (God, how had Tennyson gotten away with that!) and sent to Lancelot with a note guaranteed to make him feel like dirt. The other, the Lady of Shalott, whose name just happened to rhyme with *Camelot* and *Lancelot*, was much more interesting. She was the one I had remembered, the one who was cursed to watch the world through a mirror. "Sick of shadows," she turned to face the world, got her own self on the bier on the barge, and headed toward Camelot before she died. Nor did she carry any note. Pale, beautiful, both women drifted, lilies clasped in their hands. Neither woman was the Lady of the Lake who had forged Excalibur. But Ross Perry had been out of school almost as long as I had. Give him credit.

I looked at my sketch again. The three women in the paintings were definitely on biers on barges. And a castle was in the distance. And a redheaded woman was painting them. Who was she? Morgan Le Fey? And what did it mean?

Halfway through the third reading of "The Lady of Shalott," it hit me. "Whoa," I whispered. "Whoa." It didn't matter what the picture meant. It was who did it that was important. And that person could only have been Ross Perry.

He was the one who thought of Claire this way. It was as if he had signed his name.

I went into the kitchen and put a cup of water in the microwave for coffee. By the time it dinged, I knew who had killed Mercy and why, why Claire's town house had been vandalized, and why she had escaped death. There was one piece missing, but the police could handle that. I looked at the clock. Damn. It was too late to call Sister.

Seventeen

The phone's ringing awoke me. "Good heavens, are you still asleep?" Mary Alice asked. "Who cut up Fred's banana?"

"Fred can handle his own banana," I grumbled. "What time is it? I couldn't sleep last night."

"It's nine o'clock. I was just checking on your hand."

I wiggled my fingers. "It's swollen and aching. I hope it's not broken."

"Well, get some coffee. I'll talk to you later."

"No. Wait a minute." I sat up and pushed my hair out of my face. "I need a haircut in the worst way."

"Make an appointment. Don't try Delta Hairlines, though. They're booked up until New Year's."

"No. Listen. I know who killed Mercy Armistead."

"Who?"

"Ross Perry."

"Why?"

"They hated each other. It went back a long way. Remember, he wrote that awful review of her work, and she showed that movie he was in that's supposed to be the worst one ever made. A movie her father made, incidentally, probably because Ross was still in love with Betty Bedsole even though she had dumped him. Plus, maybe he was buying and selling Outsider art and she was running up the prices he was having to pay.''

''Then who killed Ross?''

''I'm not sure. It could have been a hunter. He was the one vandalized Claire's house and came at her with the knife, though. He painted that little picture I showed you last night. You remember him telling us he always thought of Claire as the Lady of the Lake with a lily in her hand?''

''No.''

''Well, he did. And that's what the picture is. It's of a pale, black-haired woman, actually three of them, on biers on barges floating to Camelot. It's actually the Lady of Shalott, not the Lady of the Lake, but it's easy to get them confused.''

''I can understand that. It's hard to tell one beer on a barge from another.''

I chose to ignore her. ''But what he was trying to do was set Claire up. He wanted it to look like she had vandalized her own house and stuck the knife in the door. And he figured everyone would think she had painted the little picture even though he had done it because he wouldn't do anything so obvious.''

''Right,'' Mary Alice said. ''Get some coffee before you run this by the police.''

''Hey, Ross Perry did it.''

''Could be. Let me know.''

I got a cup of coffee, put on my sweats, and went out to walk Woofer. It was a cold, sunny morning, and the Iron Man on the mountain was mooning us with a vengeance. I gave Woofer plenty of time to investigate every lamppost and tree while I tried to decide how I would convince Bo Mitchell that Ross Perry was the murderer. I certainly hadn't convinced Mary Alice, but she hadn't seen Claire's house, the knife slit in the door, or the little painting. It was too well planned, made to look like Claire had done it trying to set up Ross. Which meant that Ross had really done it.

''It was Ross,'' I explained to Woofer. ''He wanted to look so guilty that everyone would think it was Claire.''

Woofer hiked his leg and marked a tree. "That was an ugly remark," I said. "But have you considered the fact that only the kitchen wasn't damaged? Only a man would think the kitchen unimportant enough to do something to."

Woofer squirted the tree again.

"Enough," I said, pulling slightly at his leash and making my hand throb.

The chilly morning air had cleared the cobwebs from my brain and made me hungry. After I put Woofer in the yard with some treats, I fixed myself a bowl of oatmeal, poured a small package of raisins in it, and sat down at the sunny window to look at the morning paper. Haiti, Iran, Iraq. Hadn't I read this same paper five years ago? Ten? Twenty? I turned to the funnies and read my old favorites. I particularly admire Mary Worth, who grows younger, slimmer, and sharper-looking every year. Not bad for an old lady who sold apples during the Depression. Gives us all hope.

I finished my cereal and looked at the phone. Surely there was a whole team of policemen working on Mercy's murder. Unfortunately, the only one I knew was uncommunicative, sometimes sarcastic Bo Mitchell. I dialed the number.

Officer Mitchell wasn't in. If this was an emergency, Officer Black was available. If not, leave a number and Officer Mitchell would return the call. I left the number.

The sweatshirt I was wearing was hot. I pulled it off and slipped on a T-shirt that had a picture of van Gogh's cat on it. The yellow tabby looked at the world from the vividness of a van Gogh painting. On its left ear was a bandage. Sister had brought it to me from London, and she and I had laughed until we cried when I unwrapped it. Fred didn't think it was funny at all, which made us laugh all the harder.

The dining room was ready for the holidays except for decorating the antique sideboard, which had belonged to Grandmother. I have a large ceramic reindeer I put in the center and I cut magnolia leaves and holly at the last minute and lay the greenery down the length. The china, crystal, and silver were ready, though. Today I was going to concentrate on the guest bedrooms.

I opened the windows and let the cool air sweep through the rooms. I changed the beds, dusted, and vacuumed. I gathered up all the old magazines that tend to collect in these rooms and put them in a garbage sack to take to the library. I Windexed the windows inside and, reaching under, as far as I could on the outside. Some day, I told myself, I would splurge and get some of those fancy windows that flip over so you can wash them on both sides. Finally, I opened a new package of Christmas potpourri and put a small amount in a bowl on each dresser.

"Ready," I said, admiring the shining, sweet-smelling rooms. A Tiffany would be nice, but there was a lot to be said for cleaning your own house.

I dragged the heavy sack of magazines into the kitchen. I'd get them to the library that afternoon. Right now, I had worked up a sweat and my hand was hurting. I had ignored it while I was cleaning, but now I took the Ace bandage off and saw that it was swollen badly as well as discolored. I probably should go to the doctor, I thought.

I was standing at the kitchen sink drinking a glass of water and wiggling my fingers, all of which worked, when the doorbell rang.

"I got your message, and I was in the neighborhood," Bo Mitchell said.

I held the door open for her. "I'm cleaning house. Come on back to the kitchen."

"Like that shirt, girl."

I grinned. "Thanks."

The opened newspaper and my cereal bowl were still on the table. I moved them and motioned for Bo to sit down. "How come Mary Worth gets younger every year?" I asked.

"Beats me. I'm still worried about what happened to Mickey Mouse's tail."

"You want some coffee or Coke?"

"Some Coke would be nice."

I fixed two glasses and brought them with napkins to the table. "You think I ought to go to the doctor with this hand?" I held it out so Bo could see.

"It hurt bad?"

"Off and on. The cleaning this morning didn't help."

"Wiggle your fingers."

I did, but they didn't move as easily as they had before I had removed the bandage.

"Better go," Bo advised. "Now, what can I do for you, or is this just our daily visit?"

I sat down at the table and held the cold glass against my hand. "I know who killed Mercy Armistead."

"Well, do, Jesus."

"No, I'm serious. Don't start that smart-aleck stuff."

Bo stirred the ice in her glass with her finger. "Okay, who killed Mercy Armistead?"

"Ross Perry."

"Unh-huh."

"I mean it. You know that little painting on the bedroom wall? The only thing that made sense? The one of a red-headed woman painting a picture in a field?"

Bo Mitchell nodded.

"Well, I know what it means. Ross Perry always said Claire Moon reminded him of the Lady of the Lake and that's what that painting is. It's a picture of Mercy painting Claire and the twins."

"I don't remember a lake."

"There wasn't one. There was a river, and the three women, Claire and her sisters, are on biers on barges floating down to Camelot, dead for love of Lancelot. Ross just got the legend a little mixed up. They were really the Lady of Shalott or maybe Elaine. My bet is on the Lady of Shalott."

Bo Mitchell put her glass down. "You know, Mrs. Hollowell, something tells me what you're saying probably makes sense somehow. But I got lost back there drinking beer on a barge."

"Not drinking beer. You know, laid out on a funeral platform. That kind of bier. It was very romantic."

"Sounds like it."

"Wait a minute." I went into the den and got *Victorian Poetry* from the bookshelf. "Here," I said, opening it to

Tennyson's "The Lady of Shalott" and handing it to Bo Mitchell. "Read that."

"You want me to read Tennyson?"

"It won't kill you. Just read enough so you'll know what I'm talking about."

Her head bent automatically at my schoolteacher glare. In a few minutes she looked up. "Oh, my, that's so sad. And all that damn Lancelot said was she had a pretty face."

"That Lancelot caused a lot of trouble," I agreed.

"Some men are just born that way." Bo looked back at the poem. " 'Singing in her song she died.' That's pitiful."

"Well, you see what I'm talking about, don't you? How this fits the picture on Claire's wall? It has to be connected with Ross Perry calling her the Lady of the Lake."

"Could be. Who is Claire's Lancelot?"

"I don't know. Maybe Thurman Beatty. But I don't think the picture is supposed to fit the whole story. It's just to lead us to Claire as a suspect."

"But Ross painted the picture."

"Yes, but it's so obvious he did it, we're supposed to think Claire did it, trying to lay the blame on Ross. See, he was too smart to have done anything that blatant unless he had an ulterior motive, which in this case was making himself look so much like the prime murder suspect that you would blame someone else."

Bo Mitchell drank some of her Coke and looked at me. "I'm still back drinking beer on the barge," she said.

"Ross killed Mercy. Put the DMSO in her hair spritzer hoping it wouldn't take effect for several hours, which is what happened. He left the party and went to Claire's where he cut up the furniture and wrote on the walls. He also did the little painting, which was just like signing his name. You with me?"

Bo nodded that she was.

"Okay. Claire comes home and Ross goes for her with her kitchen knife. But he never intends to kill her. He sticks the knife in the door, being careful to hold the end so he won't wipe off her fingerprints. He's wearing gloves, you understand. Claire runs and he leaves. You, the police, come in and say, 'Nobody tried to kill this girl. She did this herself, and look here, here's a painting like Ross Perry would have done. But he's too smart to have done that. She's trying to frame him.' Right?''

Bo ran her fingers across her lips. ''One minor detail. Who killed Ross Perry?''

''Hey,'' I said, ''I can't do everything. You're the one getting paid for this.''

''Not enough.'' Bo pushed her chair back. ''Can I borrow this book?''

''Sure. Yeats is my favorite.''

''Thanks.'' Bo walked down the hall with me following right on her heels.

''What do you think? About my theory? It could be right, couldn't it?''

Bo turned and looked at me. ''Could be,'' she said, ''but don't start setting odds just yet.'' She opened the door and walked to her car, turning to give me a little wave. I went to call the doctor to make an appointment, giving a little triumphal skip on the way.

He put my right hand in a cast. My right hand, two weeks before Christmas, ten days before the family would descend on me. My Christmas cards weren't addressed, my shopping wasn't finished, I couldn't even make another batch of fruit drop cookies because I couldn't stir the batter.

''It's to keep the hand immobile,'' he said. ''That's about all we can do with knuckles.''

Worst of all, I was going to have to tell Fred the truth about how I hurt it. And admit I'd lied to him. There was no way I could keep up the car door story for a month.

There was a message to call him when I got in. Might as well bite the bullet. I picked up the phone and discovered immediately that you can't even punch the buttons on a phone with a cast on your hand. The ends of my fingers were free, but the cast kept hitting the phone.

''Metal Fab!'' he barked into the phone. Fred's business

is a small metal fabrication shop he has owned for twenty-five years. His shop deals in a lot of special items that are hard to find, and his customers range from the utility companies to strip joints. For the latter, he provides the metal poles the dancers slide down. They have to be brass and shiny. And smooth. God knows those poles have to be smooth. The nature of Fred's business means emergency orders sometimes. Not often, and he's paid well for them.

"It's me," I said. "You mad at the world?"

"Just busy. How are you, honey?"

"Okay." I could tell now was not the time to mention my hand.

"We've got a rush order for some valves for Chatham Steel, and when we finish, we've got to get the chemistry run on them. So don't count on me for supper. I'm not sure what time I'll be home."

"Don't work too hard."

He would. But he thrived on these emergencies. Adrenaline was crackling across the phone line.

I put on my jeans and turned the Christmas tree on. It was almost three o'clock and I realized I hadn't had any lunch. I fixed a peanut butter and banana sandwich and a glass of milk and went into the den to watch Oprah.

Oprah is like Mary Worth. She's getting younger, slimmer, and sharper-looking all the time. Today she was talking about help for abusive parents, which reminded me of the Needhams. Could they, at some point, have been helped? Probably. At least the children could have been removed earlier.

I finished my sandwich and wiped peanut butter from my cast. Damn. It was even going to affect my eating.

"I had no control," the man on television was saying. I crumpled up my napkin, thinking for the millionth time how lucky Mary Alice and I were. Occasionally Daddy would swat us on the behind when an "attitude adjustment" was called for. Mama would make us stand in the corner, the equivalent of today's "time-out."

Last night's lack of sleep, the morning's work, and the

trauma of the doctor's visit were catching up to me. I stretched out on the sofa and closed my eyes. I awoke an hour later to feel someone against my feet. I came up with a start.

"What's wrong with you?" Sister asked.

"I thought you were the Ghost of Christmas Past."

"Not yet. I see you went to the doctor."

I held up my hand for her inspection.

"Hurt much?" she asked.

"Off and on. I used it too much this morning washing windows."

"That'll do it. There's nothing like washing windows with a broken hand."

"How would you know?"

"I can imagine." Mary Alice propped her feet on the coffee table. "Did you tell the police you had solved Mercy's murder?"

"As a matter of fact, I did. Bo Mitchell took it very seriously."

"She took the bier on the barge seriously?"

"She did after she read the poem. She even took the book with her."

"Well, I guess stranger things have happened. But Ross Perry figuring out that weird way to kill Mercy? And spraying Claire's walls to make it look like she was framing him? To tell you the truth, Patricia Anne, I don't think he was that clever."

I shrugged. "He was."

"Maybe so."

"Are you and Bill working at the mall tonight?"

"We sort of lost our job. Bill's scratching made the parents nervous."

I laughed. "Did they make you give up your electric shirt?"

"I'm afraid so. I'm going to miss that shirt." Mary Alice grinned. "That's where I'm going now. Out to Rosedale to take our costumes back and pick up some presents they ordered for me at McRae's."

"You want to eat supper at Morrison's? Fred's working tonight."

"Sounds good."

"Then just give me a few minutes. How about feeding Woofer for me? You can even walk him around the block if you want to."

"I don't want to. It's too cold. By the way, did you know they're predicting snow flurries again tomorrow?"

"A white Christmas!" I squealed. "Can we stop by the grocery?"

"Of course."

Things get set in motion by the most innocent things. There we were, two old ladies having supper at a mall cafeteria on a cold winter night. Vegetable plates. Macaroni and cheese, turnip greens, black-eyed peas, and corn bread. Egg custard pie. A walk to the mall office to return the outfits. A stop at McRae's to pick up Mary Alice's purchases. Some browsing through the Christmas sweaters. One that Sister wanted me to buy, a Victorian couple sitting by a fire. It was Fred and me, she said. But I demurred. Too expensive.

We stopped and checked out the new Mr. and Mrs. Santa Claus.

"Too skinny," Mary Alice declared.

"Ho, ho, ho," Santa said weakly as a fat twelve-year-old kid sat on his lap, double-dog-dared by a group of friends who laughed on the sidelines.

We bought a cup of cappuccino and sat by the fountain watching the crowd.

"Don't burn yourself," Sister cautioned me, noticing how awkwardly I held the cup in my left hand.

It was a night like thousands of nights Mary Alice and I have shared except I remember the details clearly. I remember someone had thrown a Susan B. Anthony dollar in the shallow, clear wishing pool, probably thinking it was a quarter. I pointed it out to Sister.

It wasn't late when we came out into the well-lighted parking lot. Maybe seven-thirty or eight. Mary Alice tossed the

packages onto the backseat and we headed for the interstate.
I looked to see if any clouds were rolling in, but there was
too much light.

"I'm going to call and see if Fred's home yet," I said. "I
should have gotten him some supper."

"Fred needs a Lean Cuisine. He's getting a pot."

"He is not." I plugged the phone into the lighter and
dialed my number. My own voice answered with "You have
reached the Hollowell residence. We are unable to come to
the phone—" I hung up. "God, I sound stupid."

"You need to get some of those seasonal messages."

I didn't answer that.

We were on the elevated part of the interstate that over-
looks the old bottling plant that for one night was the Mercy
Armistead Gallery. In the distance, the Sonat Building's
wreath and Christmas stocking shone, and on Red Mountain,
Vulcan held up his torch. Traffic was not heavy.

"Look," Mary Alice said. "Somebody's at the gallery.
The lights are on. I'm going to go get you that picture quilt
of Leota Wood's that you admired so."

"Do you remember how much that thing cost?"

"I want you to have it. You worry about money too much,
Patricia Anne."

"I've never had much of it to worry about."

"True." Mary Alice swung down the exit ramp.

"What if it's the police down there?" I asked.

"Well, my Lord. We're not doing anything criminal. My
guess is it's Thurman getting the stuff sorted to send back
to the artists or maybe trying to decide what to do with the
place. It won't hurt to see. We might even get a bargain on
the quilt."

"I hope so," I said.

All of the lights were on in the gallery, but there were no
other cars parked in front.

"He probably went in the back door," Mary Alice said.

I was beginning to think this was not such a good idea.
"Let's come back tomorrow," I said.

"Don't be silly." Mary Alice got out of the car and went to the front door. "Come on," she said, opening it and walking into the building. I followed her reluctantly.

The walls that had been so bright with folk art the night of the opening were now just pale gray walls. Only a few paintings remained.

"Almost everything's gone," I said.

"I hear somebody in the back. I'll bet they're packing it up right now."

"Let's go," I said.

But Mary Alice was already on her way toward the door that probably led to a storage room and the back door.

"Hello," she called, knocking on the door and opening it at the same time.

"Mrs. Crane!" Claire Moon stood in the middle of the room, which was empty except for some cans of paint and paint thinner stacked on shelves against a wall. The smell of mineral spirits was almost overpowering. "What are you doing here?"

"Patricia Anne and I saw your lights on and hoped we could buy that quilt of Leota Wood's, the one about the sixties."

"Hello, Claire," I said.

She nodded. "Mrs. Hollowell. I'm sorry, ladies, but almost everything's been sent back."

"We'll check with her, then. Sorry to have bothered you, Claire."

"It's okay. I didn't realize the front door was open and you startled me. I'll just follow you and lock it."

"You do that," Mary Alice said. "It's not a good idea you working here by yourself at night anyway."

"I'm just finishing up."

"Okay. Good night, Claire. We'll see you later."

"Good night, Mrs. Crane. Mrs. Hollowell."

"Can you believe that?" I said as we got into the car. "She didn't even notice my hand was broken."

"Snake in the woodpile," Mary Alice said, starting the car.

"What?"

"I said a snake in the woodpile. Don't be so dense, Mouse. She's up to something. Did you see how she jumped when we walked in? And where's all the art?"

"You scared her, and they've returned it."

Mary Alice drove past a couple of buildings, pulled in beside one of them, parked, and cut the lights.

"Let's go home," I said. "I want to give Fred his supper."

"You are such a wimp. I want to see what's going on." She got out and disappeared behind the building into an alley.

"Wait for me," I said, scrambling behind her.

She was waiting at the corner. "Listen," I hissed, "this is dangerous, creeping around in the dark like this. I've already got a broken hand. Damned if I want to add a hip to it."

"Don't you want to know what she's up to?"

"Not really."

"Wimp." Mary Alice started walking down the alley. The gravel crunched under her feet so loudly I was sure it could be heard at the gallery.

I grabbed her by her coat sleeve. "If you don't go up there, I'll tell you what I did with your Shirley Temple doll."

She stopped. "You're lying, aren't you?"

"Of course I'm not lying."

"Yes you are. Look, either go back to the car or come and see what's going on. I'm just going to peek in the window."

I sighed. "Then let's walk on the grass. We sound like a herd of elephants."

There was no car behind the gallery as we had expected there would be, but all the lights were still on.

"Maybe she's left," Sister whispered. "She could have gone down the alley in the opposite direction."

"And left all the lights on?"

"She could have gone to get something and be planning to come back."

I shivered. "I'm freezing and I think we've lost our minds."

"I'm going to look in the window." Sister got down low and scooted over to the building. Her aqua aerobics classes were beginning to pay off, I noticed. I could hear her knees pop, though, as she stood up to look in the window. She had to stand on tiptoe, so there was no use my trying it. If she could barely see in at six feet, my five-one wouldn't be any help.

She moved to the next window and the next. She disappeared around the building and I was beginning to get worried when she scooted back across the pavement to me.

"There's no one in there," she said.

"Then why are you crawling like that?"

"Damned if I know. Claire must have left out of the back door like I said."

I shook my head. "I don't think she had time."

"There's nobody in there."

"Then let's go home."

"The back door's unlocked."

"You tried it?"

"Of course. Let's go see what Claire was up to."

"This isn't a game, Mary Alice. A woman was murdered in there."

"True. But you know who did it and he's long gone. Right now, I think Claire Moon is stealing all the stuff from the gallery."

"Surely not!"

"Want to bet? Come on. Let's see what we can find."

That's when I should have put my foot down and said, "Absolutely not. We're going home." Instead, there I was, following Sister just like I had for sixty years. Like I didn't have a grain of common sense.

We went up to the back door and Mary Alice opened it, quietly. "See?" she whispered. "No one here."

"What are we looking for?" I whispered back.

"Don't know. Just keep your eyes peeled."

We stepped into the room that smelled so strongly of mineral spirits. My heart was pounding so loudly, I was sure Mary Alice could hear it. I looked around wondering what in the world I was looking for.

"Let's see which pictures are still left out in the gallery," Mary Alice said. She opened the door, stepped through, and I followed her.

"Ladies, ladies," Claire Moon said beside us. "Have you ever noticed that Southern women have this failing? They just can't let well enough alone."

At least I think that's what she said. Most of my attention was riveted on the small pistol she held in her right hand. In her left hand was a five-gallon can of gasoline.

Eighteen

"We startled you again, didn't we?" Mary Alice said. "But it's just us. You can put the gun up."

"I don't think so. Let's walk into the back room, shall we?"

"Is that a real gun?" I asked.

"You don't want to find out, Mrs. Hollowell."

"Are we going to?" Mary Alice asked. "Find out?"

"Not if you do what I say. Now, go into the back room. The fumes are getting to me in here."

We went through the door with Claire right behind us.

"So much for your detective ability," Mary Alice murmured to me.

"What?" Claire was so close, the gasoline can bumped against my hip.

"My sister thought Ross Perry killed Mercy."

"Ross Perry was a bastard. Lying through his teeth about Fred's paintings." Claire put the can down. It clanged emptily on the floor. "I swear, I'd give anything if you hadn't shown up here tonight. It messes everything up."

"Messes what up?" Mary Alice asked. "And can we turn around?"

"Sure. Just not too fast."

We turned around to face Claire. Tiny, delicate, beautiful,

she looked as threatening as a doll. Except for the gun in her hand.

"Claire," I said. "What's going on? What do you mean about Ross Perry lying through his teeth about your husband's paintings?"

"He told me they were beautiful. He said, 'Claire, come to bed with me. I'll write wonderful things about these paintings. Look at these paintings, Claire. They should be in museums.' " She shrugged. "Then he told Mercy they were clever cartoons. Cartoons. She told me what he said." Claire nudged the empty gasoline can with her foot.

Mary Alice looked down. "You're going to set the place on fire?" She hesitated. "That's a stupid question, isn't it?"

Claire smiled.

"But why?"

"It was Mercy's."

Mary Alice looked at me and raised her eyebrows.

"Did you kill Mercy, Claire?" I asked.

"She killed herself. She stood in front of the mirror right there"—Claire pointed toward the bathroom door—"and sprayed curling mousse on her hair and scrunched it." Claire's voice took on a dreamy tone. "Mercy had red curly hair like my mother. My mother scrunched hers the same way. It looked like fire sometimes."

"But you put the DMSO and the digitalis in the bottle."

"Thurman and James said it would work. I heard them talking about it." Claire looked down at the pistol in her hand. "I wish you hadn't come back."

"So do we," Mary Alice said.

"I don't know what I'm going to do about you."

"We could just go home," I suggested.

"I don't think so. I'll ask Liliane. She'll know."

Mary Alice looked at me again with her eyebrows raised.

"You spray painted your house, Claire?" I asked.

"I guess so."

"The little painting of the Lady of the Lake was very clever."

"What little painting?"

"The picture in the guest bedroom of the three women floating to Camelot."

"I don't know what you're talking about." Claire seemed to sway a little. "I'm going to open the back door," she said. "These fumes are making me sick."

She backed toward the door, still pointing the gun at us. "Mercy should have shown Fred's work. It's so beautiful. I told her Ross Perry was wrong. But what did she know? She had hair that looked like fire. That crackled. She hit me, over and over."

"Mercy hit you?" I asked.

Claire looked confused. "Somebody did."

"Give me the gun, Claire," Mary Alice said. "You don't want to hurt us."

"I wish you hadn't come back. I don't know what to do."

"Just give me the gun. It'll be all right."

Claire looked down at the pistol and then at Sister. She began to raise her arm to hand over the gun. I'll always believe that was what she was doing. But at that moment, the back door flew open and hit her. The sound of the gun firing and Liliane's "Claire!" were simultaneous.

The explosion and shout seemed to linger in the air for a moment and then fall to the floor and shatter. I remember thinking of Roman candles, the loud swoosh, the arc, and then silence.

The four of us stood there, suspended for a moment in disbelief. I looked at Mary Alice.

"Damn," she said, a look of surprise on her face. And then her eyes closed and she fell. I didn't even have time to cushion her fall.

"Oh, God!" I screamed. I threw myself down beside her and cradled her head. She had fallen forward and slightly sideways. As I lifted her head, I could see blood already pooling on the floor.

"Call 911! For God's sake, call 911."

I heard the door slam and realized I was alone with Sister. "You're all right," I said, rocking her back and forth and sobbing. "You're all right. I'm going to get help."

I eased her back to the floor. There had to be a phone somewhere.

And that was when the room erupted in flame. There was no warning smoldering of smoke. Just sudden, all-encompassing fire. And I did all I could do. I opened the door, picked up my unconscious sister, and carried her out into the December night.

The 911 call came from a woman, they said. Later, when I had time to think about it, I hoped it was Liliane or Claire. When the Rescue Squad and police cars pulled into the parking lot, I was running to Mary Alice's car to call them. I didn't question the fact that they had appeared. I was just grateful.

"It's my sister!" I shouted, waving and pointing. By this time, the scream of the fire truck's siren had joined the rest of the noise. "She's been shot!"

I rushed to the back of the building, screaming, "Here! Here!" The heat of the fire burned my face.

"In the back, Jimmy! In the back!" someone shouted.

I knelt beside Sister and patted her cheek. "You're all right," I said. "You're all right."

A hand pulled me away. "Move, lady!"

Dark figures surrounded Sister. I turned my face from the heat and looked into the overgrown lot across the alley. Several pairs of eyes shone brightly in the tangles of dead weeds and sawbriars. Cats? Rabbits? Throw me in the briar patch. "Throw me in the briar patch," Mama read. And Sister and I laughed.

"I'm Leslie Morris"—a young woman in uniform touched my arm—"and we need some information. The lady's your sister?"

I nodded.

"First we need her name, age, and any medical problems she might have."

"She's not dead?"

"No, she's not dead."

The earth tilted. The woman steadied me. "Let's go sit in the car," she said.

"I'm all right." I caught my breath. "Her name is Mary Alice Crane and she's sixty-five years old."

"Medical problems?"

"She's too fat."

"No diseases that you know of? Any family history of disease?"

"She gave me whooping cough and measles."

"I'll be right back." The woman, whose name I had forgotten, disappeared into the crowd around Mary Alice. Her place was taken by a young man who wanted to know what had happened. I explained to him about Claire and the gun and the gasoline.

"How did you get Mrs. Crane out of the building?" he asked.

"Carried her."

He looked at me. "You carried her?"

"Well, it was sort of between a carry and a drag."

"I'll be right back," he said.

But I grabbed him by the sleeve. "She's shot in the head, isn't she?"

He nodded. "Yes."

I wandered over and sat on the grass at the edge of the alley. Another fire truck came roaring up. I couldn't imagine why. The old wooden building was engulfed in flames.

"Mrs. Hollowell?" A young man sat down beside me. "I'm Raymond Estes. I understand you carried your sister from the building?"

"Is she going to die?" I asked.

"Not if we can help it. Do you mind if I take your blood pressure and listen to your heart?"

I took off my coat.

"Take a deep breath," he said.

"It's going to snow tomorrow," I said.

"That's what I've heard."

"I've never seen a white Christmas. Have you?"

"No, ma'am. Take a deep breath now." I felt the biting cold of the stethoscope against my back.

"Raymond!" a man yelled. "We're taking her in."

"I'm going with her!" I tried to get up and realized I couldn't. It was as if I were paralyzed.

"Come here, Jimmy," Raymond called back. Together they helped me to my feet.

"Can you walk okay?" Raymond asked. "We'll help you."

I took a tentative step. "It's like all my muscles have frozen," I said.

"It's your body's reaction to the adrenaline surge. We're going to take you in, too."

"I want to go in the ambulance with my sister."

"Sure."

So for the second time in as many weeks, I was in an ambulance hurtling across Birmingham to Memorial Hospital. But this time I sat beside Mary Alice, whose head was swathed in bandages and whose neck was braced.

I reached over and touched the chicken pox scar on her cheek, still faintly visible after sixty years. "Chicken pox," Mama said. "Can you believe it? She came down with chicken pox the day you were born!"

Mary Alice opened her eyes, startling me. "Mouse, Claire Moon shot me, didn't she?"

"Yes."

"That really pisses me off."

"It pisses me off, too."

She closed her eyes again. I propped my head against the gurney and felt the ambulance, like time, rushing across the landscape.

They admitted both of us—me, overnight for monitoring my heart and blood pressure (they were both fine); and Mary Alice in intensive care. The bullet had entered her head just above her right temple and exited over her ear.

"She lucked out like you wouldn't believe," Haley told us when she came from the operating room. "She's lost a lot of blood, but the bullet didn't even enter the skull, just skirted along it, chipping off some bone fragments.''

The family, gathered in my room, was totally quiet for a minute. Then Debbie, who was sitting by my bed, took my hand and began to cry. "See," she said. "We've always said Mama was thick-skulled." The rest of us joined her in laughing and crying.

Before they left, Debbie said, "Okay, everybody. Aunt Pat gets to say just one time, 'She ain't heavy, she's my sister.' "

"Don't be stupid," I said. "The woman weighs a ton."

A day or so before Christmas, Bo Mitchell stopped by the house to update me on Claire Moon and Liliane Bedsole and to return *Victorian Poetry*. Frances Zata and I were sitting at the kitchen table drinking spiced tea and Bo joined us.

The two women had been caught in Nashville delivering a van load of folk art to a gallery. Liliane was out on bail and probably faced no more than a suspended sentence and a fine. We already knew that. Bo had come to tell us that Claire had been admitted to the state psychiatric hospital.

"I hope they keep up with her," I said.

Bo chose to ignore this.

"I'm glad she's getting help," Frances said.

"She's already been in a mental hospital in California for three months," I said.

"Being treated for depression," Frances said. "I'd be willing to bet you, though, that Claire's main problem is multiple personality disorder. Childhood abuse is the primary cause of it."

"Could be," I agreed. "The twins came by here the other day to see if I was okay and they talk about her as 'Good Claire' and 'Bad Claire.' Did you know that?"

"I think that's what the doctor believes," Bo said. "She has whole periods of time she doesn't remember, times when things happened like the picture being painted and Ross Perry being shot. Both of which she did, incidentally. Turns out after her husband was shot, she bought several guns and took lessons at a rifle range.''

"She must have loved Fred Moon a lot," Frances said. "I wonder if his work is any good?"

Bo Mitchell shrugged. "Don't ask me."

"Well, who got her out of the hospital?" I wanted to know.

"She got herself out. Bad Claire clicked in, stronger than the medicine. We found the guy she hitched a ride with. She went to the gallery and got Mercy's van."

"But it was Good Claire who showed up on my door-step."

"Yes."

We drank our tea and watched the birds coming to the special Christmas suet ball I had hung for them on the deck.

"You know," Frances said. "That picture Claire painted on the bedroom wall? What if it isn't Claire and the twins? What if it's three Claires?"

"Drink your tea and don't even think such a thing," I said. "One more thing, though, Bo. Who do you think our Peeping Tom was?"

"I know who it was. Liliane. She saw your Abe painting with the hair and figured it was worth a bundle. She also saw you didn't have dead bolt locks on your door." Bo pointed her finger at the door accusingly. "Fortunately, your husband was sleeping on the sofa." She took a sip of her tea. "He do that often?"

"None of your business."

Bo Mitchell laughed. "How's your sister?"

"She went home yesterday. She was wearing her T-shirt that says 'Tough Old Bird.' "

"You give her my best."

I walked Bo to the door. "You always knew it wasn't Ross, didn't you?"

"No, we didn't. You were pretty convincing."

"That's good to hear. You have a nice Christmas."

"And you."

*   *   *

And we did. Somehow we managed to pull it all together. We didn't go to Fox Glen for dinner because Mary Alice was still having some dizziness, which the doctor said was to be expected and was temporary. For an obscene amount of money, Fox Glen came to us with turkey and all the trimmings. Money well spent, I thought, looking around Sister's large dining room table at our children and grandchildren. At one end of the table, Bill Adams sat, still scratching furiously but beaming at Sister, who sat at the other end, the side of her head bandaged. We were not, she informed us, to call her Vincent. She'd gotten a bait of that in the hospital.

"She could do worse," I whispered to Fred.

"Who could do worse?" He was flirting rather sweetly with Freddie's Celia.

"Mary Alice. With Bill."

"How come he scratches all the time? He needs to take some Benadryl."

I turned to talk to Haley, who was seated on my left. She had brought Sheriff Reuse, but I didn't detect any sparks. Across the table, Debbie and Henry Lamont were sparking up a storm. None of us were surprised at their announcement as dessert was being served that they were being married in March.

"On Mama and Daddy's anniversary," Debbie said.

"Darling, that's wonderful," Mary Alice said. "When is it?" she mouthed at me as everyone congratulated Debbie and Henry. I held up the fingers on my left hand three times and then a single finger. "The sixteenth. What a sweet thought."

Freddie stood up and I thought for a moment he was going to announce he and Celia were engaged. But he held up his wine glass and said, "To Debbie and Henry."

We drank a toast to Debbie and Henry. My glass had sparkling apple juice in it, but I swear I could feel it. We drank a toast to Mary Alice's health, and to my strength, and to Celia's ability to conjure warts. We drank a toast to Bubba, whose red bow had slipped to one side, covering his ear, making him look like van Gogh's cat.

But Fred had the nicest toast of all. Just before we dived into huge slices of pecan pie, he patted my arm and stood up.

"Hey," he said, raising his glass. "We're here."

Discover Murder and Mayhem with

~&~ Southern Sisters Mysteries ~&~

by

ANNE GEORGE

MURDER ON A GIRLS' NIGHT OUT
0-380-78086-0/$6.50 US/$8.99 Can
Agatha Award winner for Best First Mystery Novel

MURDER ON A BAD HAIR DAY
0-380-78087-9/$6.50 US/$8.99 Can

MURDER RUNS IN THE FAMILY
0-380-78449-1/$6.50 US/$8.99 Can

MURDER MAKES WAVES
0-380-78450-5/$6.50 US/$8.99 Can

MURDER GETS A LIFE
0-380-79366-0/$6.50 US/$8.50 Can

MURDER SHOOTS THE BULL
0-380-80149-3/$6.50 US/$8.99 Can

And in hardcover
MURDER CARRIES A TORCH
0-380-97810-5/$23.00 US/$34.95 Can

....

Available wherever books are sold or please call 1-800-331-3761
to order.   AGO 0900

Murder Is on the Menu
at the Hillside Manor Inn
Bed-and-Breakfast Mysteries by
MARY DAHEIM
featuring Judith McMonigle Flynn

CREEPS SUZETTE	0-380-80079-9/ $6.50 US/ $8.99 Can
BANTAM OF THE OPERA	0-380-76934-4/ $6.50 US/ $8.99 Can
JUST DESSERTS	0-380-76295-1/ $6.50 US/ $8.50 Can
FOWL PREY	0-380-76296-X/ $6.50 US/ $8.50 Can
HOLY TERRORS	0-380-76297-8/ $6.50 US/ $8.50 Can
DUNE TO DEATH	0-380-76933-6/ $6.50 US/ $8.50 Can
A FIT OF TEMPERA	0-380-77490-9/ $6.50 US/ $8.99 Can
MAJOR VICES	0-380-77491-7/ $6.50 US/ $8.99 Can
MURDER, MY SUITE	0-380-77877-7/ $6.50 US/ $8.99 Can
AUNTIE MAYHEM	0-380-77878-5/ $6.50 US/ $8.50 Can
NUTTY AS A FRUITCAKE	0-380-77879-3/ $6.50 US/ $8.99 Can
SEPTEMBER MOURN	0-380-78518-8/ $6.50 US/ $8.99 Can
WED AND BURIED	0-380-78520-X/ $5.99 US/ $7.99 Can
SNOW PLACE TO DIE	0-380-78521-8/ $6.50 US/ $8.99 Can
LEGS BENEDICT	0-380-80078-0/ $6.50 US/ $8.50 Can

And Coming Soon

A STREETCAR NAMED EXPIRE
0-380-80080-2/ $6.50 US/ $8.99 Can

··

Available wherever books are sold or please call 1-800-331-3761
to order.   DAH 1000